W9-BKW-324

———————————— ★ ————————————

"DON'T YOU DARE WALK OUT ON ME NOW."

Miranda's voice was a knife-edge whisper.

Ingrid slid back into her seat.

"It's just a simple little job I want you to do," Miranda said.

"If it's that simple, why don't you do it yourself?" Ingrid glanced briefly over Miranda's shoulder, not meeting her eyes.

"I can make trouble for you if you don't go along with me on this. You must have known a few toughs with guns in Humboldt. Well, those guys look like weak-kneed amateurs next to the kind of dogs I can sic on you. Don't worry, I'll pay you."

"You might not understand this, Miranda, but there are things some people won't do for money."

"I doubt that. If not for money, then to save your neck you'll roll over, I promise you."

———————————— ★ ————————————

"...a promising debut."

—*Publishers Weekly*

"Let's hope first-novelist Murray keeps writing...."

—*Booklist*

Lynne Murray

TERMINATION
— INTERVIEW —

W✪RLDWIDE.

TORONTO • NEW YORK • LONDON
AMSTERDAM • PARIS • SYDNEY • HAMBURG
STOCKHOLM • ATHENS • TOKYO • MILAN
MADRID • WARSAW • BUDAPEST • AUCKLAND

If you purchased this book without a cover you should be aware that this book is stolen property. It was reported as "unsold and destroyed" to the publisher, and neither the author nor the publisher has received any payment for this "stripped book."

In loving memory of my mother,
Dorothy Leone Murray,
the first mystery reader I ever met

TERMINATION INTERVIEW

A Worldwide Mystery/September 1994

First published by St. Martin's Press, Incorporated.

ISBN 0-373-28020-3

Copyright © 1988 by Lynne Murray.
All rights reserved. No part of this book may be reproduced or transmitted in any form or by any means, electronic or mechanical, including photocopying, recording or by any information storage and retrieval system, without permission in writing from the publisher. For information, contact: St. Martin's Press, Incorporated, 175 Fifth Avenue, New York, NY 10010-7848 U.S.A.

All characters in this book are fictitious, and any resemblance to actual persons, living or dead, is purely coincidental.

® and TM are trademarks of Harlequin Enterprises Limited. Trademarks indicated with ® are registered in the United States Patent and Trademark Office, the Canadian Trade Marks Office and in other countries.

Printed in U.S.A.

ACKNOWLEDGMENTS

Particular thanks to Barbara Landis for her valiant
and untiring reading of the manuscript through
several drafts and her help with innumerable details
of photography and business. Much gratitude also to
Merry von Brauch for her encouragement on kindly
reading the first draft and to Jonathan Brown for
checking the photography and martial arts,
and rechecking them when I had to change them.
Also thanks to Jonathan H. Malone, Secretary of the
San Francisco Landmarks Preservation Advisory Board,
for the information on how old buildings are given
landmark status in San Francisco.
Any errors I have managed to insert despite all this
assistance are entirely my own responsibility.

Made in U.S.A.

AUTHOR'S NOTE

Serious observers of the streets of San Francisco will note that I have invented Taft Alley, a one-block alley leading off an unspecified cross street of Montgomery. Taft Alley is bordered on one side by the imaginary Bramwell Building and on the other by the equally invisible charming old bank building which is being hollowed out to hold a high-rise.

ONE

Monday, December 19

INGRID HUNTER SAT at a desk in the most remote secretarial outpost on the twelfth floor of Bramwell, Stinson & Flint. She had a tempting view of the elevators through the branches of the huge Douglas fir set up by the law firm near the receptionist's desk. Six days before Christmas, and the tree's fire-retardant-sprayed branches weren't decorated yet. It was six P.M. She had film in her camera and an appointment to photograph a woman on Pacific Avenue at seven.

But an iron-faced homicide detective had said, "Stick around a little longer. We need a few more details for your statement; then you can go."

So she waited. The lawyers had retreated at the first sign of trouble into their offices, except for a few who were holed up in the law library. The senior partner, Atherton Flint, had conveniently boarded a flight to Washington earlier in the day. His son and heir, though only a junior associate, played host, to the fury of higher-ranking associates. The young man's sun-bleached hair and yachting tan glowed in the soft economy lighting as he talked in low tones to a man from the district attorney's office. Occasionally one of the senior partners would descend from the penthouse level to the neutrality of the twelfth-floor conference room where the police had set up shop. As seven o'clock drew nearer, Ingrid began to hover near the door to this room. A knot of secretaries and messengers clustered halfway down the hall, where a water fountain in an alcove made a natural oasis.

A tall, slender woman with straw-colored hair burst out of an elevator and charged down the hall, tweed skirt and blazer flapping. She was intercepted at the water fountain by a short but muscular man with a pirate's earring. Ingrid recognized him as Max Leon, the supervisor of Word Processing. He steered the woman down the hall just out of Ingrid's earshot. Her hair was twisted into a tight bun above a face with over fifty years scrawled on it in nature's shorthand. She ducked away from her earnest informant.

"Yes, I've heard the good news about Miranda Falk, damn it. I'll believe it when I see the body."

Max, still whispering intensely and inaudibly, kept pulling her toward the nearest office door for a private talk. But she was not to be restrained.

"I certainly do want to see the body. Let go of my arm, Max. If that woman is honestly dead, it will be the first honest thing she's ever done."

Max continued to plead with her softly; perhaps he was telling her that the body had never been in the Personnel office—where the woman now seemed to be heading. And furthermore, the police had taken the body away. Everyone had leaned out the Bramwell Building's big, old-fashioned windows to watch, threatening to increase the day's body count as they did so.

Ingrid strained to hear Max's words, but he was speaking too softly. Tanya Hawkins, the young black woman Ingrid had sat next to all day, stood on the fringes of the group near the water fountain. Tanya was the only person here Ingrid knew at all well, except for Miranda Falk. And she was dead. Ingrid joined Tanya, and they both listened intently but heard nothing more.

Max now pointed discreetly to Ingrid, no doubt explaining who had found the body. He was not the first person to point to Ingrid since the moment that afternoon when she had walked into the office, time card in hand, and discovered that the head of Personnel was out. Permanently. For all her trouble, Ingrid still hadn't gotten her time card signed.

The blonde looked at Ingrid for several seconds, as if about to demand an eyewitness account. But her friend's persistent tugging at her arm dissuaded her.

Turning to follow Max into an office, she glared at the small group near the water cooler. "I see you laughing, you crowd of vultures. You deserved her and you got her. I only hope you get someone much worse this time." With that, the office door closed after her.

There was a momentary hush among the waiting group. None of them had, in fact, been laughing. But several people rolled their eyes at the woman's outburst.

"Who was that?" Ingrid asked Tanya.

"Nell Scott. She was Flint's secretary for over twenty years. He kicked her upstairs to Personnel and put Miranda in her job. Then when Miranda wanted to take charge of Personnel, old man Flint kicked poor Nell all the way down to the basement to write style manuals. I feel sorry for that lady."

"She must be tight with the guy with the earring. Max, isn't it?"

"Max Leon. The grapevine says Miranda fired him today."

Ingrid's name was called, and she went into the conference room to confront a weary-eyed man in his mid-forties. His chocolate-brown wool jacket was draped over the conference table next to him, as if for the express purpose of soaking up the coffee that threatened to spill from the small raft of plastic cups nearby. Ingrid's eyes kept returning to the coat and the cups near it as they talked. She explained that she had a seven o'clock appointment.

"Sorry to keep you so long, Miss Hunter—or is it Mrs.? Or Ms.?" His voice had an ironic twist to it.

Ingrid shrugged, refusing to be baited. "I was born Ingrid Hunter. I was married to Victor Nagel, but I've been divorced for over two years now, if that's what you mean."

He noted all this in a small, spiral-bound notebook. "Your husband's full name?"

"My ex-husband's name is Victor Calvin Nagel."

The detective showed no signs of recognizing the name. Ingrid sighed in silent relief. Maybe the homicide and drug divisions of the police force didn't always keep in touch.

"And your former husband's current address?"

Maybe he *was* interested in Vic. "I don't know and I don't care."

"Still sore, huh?"

"Did you ever meet anyone who was divorced who wasn't just a little bit bruised?"

"Come to think of it, no."

The latest rumors Ingrid had heard placed Victor in prison, but he could just as easily be in Pakistan or a penthouse in Peru now for all she knew.

"They say here you knew the deceased..." He consulted another page of his notebook. "Ms. Falk?"

"She and I went to the same girls' school, even the same college for the first year."

He took down the addresses of Valley School and the private women's college. "Prep school, huh? For poor little rich girls in trouble?"

Ingrid almost laughed in spite of herself. "Maybe so. But why don't you call the school yourself?" She told him the year she and Miranda had graduated.

There was an odd gleam in the man's eye. It might have been suspicion or simply a taste for divorced women of thirty plus with curly dark hair showing distinct salt among the pepper. Whatever it was, it threatened to stretch on past seven o'clock.

Ingrid was a tall woman with a short mop of black curls generously laced with gray. "Premature gray—an old family tradition," she told people. Telling them took less time and money than the hair-dye routine. But she also knew the silver streaks set off her turquoise eyes and contrasted strongly with the childishness of her face. Yet her prettiness always seemed to bring her more unwelcome than welcome attention. Witness the detective. Did he see her as a suspect or a date?

"You say you went to high school with Ms. Falk. I'd appreciate any light you could shed on her background."

"Well, her name was Mary Valkevich back then. I only knew her for two years. She boarded at the school and I commuted. All I remember about her situation was that she seemed to be on some sort of scholarship."

"You drifted away, in spite of all those great long-distance telephone rates?"

Ingrid shrugged. "Maybe someone from the school kept in touch, but..." She thought hard while he waited, but she

couldn't recall anyone who had been close to Mary Valkevich in school. "She didn't have many friends there. I
didn't know she was in the Bay Area. When I came here
today on the temp job, I didn't even recognize her at first."

She had been surprised to run into Miranda again after
so many years, but the encounter had dissolved so swiftly
into a barrage of threats that Ingrid suspected Miranda had
engineered the meeting for some reason of her own. Her
fall from the twelfth-floor window had short-circuited
Miranda's plan, whatever it was. Once the initial shock of
discovering the body wore off, Ingrid had to admit she was
relieved to think that Miranda couldn't make any more
trouble for her. The thought was immediately followed by
a mild backlash of guilt.

She did not admit her relief and definitely not her guilty
afterthought to the homicide detective, who was regarding
her with the slit-eyed patience of a crouching cat. He relaxed a bit, lit a cigarette and asked for her I.D.

As she opened her wallet something dropped out. She
picked it up. It was the key she had come away with after
her disastrous luncheon with Miranda.

Suddenly Ingrid felt as if she were standing on a narrow
sliver of ground with one foot poised over the abyss. Deep
canyons yawned on every side. She didn't know which way
to step. She looked up, meeting the eyes of the homicide
detective. Eyes that were suddenly clouded with suspicion.
Her hand shook as she put the key away, took out her
driver's license and handed it to him.

"I'll be right back."

He was going to check it by phone through the police
computer. Of course he would suspect her. Was it too late
to tell him about the key? How had she gotten into this
mess? Her mind went back through the events of the day as
she searched for something she could say about Miranda to
help the investigation without incriminating any innocent
people—such as herself.

But the past morning seemed impossibly far away to her
now.

TWO

INGRID HAD SPENT the first few hours of her Monday morning—or perhaps it would be more precise to say the last few hours of her weekend—in a state of remarkable insecurity, despite the high-tech burglar alarms of the Sea Cliff district mansion where she had spent the night.

Two stone posts at Twenty-fifth Avenue marked the barrier between the stately homes of Sea Cliff, where live-in Guatemalan maids and Japanese gardeners performed wonders, and the mundane home across the street in middle-class San Francisco. The small seal face on each stone pillar pointed like a granite tongue at its lower-rent neighbors. Around the corner on Twenty-fifth Avenue North the stone wall around Jason's house was several inches thick and bore a discreet plaque announcing electronic surveillance. By dawn, the lights in the upper story of the stone house gleamed from their slits, visible only to ships passing under the Golden Gate Bridge.

She had to frown when Jason Grapelli offered to share his toothbrush. Shouldn't the wealthy have spares for overnight guests? A brief shuffle through her shoulder bag revealed a camera body, flash and two extra lenses but no toothbrush. The more she learned about Jason, the more she wondered how many other women had used these innocent-looking bristles even within the past week. She made a mental note to buy another folding travel toothbrush. Though this was not her first sexual adventure since her divorce, it was the first one worth staying for a morning shower.

She had admired Jason's artwork, which he playfully signed "j g graffiti." His painted collages all included fragments of mirrors. The other materials came from the streets (with a little scribbled list of where they were found serving as the title for each collage). The artist was even more intriguing than the paintings. Jason had the coiled energy of a newly captured wild animal and eyes the color of pale beer.

Ingrid had expected a Potrero Hill warehouse when he had invited her to his place. Yet he had walked into the walnut-paneled hallway as if he had always lived there. He took it all for granted—just as he took for granted his magnificent hair and skin—the same golden color as his eyes.

She was glad she had a temporary job to get to by nine A.M.; the prospect seemed somehow restful after the rough-and-tumble action of the night before. She was physically exhausted, but not too sore to sit at a typewriter. Jason didn't seem to have a schedule for the day. When, after a few words on "sex as an aerobic sport," he went on to say that he also wrote poetry, she decided to leave immediately.

In the gray light of dawn, the small bedroom had an old-fashioned, quaint look that clashed with the unframed watercolors that were propped against the walls, scraps of newspapers and political posters sticking up off their surfaces, each protected by a sheet of glass. Suddenly Ingrid realized that this was the guest bedroom, or possibly a servant's quarters. The mists of sleeplessness cleared and her mind became more alert, stretching toward conclusions.

She had glimpsed a long staircase in the center of the wood-paneled hallway before being hustled in the other direction. The stairs must lead to the main bedrooms of the house. Whose house was it, and how had Jason come to live here?

Ingrid's '68 Mustang coughed several times in protest but at last roared to life and sputtered into its five-minute warm-up. Down the block a brown van also started up. The driver followed when Ingrid turned east on Lake Street. There was very little traffic in front of her. The van stayed several car lengths behind her, as if the owner were anticipating a breakdown. Ingrid paid little attention.

The brown van drove past as she reached the high stone stairs in front of her Oak Street apartment building. The glimpse she got of the driver made her turn back and stare.

No. It couldn't be.

Perhaps she was experiencing a new type of hangover. Ingrid shied away from alcohol, reasoning that her alcoholic parents had drunk her share several times over. Perhaps the sleepless night and Jason Grapelli's toothbrush were somehow having a bizarre effect on her perceptions. The driver had looked like her ex-husband. She hadn't thought of Victor in so long. That slightly flattened nose. The wave of black hair over a long forehead. But it couldn't be. Victor would never wear a beard.

THREE

INGRID'S APARTMENT WAS at the end of a long, twisting hallway facing the alley behind the building. The rent here was cheap, so she could afford to buy darkroom chemicals and pay the outrageous water bill for the cubbyhole behind Ito's Aikido School where she developed her pictures. Ito threw in free lessons, so it was a bargain.

She had started martial arts lessons when she had left Victor. Every so often while they had been married, he had hit her. Ingrid's first few aikido lessons had been marked by cheerful fantasies of smashing Vic a few times in retaliation, despite the warning of her teacher, Ito-*sensei*, that aikido was "defensive, neh?—no punching, no kicking."

At a right angle to Ingrid's door was the rear entrance, which displayed a sign reading: "Fire Exit. This door must remain locked at all times. The Management." Ingrid agreed with the manager, Mrs. Phelps, who lived in Apartment 1. MacHarg's Bar was not far away, and sometimes there were fights in the alley outside. She kept the dime-store curtains on her window securely shut. Their fiercely cheerful orange and yellow hues echoed the bedspread and contrasted sharply with the thin gray carpet. She swept the carpet daily; its flattened fibers gave up the dust without argument.

Ignoring the temptation of her narrow bed, Ingrid put a pot of water on the stove in the kitchen. Stripping off her thrift-shop lace shirt and painstakingly aged blue jeans, she carried the electric heater into the kitchen and stood in front of its humming orange bars while she brushed her teeth properly with her own toothbrush at the kitchen sink. There was nothing on the counter or in the sink. Ingrid rarely cooked.

Changing into clean underwear, she yawned, stretched and bent over to touch the floor. No time for any aikido, just the simplest stretching exercises.

When the phone rang a few minutes later, Ingrid was already dressed in her muted gray skirt and blazer with an ivory turtleneck sweater.

"Ingrid Hunter. Good. I've reached you at last," announced a raspy voice of no discernible sex. The voice continued, with the clear expectation that all within earshot would recognize and instantly obey.

Ingrid held the telephone receiver between chin and shoulder, spooned instant coffee into a cup and added boiling water. "About our photo session tonight," the voice went on. "I've got you down for six P.M. My afternoon conference is going to run late. How about making it seven o'clock?"

The shoot with Rosemary Tanner, of course!

"Seven tonight, let's see." Ingrid tried to sound as if she were checking an appointment book. "That will be fine."

She had volunteered to take Rosemary Tanner's picture for the newsletter of the Professional Women's Network, a group Tanner had founded for upwardly mobile businesswomen. Her organization did not welcome secretaries or clerks; most of its members were newly hatched managers, anxious to set themselves apart from the fieldhand stigma associated with clerical work. Ingrid was not ashamed of the way she supported her photography habit, but she never mentioned it to any of the Professional Women. She dreaded a chance meeting with one of them on a temporary assignment and her exposure as a "mere" secretary.

At the door, Ingrid checked her gear to make sure one camera was loaded with black-and-white Tri-X for the newsletter mug shot. The other camera body held Vericolor-3. Rosemary had just decorated her office; no harm in a few color shots. Ingrid debated the extra-weight issue, then threw in her wide-angle lens as well as the 105mm in case she ran into an interesting outdoor picture.

The camera bag already contained several rolls of exposed film. Her Sunday-night escapade had taken up her darkroom time.

Her last act before leaving was, as always, to unplug the electric heater and stow it in its nook beside the door. It had a habit of turning itself on at odd moments when its thermostat decreed that things were too cold. It had awakened her a few midnights with its abrupt, resonant hum and splash of orange light; after that she had decided not to let it live a life of its own.

The day looked cloudy, but no rain was falling. San Francisco always reserved the right, Ingrid knew, to deal out cold rain and fog or sunshine any day of the year without notice.

As Ingrid reached the foot of the front steps, Mrs. Phelps disappeared around the corner of Oak. By the time Ingrid passed the doorway of MacHarg's Bar, Mrs. Phelps' pink sweater glowed out from the dark interior as she settled herself on a bar stool to breathe the slow air and blunt the seventh hour of a Monday morning with the first drink of the day.

Remembering her childhood, Ingrid shivered and hiked her camera bag up higher on her shoulder.

THE BRAMWELL BUILDING, twelve floors of tan brick and a bunker-like penthouse, stood on a narrow L-shaped strip of land. The shorter wing of the building faced Montgomery Street, which ran through the heart of the financial district. The long wing stretched along one of the major tributary streets.

A thunderstorm of heavy equipment surrounded the building. The front pillars and walls of a fussy brick bank next door had been declared historical, and builders had hollowed it out, leaving the shell, the four walls, intact. The process of inserting the fifty-story high-rise into its two-story socket was about as graceful as standing a lamppost on a layer cake.

Studying the new construction, Ingrid decided the developers must have wanted the entire half block, then had to grit their teeth and settle for whatever odd-shaped par-

cel they could get, even if that meant their architect had to
do backward handsprings.

Stone sunbursts and eagles trimmed the Bramwell
Building's doors and windows and adorned its rooftop
penthouse. It was a handsome building, but Ingrid had
liked the gutted bank better.

As the door closed behind her, the sudden hush in the
Bramwell's lobby lapped over Ingrid. There was only the
sound of her footsteps echoing from the marble floor up to
the vaulted bronze ceiling. Originally built by a wealthy
client in 1912, the building had been purchased by the
firm's founder, Eugene Bramwell, whose marble bust
looked out over the lobby. Ingrid remembered it from her
last temp job here. She greeted the statue with a smile and
headed for the elevators.

Ingrid heard a rush of running footsteps and was struck
from behind as a beefy hand closed around her arm. An
arm in a blue shirt draped around her shoulder. She could
smell sweat and the residue of a ham-and-eggs breakfast on
the man's breath.

She lowered her body instinctively, her camera bag sliding off her shoulder and hitting the marble floor. Silently
praying that nothing had broken, Ingrid reached across to
grab the right hand that gripped her arm, now pressing
suggestively against her breast. She dug her knuckles into
the back of the man's hand to break his grip.

As he winced away from her in pain, she pivoted with
him to face him and twisted his elbow in the opposite direction from the wrist, locking the joint. She was about to
push against the locked elbow and put him down on the
floor when the man groaned loudly. She dropped his arm
and stepped back several paces. She saw now that he wore
the uniform of a security guard. He was perhaps twice her
age, and quite overweight.

She realigned herself on the slippery floor, checking to
see that her posture was balanced. The shakiness of her
high-heeled shoes made her aware of her vulnerability. She
backed away, watching him rub his elbow as he stared at
her.

"Excuse me, ma'am," said a voice close to her shoulder, but not close enough to touch.

Ingrid flinched, instinctively opening her stance a little more to include the owner of the voice. Her teacher, Mr. Ito, would have rebuked her lack of attention even though she had repelled the attack. She had been taken unawares for the second time in a row—she needed more hours of practice.

"Don't hurt us now, please, ma'am," the voice continued. "Claude here doesn't get paid enough to suffer."

She glanced around, blushing as she looked into the most whimsical set of down-tilted blue eyes she had ever seen. The drooping eyes belonged to a man half a foot taller than she, perhaps her own age or a little younger. He wore the lawyer's uniform—a three-piece suit—and carried a gleaming alligator briefcase.

The man was handsome, impeccably groomed and flawlessly male, with white-blond hair that was as curly as sheep's wool. His glowing deepwater tan could only have been acquired on a sailboat. When a woman in San Francisco sees such a man, she tells herself, "Probably gay," and commands her pulse rate to slow down.

Gay or straight, he was tremendously amused, barely concealing his laughter. He had picked up her camera bag. He handed it to Ingrid, swinging it slightly as if to emphasize its weight.

Ingrid saw the humor in the situation and began to giggle. When he saw that she had relaxed, the man motioned her to follow him to the guard's desk near the entrance. She did so, grateful to this gorgeous stranger for defusing the situation.

"Sorry about the confusion," he said as she approached. "It's a new policy that you need a visitor's badge to go in. We've had some thefts lately. Just by looking at you I can tell you've got an appointment with someone; I'm only sorry it isn't with me."

She consulted her notebook, avoiding the man's eyes as she realized how foolishly she had behaved. She explained her agency assignment.

The security guard smoothed his hair back and returned to his post, circling widely around Ingrid, unconcealed hatred in his eyes. "Here, Mr. Flint, I'll call the twelfth floor."

The man with the briefcase drew Ingrid aside. "Just ignore Claude," he said softly. "He's been here only a few months, and already he's famous for accidentally grabbing all the best-looking women—purely in the line of duty, of course. It's high time someone blocked a few of his moves. I'm the boss's son and I've got to watch it around here, or I'd do it myself. If you need anything, call Tony Flint. I'm in the directory." He shook hands with her solemnly.

He was halfway to the elevator bank before Ingrid thought to wave. He waved back and stepped into an elevator that seemed to have been waiting for him by prior appointment. The doors closed, and Ingrid stood staring at them for several seconds.

She turned back to see Claude holding out a building pass at arm's length.

THE PERSONNEL OFFICE, at the end of the hall looking out over Taft Alley, was deserted except for a very young woman who sat at the reception desk. Ingrid stood by and waited for her to look up, but she was gazing into a folding mirror and randomly sticking bobby pins into the flood of dark-brown hair she had halfway pinned up on her head. It was already slipping down, but she had a big stack of pins in front of her and seemed determined to use every one.

Abruptly, the door opened, causing one of the inner doors to slam as a woman darted in, quick as a hummingbird.

"You must be Mr. Flint's temp for the day," she said, slipping her coat onto a hanger just inside the door and looking Ingrid over from head to toe as if measuring her with an invisible tape measure. Ingrid waited for her to finish and returned the inspection.

Where had she seen this woman before? Another temp assignment? She had the underworked, professionally flirtatious air of the token female manager. There was perhaps a greater smack of relish about it than most, as if her slick surface were the first in a succession of polished shells that would peel away like onion layers, revealing nothing but the tears of the explorer.

The scarlet designer scarf and cashmere sweater dress must have cost more than Ingrid's entire wardrobe. Never mind the snakeskin boots. No. This was someone's girlfriend playing at office life. Real personnel women didn't make *that* much money.

"Mr. Flint will be waiting—let's go up." The woman's glance at her watch conveyed the subtle but practiced implication that Ingrid was late, when in fact she herself had just arrived. "Let's go up to the penthouse level and see what kind of work he's got for you. It's just one floor, but why walk?" the woman said as they got on the elevator.

"Is this Flint Junior or Senior?"

"*Mister* Flint Senior. He's quite particular about his work. You've worked for him before, I saw from your file card..." There was a slight edge to her voice.

"He's still around?" Ingrid said. "No one's murdered him yet?"

For one hopeful moment it looked as if her irreverent remark might cost Ingrid the assignment. Her bus transfer was probably still good. But no. The woman simply flashed her teeth in a smile that could have been a warning. "Don't I *know* you from somewhere?"

The elevator opened on another marble-floored lobby, and their heels clacked as they stepped out.

"You look familiar too, but..." Ingrid shrugged. "Are you from L.A.?"

The woman looked as though she might have just gotten off a commuter flight from Burbank. Almost a head shorter than Ingrid, she had the winter-corn hair, big dolly eyes and small nose and mouth that signaled the Hollywood mills. In the Los Angeles area where Ingrid had spent much of her life, such faces are epidemic among both sexes, often resulting from cosmetic surgery and occasionally from inbreeding among actors.

"Remember Mary Valkevich from Valley School?"

"Oh, yes, it's coming back to me."

The nose had been surgically changed. The Mary whom Ingrid remembered from Valley School had been convinced that only half an inch of nasal cartilage and a comparable span of hymen had kept her from true happiness—which she had defined as popularity. Aside from Ingrid and the terminally nosy headmistress, no one had listened to Mary's problems. After high school she and Mary had simply stopped calling one another. Ingrid forgot who had stopped first. The next year, while taking pictures for the program of the local Tri-Colleges Shakespeare Festival, she had seen Mary again, still with the nose but minus the troublesome hymen. She had discovered sex with a vengeance—sex as revenge.

Rumor had it that Mary had next surfaced in Hollywood on a daytime TV soap opera. Ingrid had not seen Mary on the show, nor had she heard her name again in fifteen years.

"My name is Miranda Falk now." She paused for a reaction, but not long enough for Ingrid to do more than nod. "You're still Ingrid Hunter? Didn't you get married?"

"I was married for several years. But I came back to Hunter after the divorce. Suits me better."

Miranda nodded complacently through all this, as though it confirmed what she had guessed all along.

Small unpleasant details from those teenage years began to filter back to Ingrid. Miranda had pretended an innocence so wide-eyed as to verge on mental retardation.

"How did we ever wind up here, Ingrid?" Miranda shook her head disbelievingly.

It didn't seem so unusual to Ingrid. Most of the other women she knew with liberal arts degrees did secretarial or clerical work. With degrees from prestigious schools they did the same sort of work, under the title of Administrative Assistant.

"Well, Miranda, at least you're making something of yourself." *What,* Ingrid declined to speculate.

Miranda nodded energetically. "I've done okay. And I'll do better still. I must talk to you, though. I know you'll agree to help me. It's in *both* our interests. We'll talk later.

Your desk is down the hall, but I have to stop by Word Processing first.''

Behind the closed door where "Word Processing Center" was painted in chipped gold letters was a room with several computer terminals screened by tall sound screens. At the back of the room a group had gathered around a printer on a small stand. They fell silent when Miranda entered, Ingrid in tow.

"You again?" A short, slender man with the muscles of a bantamweight boxer and an earring in one ear detached himself from the group and approached Miranda. "We're going to have to lock that door." He spoke with a petulant, cynical drawl that passes as a man's gay accent in San Francisco.

"What about a security buzzer, Max?" one of the women in the group called. "That might slow her down."

Ingrid restrained a laugh, but Miranda was clearly taking names.

"I see you guys have got the envelope-feeding printer," Ingrid volunteered, wishing she could stay here instead of outside in the secretarial torture pit.

The short man with the earring looked blankly at Ingrid for a moment, then smiled like a conspirator with a flash of very white teeth against dark olive skin.

"Yes, we just got a new model in yesterday." He ignored Miranda, speaking only to Ingrid. "Watch this—print another one, Louise!"

Louise, a heavyset black woman in designer jeans, bent over her keyboard to type in an instruction. In the sudden silence the *clip-clip-clip* of the keys was clearly audible. There was a brief pause, then an abrupt *brrrrrip-zip* Bronx cheer erupted loudly from the machine, startling Ingrid and Miranda into sudden flinches and sending the operators into further fits of laughter.

Max was highly amused. "See? You put the envelopes in the hopper on top of the machine, here where it looks like the bleach feeder on a washing machine. Then the machine sucks it up with that funny noise, prints and watch this, this is hysterical."

The envelope rode the rollers 180 degrees and leaped out of the slot at the top of the machine like a small, belly-flopping diver.

Ingrid laughed. "I love it." She turned to Miranda, who was drumming her nails on the nearest table. "Well, don't worry, Miranda, word processors are easily amused; that's why we're so much happier than personnel directors."

There was a murmur of appreciation and agreement, and the operators disappeared, as if by sudden signal, behind their sound screens. The click of plastic keys being struck filled the silence. Max crossed his arms and stared up into Miranda's face. He must be quite short, Ingrid thought, because she could not have been more than five feet three inches in her high heels. Ingrid looked at the tops of their heads and waited for them to finish.

"Okay, Max. I want to see you at one o'clock in my office. You know what it's about."

"I certainly do, missy, and you'd better have my check, with vacation pay and severance pay and that Christmas bonus, ready for me when I get there."

"Don't worry. You'll get what you deserve."

"So will you, honey. So will you." He turned back to the desk just inside the door with the name plate Max Leon on it. He opened the magazine on his desk top and did not look up again as they went on.

"Termination interview," Miranda said casually. "Not my favorite part of the job, but not the worst part either. I'm very good, Ingrid. If we had another few years at it, we might just whip this place into shape." Ingrid wondered who "we" referred to, but Miranda wasn't finished. "You still take pictures, don't you? I'll bet you've got a camera in that shoulder bag, haven't you? Same old Ingrid."

Ingrid had a sinking feeling. "Well, yes but—"

"Good. Okay. Now I have a little job for you. Just an errand, really, but it pays amazingly well. You can feed that hungry camera of yours. Come by my office later. We'll go for lunch. Make it eleven thirty so we can talk." Ingrid hesitated, which was a mistake. "Good then, that's settled. Don't worry about the check. It's a business expense. The firm will pay, believe me." Miranda continued down

the hallway, past the glass-windowed office doors. The
smell of aromatic pipe smoke, like roasting marshmal-
lows, wafted out from one of the offices.

They reached the northwest corner of the building, where
the office overlooked Montgomery Street. "You know Mr.
Flint's office, of course." She gestured at the pair of ceil-
ing-high solid-oak doors. Ingrid had almost expected a
butler to come out the first time she had seen them.

The secretary's desk shared an alcove fenced by sound
screens with another secretary's desk just a few steps outside those massive doors. Flint's corner penthouse office
commanded the best view of any in the building.

"Tanya, hi," Ingrid greeted the black woman in her mid-
twenties who turned from her keyboard.

"Well, hello again, Ingrid," she said. "I still have that
picture you took of me outside the lunchroom. Has it been
a year?"

"Longer. It was September of last year. Your son must
be walking and talking like a veteran by now." Ingrid
hadn't met her son, but Tanya had pictures tacked up
around her desk showing him smiling, sitting, creeping and
shakily standing.

Tanya smiled and tapped a stack of pictures. "I'll show
you the walking ones later."

"Okay, you two have already met." Miranda brushed
past Tanya's desk. "You'll sit here. You know where everything and everyone is. Let's just see if Mr. Flint's phone
light is lit. I know he's in—he's always here by seven A.M."
She leaned over the desk and looked at the row of buttons
on the telephone. One button was lit, but the light went out
a second later.

Then, like a fighter throwing off his robe, Miranda
stripped off her blazer and draped it across the chair where
Ingrid would sit. She pulled her sweater dress down with a
motion that made it hug her breasts more closely and
showed that she wore no bra. Her small nipples pushed out
through the cashmere. Then she led the way into Flint's
office. Ingrid followed, exchanging a glance with Tanya,
who shrugged and pointedly turned back to her typing.

Flint Senior sat at his desk in the middle of the large, carpeted room. Ingrid hadn't taken in many details the last time she'd worked for him. The man had made her angry enough to want to avoid his office as much as possible. She had only vague impressions of the walls lined with floor-to-ceiling bookshelves.

The door behind Flint's desk betrayed the ultimate American executive's toy—a private bathroom. Persian carpets marched to the Montgomery Street window. A set of tall, varnished wooden shelves pressed against the angle of the window and continued on to cover two walls. On the shelves a ceramic army of tiny pots contained grayish-green vegetation. How could Ingrid have forgotten the plants?

Flint Senior, a plump, elderly man, wore a suit of such a dark banker blue that it was almost black. He had the pink skin and spiky white hair of an albino rat. There was a cunning gleam in his eyes, which Ingrid now noticed were brown, not his son's intense blue. A pink tongue crept out to wipe his lips occasionally. He stared fixedly at the papers on his desk as if determined not to look up.

When Ingrid had worked for him before, he had kept his eyes riveted on his work and had spoken so softly that she had been forced to come very close to the desk and had strained to hear him. When she bent close enough, he would bark a sudden gruff order and smirk when she jumped.

Miranda foiled him this time by making such an extraordinary cooing sound that both Flint and Ingrid turned to stare at her. She rushed over to the shelves, climbed up on a gray metal step stool and cupped her hands around a pot that was just above her eye level.

"Oh, your Midget Midnight is blooming!"

Looking at the plants more carefully, Ingrid could see that each pot in the regiment contained stubby leaves. Small velvety flowers bloomed in a variety of violets, pinks and lavenders. Involuntarily she took another step forward. Flint rose from his desk as if coming to the plants' rescue. Standing next to him for the first time, Ingrid realized that he was not a tall man, which was odd because his blue-eyed son was extraordinarily tall.

He was at the best height to examine Miranda's cashmere soft breasts as she stood on the stool to reach up to a higher plant. She cupped her hands around it as if absorbing some sort of warmth. A tiny blue-violet flower poked up out of the fuzzy, furrowed leaves.

The flowers brought out a different side of Flint. "This winter there are hardly any blooms worth looking at," he said petulantly. "It's those damned new buildings like that Helmut Kubler's atrocity next door cutting out the light. I may have to move the whole lot of them. The plants, I mean. I wouldn't mind moving the skyscrapers if so many of my best clients weren't located in those monstrosities."

This was the longest, most personal speech Ingrid had ever heard from the old man. He had confined all his previous communications to pointing out her mistakes with the resentful air of one who has been deliberately sabotaged.

Miranda turned to Flint Senior and said archly, as if they were alone together, "Come on down and look at mine sometime. My little plantsies just love the east window, even with all that construction outside. I just keep the window shut, and my itsy bitsy babies just bloom and bloom. You will come soon, won't you." She made a few small stroking gestures on his old-fashioned vest.

Flint sputtered something halfway between a groan and a choking sound and reeled back toward his desk, patting his impeccable necktie straight as he sat down. His eyes almost met Ingrid's before sliding away like startled fish. Suddenly he was flushing furiously. He cleared his throat and began to rattle a thick packet of yellow foolscap sheets covered with his unusually large, shaky but very clear handwriting.

All his work seemed to be headed "Confidential and Privileged." He dealt out a series of paper-clipped stacks into Ingrid's hands and then turned back to his open tablet and began to write.

Ingrid glanced at a pile of microcassette tapes in his outbox and looked away in horror. She hated transcribing dictation. With some relief she noted that Flint made no move to hand them to her. Then she saw that "PRIVATE" was inked on the label of each microcassette in

Flint's huge block letters. Wouldn't trust that stuff to a temp, Ingrid decided. At any rate she hoped they wouldn't.

It was several seconds before Ingrid realized that they had been dismissed; Miranda was on her way through the doors.

"He's so shy," she whispered to Ingrid as they stopped outside. "I used to get him acting almost human when I was his secretary. He's an old silly."

"You must have been out sick when I was here last year," Ingrid said.

"I may have been away on business; I'm never sick," said Miranda with a blinding smile as she gave Ingrid's arm a grab. She had always been more of a "toucher" than Ingrid, but now she was gripping her arm painfully.

"He has a new secretary now. Boys will be boys. She's very pretty. Very young. She's a little wild, probably late getting back from a strenuous three-day weekend."

Ingrid hoped Miranda wasn't going to try to corral her as the wild young secretary's permanent replacement. But Miranda's attention had already turned to other prey. Halfway down the hall, Tanya was talking to a black man, also in his mid-twenties, who had parked his mail cart.

"Oh, Franklin, would you be in my office by two for that interview? You can go right to payroll after that. They'll have your check and severance pay," Miranda said calmly.

Tanya gasped in shock, but Franklin simply nodded.

Miranda turned and grabbed Ingrid's hands warmly. Ingrid decided she was playing for the benefit of an audience. "Take good care of Mr. Flint, Ingrid. You know where my office is. I'll see you at eleven thirty. We'll talk about old times."

She left, and Ingrid turned to meet the hostile glares of Tanya and Franklin.

FOUR

WITH A SHRUG Ingrid sat down at her desk for the day. "I had the misfortune of going to high school with her," she said to Tanya and Franklin.

"Yeah." Franklin handed her Flint Senior's mail. Clearly his opinion of anyone who might have shared a classroom with Miranda was unprintable. He sighed. "Well, Tanya, if you look for me between mail rounds, I'll be scrubbing the walls in the restrooms."

"The *walls!* Whatever for?" Tanya paced back and forth nervously. She seemed too upset to sit down.

"Her highness says the janitors' union won't let them wash walls, and they're too cheap to pay for an outside service. Sooo, since the mailroom people have so much free time... You ladies look out, they see you filing your nails, next thing you know, you'll be out on the ledge washing the windows."

"Sorry, I don't do windows." It was a corny remark, but Ingrid couldn't resist. Franklin and Tanya both smiled mournfully, and the ice was broken somewhat.

"Let me talk to Junior, Frank. She can't do this to you." Tanya followed him down the hall.

Ingrid switched on her computer. She fed the program into the disk drive, formatted a document and began to convert Flint's bold scrawl into little green letters on the screen in front of her.

Time passed in a flow concentration. Soon she was ready to print out the copy, politely looking up first to see if Tanya needed to use the printer.

"No. You go ahead."

She was relieved to see that Tanya seemed to have forgiven her for knowing Miranda. People sharing a printer could make life difficult for each other if they chose. Back at her desk, Tanya was now applying royal-purple polish to her two-inch-long nails.

"Old man Flint sure puts out more work than his son. True, Lucinda, his so-called secretary, has been sick. Anyway, she can't type her way out of a paper bag. I help out when I can. And I usually can. Nell Scott comes in early and takes away all the real work. She gives me the overflow typing. Same thing when Miranda was his secretary." Tanya snorted. "She'd be on the phone all day or out on personal business. Don't know why they needed a temp today. You count on it, she has some little plan for you. She always does."

"You work for Flint Junior now?" When they'd had time to talk before, Ingrid hadn't asked a single question about work, and Tanya had seemed glad to forget about it. "Didn't you use to work for three or four hotshot junior associates? I remember they kept bringing you tons of work."

"Oh, well, I *am* good. But when Junior finally joined the firm last year, they said they'd pay a little more and asked me to keep an eye out for him, sort of baby-sit him. He's not a hard worker like some of those young kids. *I* think he's afraid he'll run into the old man in the halls or the library. So he hides out. When he wants to write a letter or a memo, he just buzzes the intercom and I go into his office. What work he does have he dictates." She laughed when Ingrid shuddered at the very thought of dictation.

"I don't know how you stand it, Tanya." She mimicked an ego-drunk executive: "'Just step in here and take down my Very Important Thoughts, Miss Hunter. Oh, and cross your legs, won't you? The view is so inspiring.' It just sums up everything I hate about secretarial work."

Tanya smiled serenely. "No, I don't mind. That man is just like a very tall two-year-old, that's all. Besides, I like to keep up my shorthand. Gets me up and out of the chair for a walk. See, his office is way down there." Tanya pointed to a door down the hall, just visible before the hallway curved around toward the elevators. "You just know his daddy put him on the same floor to make sure Junior came to work every day."

"I met Junior on my way in. Is he in there now?" Ingrid looked at the closed door and thought of the disarming blond man.

"No way to tell for sure. Say, you kind of like him, don't you?" Tanya was clearly tickled by the thought.

Ingrid smiled and surprised herself by asking, "Is he married? Don't tell me—he must be gay."

Tanya considered the question seriously. "I don't know, but don't get your hopes up. Junior's nice enough, but he's a snob. At first I thought he knew *your* friend Miss Falk."

"Oh, no, marked for life as a friend of Miranda Falk. What makes you think Tony Flint knew her?" Ingrid loaded yellow draft paper into the printer drawer, pressed the Print button and walked over to Tanya's desk.

"She knew Tony from where she used to work. When he first came in to work here she kept grabbing his arm"—she mimicked an overfamiliar Miranda so well that Ingrid laughed—"so we all thought they were close personal friends. Then something happened just lately and they started ignoring each other."

"What happened?"

Tanya shrugged. "Anyway, watch yourself with Junior. My bet is if he ever gets serious, he'll pick someone with enough money so he won't ever have to depend on the old man again. I think he lived for a few years on his yacht after he finished school. The old man forced him back and sold the boat, but he hates it here. It's written all over him. He needs a rich wife."

"Don't worry about me, Tanya, I just met him this morning. But I must say he *is* pretty charming."

"Yeah, Junior's nice. I feel sorry for him. I wouldn't work for his old man, though, not for a million dollars. He gives me the creeps."

Ingrid's documents finished printing, and she took them in to Flint Senior, who wrinkled his nose. "This is very good," he said, so softly that she had to bend close to catch the words. He picked up a magnifying glass and examined the page carefully. Then he glared up at her suddenly; she jumped back almost a foot at the indignant flash of brown eyes.

"It's so good that I must ask you why it isn't better. Look at that right margin. Straighten it out, why can't you?"

"Well, you said is was going to be typeset. You didn't ask for a right-justified margin."

"You might have enough intelligence to make it look like a printer's margin. I indicate here that it's part of a stock prospectus. You should know what such a document looks like. See if you can't do better next time. When you finish on these, run over to the travel office and pick up my tickets, will you?"

Ingrid held back all the various replies that occurred to her and picked up the next sheaf of yellow paper carefully, to avoid swatting him with it. She was beginning to feel a good deal of sympathy for the rebellious Flint Junior.

The rest of the morning passed as quickly as she followed the flow of green dots on the glowing screen. At eleven thirty Ingrid realized she had worked all morning without even a cup of coffee. She went to find Miranda before Miranda could come in search of her.

FIVE

MIRANDA CHOSE Le Choux D'Or, a French nouvelle vegetarian restaurant that presently enjoyed the status of *the* new, veggie-chic lunch place in town. It was a few blocks east on Battery Street. Ingrid knew how hard it was to get a lunch reservation there on the same day you called: secretaries were frequently asked to perform such miracles. Miranda and Ingrid walked there on streets that were slick from the midmorning rain. The clouds kept the worst cold out, and a pale disk of sun winked off and on as the clouds traveled across it.

At the stoplight a bicycle messenger in an orange plastic rain suit brushed past them as he rocketed into the streetful of traffic with a blood-curdling yowl, narrowly avoiding death under the wheels of a Muni bus. Down the street another messenger howled in answer to the first.

"Idiot!" Miranda called at him, jumping back to safety on the curb.

"Can you hear them when you open your office windows?" Ingrid desperately wanted to take a picture but realized she would have missed the best one anyway. "I remember them best from a temp job I worked in the Russ Building with windows right on Montgomery. The sound echoed off the buildings like the cries of the damned in hell."

"Never noticed," Miranda said firmly, crossing Battery against the light amidst a comfortable crowd of fellow jaywalkers.

Ingrid could see this lunch would be difficult, but her stomach was empty and the food was free.

"You've started curling your hair," Miranda remarked as she settled herself at the table. "You always were a little strange. Why let it go gray and then get a permanent?"

"I'm afraid this is no permanent. The frizz you see is the real me." Ingrid pulled a lock of her short-cropped hair out to demonstrate. "The rain in the air brings it out more."

"Back in school your hair was straight."

"That was because I straightened it with an iron. Hot rollers. Things I don't have time for right now." The waiter took their orders and left. There was an uncomfortable silence.

"I subscribe to the Professional Women's Network Newsletter, Ingrid. I saw your pictures there. I thought it must be you."

Ingrid doubted this; no one looked at photo bylines except photographers and relatives of photographers. "I've never seen you at any of their meetings."

"Rosemary keeps inviting me and I keep meaning to go. I thought I might run into you there. Then when I saw your name on our list of people Mr. Flint would consider accepting as a temp again—well, I was a little shocked. I didn't know they even let secretaries *into* the Professional Women."

"Maybe they don't. I doubt if they'll kick me out when you tell them, though. They've gotten used to the free photographs." Ingrid sipped her glass of ice water and tried to look unconcerned.

"Oh, I wouldn't dream of revealing your little secret. At school, you know, you were always a role model to me."

Ingrid choked on a mouthful of water and coughed for several seconds.

"Oh, really?" she managed to say at last when her continued breathing seemed ensured.

"I liked you in school," Miranda continued blithely. "You were the closest friend I ever had."

Ingrid sighed noiselessly. If she was Miranda's best friend in high school or ever, Miranda was in bad shape. "Well, things were pretty crazy for me back then," she said cautiously. "You boarded at school, didn't you? Your parents were always traveling or something. Must have been a rough time for you."

Miranda nodded. Her eyes seemed to glitter. "You told me your parents were career alcoholics."

"I did?" Ingrid bit her tongue and successfully avoided saying, I said that to *you?* "I was pretty frustrated about it back then—and pretty brutal."

"I liked that a lot about you. Your brutality. I couldn't talk about my...problems the way you did. Even now. My parents got divorced before I was old enough to know my father—never met him. My mother's parents doled out an allowance to her—well actually, for both of us—but whenever she got her hands on enough money to travel, she was gone. She'd leave me somewhere and just forget to pick me up. Once someone gave her enough money to go off for five years. I just stayed with this woman—not a relative, a nurse's aide—and she took care of me. I told you about it in school—maybe you don't remember."

Miranda paused, then continued a fraction of a second before Ingrid could think of any way to pretend to remember. "By the time I hit Valley School, my mother was on a full-time campaign to marry a rich lawyer."

"What happened?"

"Honestly, I don't know what happened to her." It didn't sound as though Miranda much cared, either. She shrugged. "She's dead now, that's all I know."

Completely at a loss for a reply, Ingrid turned to what she knew would be a favorite topic. "So, what about you? Are you campaigning to marry a rich lawyer?"

"It's different for me." Miranda bent forward earnestly as if trying to talk through a wall. "I never believed in all those rules. You can make a lot of money on your own, if you snap up every opportunity. You have to be careful and tough. You can't faint at the sight of blood. Like those termination interviews today. You do what you have to."

"And you have to fire people?"

Miranda smiled pleasantly. "Some of them, like Frank Bates, may never find another job. He has a prison record, you know."

"Cheer up—maybe he'll sue for discrimination."

Miranda laughed as if quite amused. "What? Sue a law firm? For refusing to employ an ex-convict with a record of substance abuse? Hardly a wise course of action; sort of like lying down in front of a steamroller, don't you think? Expensive, too."

Ingrid raised her eyebrows. "Why, Miranda, you've gotten so tenderhearted with age—you didn't use to be such a pushover."

Miranda sidestepped the irony. "Who cares? Nobody helped me. Why should I help anybody else?"

"What about your scholarship to Valley School? And somebody must have paid for your... cosmetic surgery."

Miranda stroked her new nose. "Believe me, I earned every penny that was spent on me. Every penny. Some kids get a nose job as a graduation present. Me, I had to try suicide before anyone would fork out—story of my life. You didn't know that I tried to kill myself, did you?"

"No. How did you do it?"

"Very dramatic, of course. I took an overdose of pills and called a suicide hotline. They kept me talking. I kept telling them my appearance was so distressing that I didn't want to go on. They got in touch with my father somehow. He didn't want to meet me, but he offered to get me some therapy. I told him a nose job was more to the point."

"Well, how about this job at Bramwell? Didn't knowing somebody, some contact or reference, help you get the job here?" Ingrid struck out in exasperation, puzzled at the turn the conversation had taken. She really wanted to ask whether Miranda was Tony Flint's lover, or Flint Senior's lover, or both.

Miranda's eyes flashed. "Are you accusing me of getting my job by underhanded means?"

"Now that particular thought never occurred to me till you mentioned it just now."

Miranda glared at her silently, then grimaced and waved her hand as if to push the anger away. The waiter approached just then with the tray of food; he saw the gesture and hesitated a moment before coming up to the table.

"Sex is the first thing to go in a relationship when people have nothing in common," Miranda said, ignoring the waiter, who had to work hard to keep a straight face as he set out their dishes. "Why should you condemn me for taking what someone else has already thrown away?"

Ingrid turned to the waiter. "What do *you* think?" He dropped a quick smile on each woman and dashed back to the rest of the lunch-hour crowd. "You're imagining things, Miranda, if you think I'm condemning you."

The food was vaguely French, certifiably vegetarian and most fashionably arrayed on the plate. Ingrid's tofu mock-trout filet looked elegant and virtuous, if a bit shrunken.

"Well, what *are* you thinking then?"

"I don't think you care about my opinion, Miranda." Ingrid tried a bite of faux trout, which had neither taste nor texture.

"Speaking of husbands, I heard your husband's dope business went sour up in Humboldt." Miranda toyed with the parsley on the edge of her plate. "Is he in or out of prison these days?"

Ingrid put down her fork. She could tell her hand was shaking. She took a deep breath. Then another. She looked down at her plate and decided to finish her lunch before walking out. The vegetables on the side were good enough to make up for the tasteless tofu.

"Actually it was organic vegetables that Vic grew up there in Humboldt."

"Sure it was." Miranda picked up her fork and cut a slice of carrot in half. "Pot is kind of old-fashioned, don't you think? Did you know about the pot scandal at Valley School, the year we graduated?"

"No." Ingrid was glad to turn the topic away from her ex-husband's underground business efforts. "I was an outsider. No one ever told me the gossip."

"Of course not. You looked pretty virtuous. *We* had no way of knowing you'd just spent your summer in Haight Ashbury."

Ingrid wondered where Miranda had gotten all this information.

Miranda continued to slice the carrot into smaller and smaller pieces. "Did you ever wonder why you won all those awards at graduation?"

Ingrid shrugged. "In a class of twenty debutantes it's no big deal to be the best at one thing or another. I assumed I exceeded their rather modest expectations."

"Well, you assumed wrong. They caught the officers of the senior class smoking marijuana in one of the girls' rooms. There was never any real question of going to the police. At first the idea was to bar them from standing up to graduate with the class—which was a big deal at Valley, if you recall."

"Yes, I recall." Ingrid smiled, remembering the long white dresses and gloves they had been forced to purchase, and the bouquet of roses each graduate had carried during the ceremony.

"Finally the school relented. Of course, they couldn't give the officers any academic honors. So they gave most of them to you. No one knew you and you seemed conservative. Isn't that funny?" Miranda was not laughing. She was looking at Ingrid carefully.

Miranda had hardly touched her food. Ingrid had cleaned her plate.

"Look, Miranda, those silly prizes meant nothing to me then and they mean nothing to me now. But it bothers you that I won them. Why is that?"

Miranda toyed with her fork for several seconds before replying. "I lived in the dorm. I was the one who told the headmistress what was happening and when and where she could see it for herself. Does that surprise you?"

Not in the least, Ingrid thought grimly. She decided to conclude the conversation as quickly as possible. "Well, you always seemed more fragile than the rest of us, somehow. I guess you thought it would be a good idea to get those girls off that evil weed."

"You know, I'm not sure even now why I did it. But I know I lost more than any one of those other girls. They punished me as if I had been the ringleader." Miranda mimicked a tone of excessive gentility. "'We're sure you wouldn't want to profit from exposing your fellow students' weaknesses, *dear*.' Ha!" She spat out the word.

"Maybe they were afraid the other girls would take it out on you if they found out who turned them in."

"They just didn't want to give me the satisfaction. Oh, I understood, all right. They didn't want their kids using drugs, but they also didn't want some outsider telling them about it. I was better than you in history and French, too. I deserved those awards. To get back at those bitches." Miranda diced her tofu into several pieces, then looked up, suddenly cheerful.

"Hard to escape the past, isn't it? Maybe it's time you paid for some of your past privileges, Ingrid. There's an opportunity coming up this afternoon, and I'd advise you to take advantage of it. All I need is a few hours of your time. If you do what I want you to, you won't get hurt. If you don't cooperate..." Miranda shrugged and ground her fork into the tofu, mashing it flat on the plate.

Ingrid began to gather up her things. She had to get away from Miranda. "Well, it's been nice seeing you again," she said, rising to her feet. But suddenly, over Miranda's shoulder, she saw a woman staring at them through the restaurant window.

"Don't you dare walk out on me now." Miranda's voice was a knife-edge whisper.

Ingrid slid back into her seat and inspected the tablecloth. She waited. The woman was entering the restaurant now. She was a very large, fresh-faced woman somewhere between twenty-five and forty-five; her weight made it difficult to place her age with more precision. She wore the kind of fat fashion-boutique clothing that earnestly strives to make a yellow onion look like a green onion and succeeds in producing a stuffed green pepper look.

"It's just a simple little job I want you to do," Miranda said.

"If it's that simple, why don't you do it yourself?" Ingrid glanced briefly over Miranda's shoulder, not meeting her eyes.

"I can make trouble for you if you don't go along with me on this. You must have known a few toughs with guns in Humboldt. Well, those guys look like weak-kneed amateurs next to the kind of dogs I can sic on you."

The large woman was now pulling her voluminous sweater down over her hips, an action that seemed to parody Miranda's breast-enhancing wriggle. She gauged the path between tables, set her sights on Miranda's back and dove in.

"Don't worry, I'll pay you. A lot of money for very little work. I need someone I can trust. And once you hear some of the alternatives, Ingrid, I think you'll agree to work with me and to be discreet."

"You may not understand this, Miranda, but there are things some people won't do for money."

"I doubt that. If not for money, then to save your neck you'll roll over, I promise you."

Fascinated by the new arrival, Ingrid did not reply, but tried to stare at her water glass to avoid spoiling the large woman's entrance. Out of the corner of her eye, Ingrid could see her squeezing between the tables with her eyes more often shut than open. Once she bumped into the back of a seated diner to avoid brushing against a waiter with a loaded tray. He shot her a look of alarm as he slipped past.

"You understand what kind of money I'm talking about here," Miranda went on, misinterpreting Ingrid's silence. "I've been very careful, and I'm almost ready to go to South America or the Caribbean—it wouldn't do to say where—and live off the interest. All I want you to do is pick something up and deliver it for me this afternoon. You'll be able to make enough money in a few hours to take a year off to travel. Go and take the kind of pictures you can actually sell somewhere."

By the time she reached Miranda, the large woman seemed in imminent danger of exploding. She planted herself solidly against the back of Miranda's chair and grabbed her shoulder roughly.

"All right, Miranda,' she said in a low, tight voice.

Miranda flinched violently at the sudden, unexpected attack. "Oh, hello, Stella" was all she said.

The large woman was on the verge of tears, her words coming out in a rush. "I'm sick of waiting outside. I did what you wanted, but that's the last time. I want my daughter back. She's just a kid and you corrupted her. Don't pretend you don't know where she is." Ingrid noticed that there were dark circles under her eyes.

"Stella, sit down. People are looking at you."

This was quite true. The lunch crowd had not seen such an interesting diversion since the last mountain climber had assaulted the TransAmerica Pyramid Building. But Stella stood fumbling in her purse and did not seem to hear. She extracted an envelope that bulged with a stack of currency.

"Take it all back," she said, slapping it down on the table. "I'm sick of it."

Several bills spilled out onto the tablecloth. Ingrid saw something small and shiny bounce once on the white linen and then disappear from view. Miranda instantly swept the bills back into the envelope and pocketed them, but not before Ingrid noted that the bill on top was a hundred.

Miranda stood up, put on her coat and handed her purse to Ingrid, bending down to hiss, "My friend here is ill. Just pay the check and bring my purse and the receipt to my office after lunch. Make it a little after two. I've got those termination interviews at one and two, but they won't take long. I still want to talk to you, though. You'll cooperate, I'm sure. Once you realize the alternatives, I think we can do business."

The large woman turned to Ingrid, her voice tight with tears. "It's a dirty business, anything she touches. She'll just set you up and ruin you like she's done to me and my daughter."

Miranda took the other woman's arm and said in a grimly solicitous voice. "Don't get too upset, Stella—you'll talk yourself into a stroke."

"You wish."

Ingrid watched them go. Miranda propelled Stella out of the restaurant as though she were a tugboat pushing an ocean liner. They exited one jump ahead of the maitre d', who hovered for a split second, wondering whether to confront the exiting troublemakers, or Ingrid, who still remained at the table. At last he decided that collecting payment for the meal was his first responsibility. He bobbed up at Ingrid's table to inquire if everything was all right.

Ingrid inhaled deeply and realized for the first time that she had been holding her breath. She smiled and said it was fine and whenever her waiter was free, she would like to have a cup of coffee and the check.

The lunch crowd lost interest in Ingrid as she sat staring into the middle distance for several minutes, drinking her coffee. Casually she examined the contents of Miranda's purse.

She could not recall examining another woman's purse before. It was a disappointing experience. The purse was very soft calfskin; the wallet inside matched. The keycase also matched. There was no identification aside from a driver's license and two local credit cards. No other cards or personal address book—maybe Miranda was one of those people who memorized telephone numbers and addresses with ease. There were two hundred-dollar bills and three twenties in the wallet. A small makeup case. Birth control pills. A codeine prescription in the name of one Wanda Sikorski and a tinted vial of unidentified tablets. A contact lens holder and bottles of cleansing and wetting solution for hard contacts. A beautifully embroidered, slightly soiled Kleenex holder. A handful of change in a cheap plastic coin purse.

After she paid the check and left a tip at the table, Ingrid noticed the waiter hovering discreetly in her path. "You left your key miss," he said, holding out a silver door key. "It was next to your plate."

"Oh." Ingrid took the key. "Thank you."

He gave her a conspiratorial smile, and she smiled back uncertainly. She started to put the key into the coin purse section of her wallet, a rectangular snap affair that included her checkbook and a small address book. Then she paused a moment to look at it: an ordinary house key with no chain, a blue plastic Dymo label bearing the raised white numbers 10-12.

"Ten twelve what?" she muttered as she went out the door.

SIX

INGRID STOOD for a moment across the street from the Bramwell Building and took her camera out of her shoulder bag. If she could just take a picture, it would help her feel better. She took out her Nikon, which was loaded with Tri-X, and fitted it with the 105mm lens for outdoor shots. As she took the lens cap off, Flint Senior came walking out of the building as if on cue. He walked slowly and unsteadily—perhaps he was slightly ill or drunk—but with the same absorbed detachment that he displayed sitting at his desk.

Ingrid held her breath, guessed at an exposure and pressed the shutter once. Then she realized that the 105mm was taking her too close. She wanted to get the construction site in the background. She fumbled to put on a normal 50mm lens.

Although he was on the other side of the street, Flint Senior was so shy and wary that she feared he heard the click of her shutter and the whirr of her motor drive as she took several frames of his progress down the street and across Taft Alley. He crossed the barricade of sawhorses that closed off the alley between the Bramwell Building and the hulking metal skeleton of the building next to it.

She hoped the one with the alley in the background came out. She even felt better, especially since the rain began to pour down again as she entered the lobby.

MIRANDA'S DOOR was closed, and the receptionist in Personnel was typing very slowly. There was an African violet that seemed new on her desk. Had it been there before lunch, or were the things springing up with the rain like frilly purple toadstools?

The receptionist pointed to a DO NOT DISTURB sign hanging on the door. It fit around the doorknob, and on the part hanging down a cartoon man held a finger to his lips; "Shhhhhh!" was written above his head, and DO NOT DISTURB was in red underneath the caricature. "She puts that thing out sometimes. Pretty tacky if you ask me," she said. "Her phone light is on, but it must be private, because usually I can hear it when she's got the speaker switched on. Try coming back after two. She's got a two-o'clock appointment and they never stay long."

"That's fine. What's your name, by the way? I'm Ingrid."

"Thanks for asking. Most people never think of it. It's Pam. My friends call me Pammy."

"Does she use that Do Not Disturb sign much?"

Pammy wrinkled her brow. "She's used it a few times since I've been here. She said she hates to be disturbed when she's on the phone or with someone. There. Now she's on a conference call. If you listen you can hear the speaker phone." They listened for a moment and a male voice could be heard through the open transom over the door. The tinny amplification of the speaker phone gave the man's voice a faint echo.

The rainy afternoon gave the penthouse level an air of tranquil smugness, of being warm and dry while others were wet and cold.

"Senior went out half an hour ago," Tanya said by way of greeting. "He said he was off to D.C., so you won't have to worry about him anymore." She seemed angry at Ingrid's lateness but would not stay to hear an apology. She handed Ingrid a few pink slips of paper. "I've got to eat something—I'm starving. Can you catch Junior's phone if it rings? He should be back from lunch real soon, and he always wants to know who it is before he'll talk to them."

Ingrid settled down at her desk. There seemed to be no more work. The huge double doors of Senior's office were closed. She checked the clock on Tanya's desk. It was nearly one thirty. She carefully cleared her desk and straightened everything twice. The key to Flint Senior's office was in the desk drawer. She took the three pink message slips and approached the double doors.

There was no one in sight. She unlocked the doors and walked in. The blinds were drawn, the lights off. The pale shelves loomed at the far end of the room, their row upon row of small fuzzy plants giving the place a laboratory atmosphere. Ingrid shivered.

She put the messages under a paperweight—it was the only thing on the huge polished mahogany desk. A rattlesnake's head gaped inside the plexiglass egg. Ingrid examined it for a moment and suddenly thought of Tony Flint's alligator briefcase.

Ingrid couldn't resist peeking into the executive's bathroom. The door opened easily enough, and she found herself in a thickly carpeted bathroom that looked as if it had never been used. She glanced at the wastebasket and winced, realizing that it had once been the foot of an elephant.

What she saw lying in the plastic liner of the wastebasket stunned her so much that she forgot her original idea of trying the door on the other side of the bathroom, which must lead into the conference room.

Ingrid heard the outer double doors opening. She bolted back into the office and stood near Flint's desk, which fortunately was only a few feet from the entrance.

She must have left the office doors ajar. Flint Junior was peering inside with lively curiosity. His platinum hair seemed almost luminous in the dimness. He smiled at her, revealing beautiful teeth. He stepped into the room with a certain teasing sensuality, as if he would just as soon close and lock the door behind him and attempt a seduction on the spot. If he was gay, he was not exclusively gay. Incredibly spoiled though, with those lazy good looks, hot blue eyes and the law degree as well. In a city like this he could take his pick, men or women. He was like a kid with a credit card for the candy store.

"My father isn't here," he said after staring at her for several seconds with the leisurely fascination of a cat who has cornered a mouse.

"No." Ingrid discovered that she was short of breath. Her heart beat violently. There was something oddly irresistible about this man; and she feared it might be his veiled air of brutality.

"I was looking to see if he had left any more work. For me to type." She stopped and said no more.

Tony looked at the bathroom door and grinned. So he had seen her. He flung the double doors open and gestured for her to go ahead of him out into the secretarial area. Ingrid went to her desk and nervously began piling her purse and Miranda's into one corner of the kneehole of her desk.

"Where's Tanya?"

"She's taking a late lunch. Can I take a message?"

"You're the new girl, aren't you? The one who tangled with the security guard this morning?" He sounded distracted, as if that memory had led to an entirely different train of thought. "Could you come into my office?"

Ingrid looked at the pile of possessions at her feet, hating to go. "Well, Mr. Flint, I'm not too clear on where that is. I really should stay out here to catch the phones."

"No one showed you how to roll them over to the switchboard? I'll show you." Beaming down at her as he stood over her desk, Flint Junior looked formidable. He certainly didn't have his father's problem with eye contact.

"You've got a camera, I see," he said.

Ingrid looked down at her camera bag and realized it was gaping open. She thought she had left it zipped shut. Automatically she checked the contents of Miranda's purse as well to make sure nothing was missing. As far as she could tell, nothing was.

"I take pictures myself," he continued, gazing at her tolerantly. "Sometime I'll show you my prints. There are a few in the office, but I had something else in mind for just now."

He picked up her Nikon and turned it in his hands as if he were about to open it up and expose her new roll of film. Ingrid stood quickly and took the camera away. He surrendered it reluctantly, and their hands brushed as she freed it from his grasp. His hand was warm, and she caught a sudden whiff of bay rum after-shave lotion.

"Okay, now I'll show you how to program the phones so we won't be disturbed." He smiled, leaning quite close to her, and punched in a series of digits on the telephone's button pad. "That should do it." He seemed in no hurry to straighten up and move away. Ingrid felt hypnotized.

"So. Your name is Ingrid." He moved away at last, and Ingrid feared she might lurch sideways, as if she had been leaning on his presence for support. "I get quite a lot of work done around here, Ingrid, contrary to popular opinion. Not when my father's around though—don't want to spoil the old playboy image. If he didn't have me to worry about, I don't know how he'd get through the day. It may drive him crazy, but it makes him feel *so* superior. Come on, bring your pad. I want to dictate a memo."

"Now I really wish you hadn't said that." Ingrid realized she was starting to relax a little around him with all that chatter about his playboy image. But you had to draw the line somewhere. "I'm sorry to disappoint you, but I don't take shorthand."

He had turned to go back to his office. Now he turned back, stared at her and raised an eyebrow. "Well, suppose you just try writing *real* fast."

Ingrid smiled grimly. "Nope. Sorry. Every time someone asks me to write down his thoughts—and it usually is a he—it just never works."

"Look, it's just a few things off the top of my head."

"It really is a few things? Good. Then it won't take you long to write them down yourself. It will help you get your thoughts in order. Don't worry if your handwriting is bad. I'll put it on a diskette. You can have as many drafts as you like. But dictation? No. No way."

"Look, your time is worth what, ten or fifteen dollars an hour? My time is currently billing at a hundred fifty dollars. Let's not waste our time, okay?"

"You're the one who's wasting time right now. Dictation is ego massage, and if I wanted to get into that line of work I'd charge more than fifteen dollars an hour."

"I'll bet you do. But I won't pay it."

They stood facing each other for a second.

Tanya came in and stared at them in amazement. "Tony, I need to talk to you about Frank Bates—you know, the messenger," she said, edging between them. "That woman in Personnel seems to think she can fire him."

Ingrid was the first to break eye contact. "Hi, Tanya. You can have your boss back now."

Flint Junior turned on his heel, "Come on, Tanya. We'll talk in my office. Oh, and bring your pencil. I need a little secretarial assistance."

Tanya took a stenographic pad and pencil from her desk top. "What is going *on* here?" she murmured softly as if to herself. "Everybody's gone crazy today." A moment later the office door closed behind them.

Ingrid sat for a few minutes, trying to calm down. She was so rattled that it took her a few seconds to realize what had upset her originally, before Tony Flint had interrupted her.

What was a disposable hypodermic needle doing in Flint Senior's wastebasket? Ingrid recoiled from needles with a primitive reflex. Had Junior come in to retrieve the needle, or had he seen her go in and come to prevent her from finding it? Or did it belong to the old man?

Ingrid was too restless to sit still for long. With the phones programmed to ring on the switchboard, she could safely leave the area and try again to return Miranda's purse. It was just two o'clock now. She had to either get her time card signed by five o'clock or agree to come back the next day if she meant to pry a paycheck out of her agency.

Pammy smiled a bit stiffly when Ingrid returned to Personnel. She seemed to have picked up a head cold or an allergy in the past forty-five minutes. She was rubbing at her nose with a Kleenex. She seemed nervous now, ready to jump at the slightest noise. She pointed to the closed door with the DO NOT DISTURB sign. Glancing around, Ingrid saw Franklin Bates fuming in eloquent silence in a chair at the far end of the reception area.

"She's *still* on the phone?" Ingrid exclaimed in mock horror, hoping to lighten the atmosphere.

"Uh, no," Pammy said nervously. "She finished that one, but now she's on her private line."

Indeed, the speaker phone had stopped its echoing amplification. "Something important must have come up," Pammy said. "She hardly ever uses that private line. She's even missing her two-o'clock appointment," Pammy said, indicating Franklin Bates, who was now staring at an invisible spot on the carpet, restraining an obvious urge to break the table.

"I don't know what to tell you," the receptionist said, holding back a nervous giggle. She almost seemed to be high on something. "I hope she finishes soon," Pammy continued, "but that silly sign was out again when I came back from the john." She indicated the cardboard sign.

Ingrid wondered what had happened to the angry Stella. "Was anyone with her when she came back from lunch?"

"No. She had a one-o'clock interview with that guy with the earring from Word Processing. *That* only took a few minutes. She had that conference call, the one she was on when you came in before. Then she came out of the office to put a package in the out basket for messenger pickup just as I went down the hall. I couldn't have been gone more than a few minutes, but she said she'd catch the phone till I got back. She must have put the sign out again. When I came back in her office door slammed shut—really slammed. The minute I came in." She was indignant.

Ingrid nodded sympathetically, although she doubted that Pammy's feelings had been too hurt.

"It does sound rude. Maybe she tried to close it and it just slammed by accident," Ingrid said gently.

Pammy looked doubtful. "I had to turn away that older woman, the blonde with the pursed lips? Nell something. She called up just as I came back and asked me to buzz Miss Falk. I wasn't about to bother Miss Falk after she'd just practically slammed the door in my face. I mean I just walked in; it wasn't as if I sneaked up to listen at the crack. I told her she could come up and buzz in herself if she wanted to talk to Miss Falk. She said it could wait."

"Well, I'd better wait here, so as not to miss her," Ingrid said.

Something crashed behind Ingrid and both women flinched. It was Frank Bates smashing his fist into the coffee table in front of him. He cast a corrosive look at both women and stood up. "I'll be leaving now. She can reach me at home." He closed the door behind him carefully and firmly.

Pammy cast Ingrid a look of desperate relief. The girl even got up from her desk and they both inspected the table for damage, finding none. From the way she dabbed at her nose, with a tissue, Ingrid wondered if Pammy had shed a few tears. It couldn't be that scary. Frank Bates wasn't angry at *her*.

"He was early for his interview, he'd been waiting twenty minutes," she said, pushing a hairpin into one of several strands of hair that had crept down onto her neck. "It's so quiet here, it's getting on my nerves. Miss Falk hasn't buzzed or come out since I came back in. The phone light is still on except . . . It's so quiet. I guess I'm used to the speaker phone."

Ingrid stood close to the door and listened. She heard an odd sound, like something rocking randomly back and forth on the hard surface of a desk.

SEVEN

"IS IT LOCKED?" Ingrid indicated the door.

"I don't know—I didn't try it."

"Okay. Let's see." Ingrid turned the knob. "Not locked." She went in. "Miranda?"

Miranda's office was at the opposite corner of the building from Flint's. Ingrid could see the ironwork of the construction project through the eastern window to one side of Miranda's desk. The room was cold. Raindrops dotted the sill of the open window.

Abruptly, the door slammed shut behind Ingrid. She flinched and looked behind her. Nothing. The wind through the open window jangled the venetian blind.

"The draft," Ingrid said aloud.

There didn't seem to be anyone there to hear her.

She decided to put Miranda's purse on her chair. But where was Miranda?

The only movement she could see as she cast around the room was that of a coffeecup lying on its side at the edge of the desk, rocking slightly in the wind. That was the faint sound she had heard. The coffee had spilled down the side of the desk and soaked into the rug. The telephone receiver had been taken out of its cradle and lay on its side unattended.

Pammy opened the door cautiously and went for the phone with a receptionist's trained reflexes. She gingerly put the receiver to her ear as Ingrid moved farther into the room, chilled by the open window.

The wall on one side of Miranda's desk was covered from floor to ceiling with mirrored tile. The wall on the other side displayed a chart with SUPPORT STAFF VACATION SCHEDULE lettered on top.

Approaching the window, Ingrid noticed a white metal cart with several shelves full of African violets. The cart wide-angled clumsily away from the open window. The violets were immaculately tended; most of them were blooming.

The old-fashioned side hinges allowed the windows to open outward like double doors by means of a metal crank at the corner of each casement. A thick steel rod extended from the lower sill to the frame of each windowpane to prop it open; there was also a simple lock along the side to pinch it shut. Each of the two casements was five feet tall and nearly three feet wide. They were separated by a few inches of window frame, and a honeycomb pattern of embedded wire mesh reinforced the glass.

Ingrid looked at the skyscraper going up across the alley. It would have unopenable windows and canned air, but the building's huge steel skeleton looked close enough for a workman to be able to lean out from his girder and swing into the room.

No workers were visible on the twelfth floor of the construction project. Had the rainstorm driven them home, or were they merely obscured from view?

The spilled coffee and abandoned phone made her uneasy.

"Ingrid?" Pammy was holding Miranda's telephone receiver out and staring at it in puzzlement. "Listen to this."

"What is it?" Ingrid returned to Pammy's side. For some reason, she hesitated to touch the receiver, but as she came close, she could hear the precise, ladylike monologue that issued from it: "The time is two thirteen exactly. Beep. The time is two thirteen and ten seconds. Beep. The time is two thirteen and twenty seconds. Beep."

The only other sound in the room was the rattle of the venetian blind in the wind. Ingrid shook her head at the time lady's voice and went to close the window.

She glanced down as she leaned gingerly out over the knee-level sill. A dozen floors down in Taft Alley something colorful rose up for a second in an updraft of wind. A speckling of rain made Ingrid blink. She saw the crumpled figure in the alley below the fire escape. That flutter must be her red designer scarf.

Ingrid backed away from the window in such a hurry that she almost knocked over Miranda's typewriter stand.

Then she saw it. A handwritten note on Miranda's buff memo paper had been rolled into the platen of the typewriter. Despite its place in the typewriter there was no typing on the note—only handwriting.

A bold scrawl in felt-tip pen read, "I'm sorry to have to do this but I have no choice. As Ever, MF."

EIGHT

THE GRAY-FACED DETECTIVE handed Ingrid her driver's license and sat staring at her discontentedly. "No priors," he said at last. "I'm not real happy with you, Ms. Hunter. You seem to think you're some kind of hotshot women's libber assaulting a security guard. Claude's a retired cop, you know."

"Well, Claude should retire from copping feels on women he hasn't been properly introduced to. I defended myself. Other people may do the same. You're not going to suggest that he thinks he has an assault case against me."

The detective cleared his throat awkwardly. "Hard to say on that one, could go either way. But yes, we've heard about his reckless handling of the ladies. Let's get back to Ms. Falk. She never married, did she? Did she seem at all depressed to you during your lunch?"

Ingrid frowned. Of course he would imagine that Miranda would kill herself for lack of male companionship.

"We talked about her job. About how things had changed since the last time we met."

"She didn't say what she had been doing or mention any names?"

"No." Ingrid couldn't bring herself to bring up the key; that would have gone against almost two decades of passive resistance to anyone in authority.

"Did she say she'd been lonely these days, or hint about any problems?"

"We did talk about how she faked a suicide attempt once. To force her father to give her the money to have her nose fixed."

Suddenly the detective perked up a bit. His mouth twitched into something approaching a smile.

"Why didn't she get her boobs done? She could have made a lot more money that way."

As far as Ingrid was concerned, the interview was over. She felt like leaving, but remained where she was more from exhaustion than anxiety. She was almost too tired to care whether they believed her or arrested her. She answered the rest of the questions as minimally as possible. The detective seemed to be listening for some distant message.

Ingrid mentioned Miranda's encounter with Stella, which came out sounding like a tiff between bickering girl friends. He brushed the money in the envelope aside. "What we didn't find on her purse, we found on her person," he said. "Looks like somebody cashed her Christmas bonus check, huh? Well, she didn't kill herself for lack of money."

"It sounds as if you think she killed herself?"

"Hard to say. But it points in that direction. There aren't too many options. She jumped, she fell or she was pushed. We'll check the note with samples of her handwriting. You say she tried suicide before. We'll check the records in L.A. on that and check the hotline up here. You say she stayed on the phone line throughout her first suicide attempt. Maybe she was bluffing someone this time and they called her bluff. Maybe listening to the time lady reminded her she was getting older every day." He winked and consulted his notebook. "Maybe we can find out who she was talking to earlier. Maybe someone saw her take the dive. So far it looks as if those construction workers across the way were all near the center of the structure, keeping out of the rain when it happened, but we'll keep checking." He shrugged. "If the receptionist is right and no one came in all . . . Hell, maybe she just got depressed. Happens a lot around the holidays. Ugly way to do it, though. . . . Someone will have to clean that alley up some."

Ingrid shuddered.

The detective seemed properly encouraged. He tried once more. "You're sure Miss Falk didn't mention any boyfriend or roommate?"

"No."

Ingrid was released after promising to come in and sign a statement and exchanging a business card with "Ingrid Hunter—Photographer" printed on it for one of the detective's cards with the Homicide Department number at the Hall of Justice. She left him holding her card by the edges. He stared at the card as if it might have bloody fingerprints.

When Ingrid reached the street level, she realized that her time card was still unsigned. She sighed, printed "supervisor unavailable" and signed her own name underneath. Two policemen checked her off a list and unlocked the street door to let her out. She was glad Claude was not on duty. Attack on a security guard, indeed!

The afternoon rain had stopped, and the air was warmer under the shelter of clouds. The streets shone black as polished leather under the streetlamps. Taft Alley was sealed with a yellow plastic ribbon with black letters POLICE LINE DO NOT CROSS chasing each other over and over again.

Small knots of people strolled past. In the Union Square area several blocks away, Christmas shoppers were massing for an assault. By contrast the financial-district crowds looked relieved. They had worked late and now were free for the evening or at least for a dinner break. They were on their way to or from pleasure, chattering as they crossed Ingrid's path with umbrellas furled and raincoats flapping.

She walked up Montgomery rapidly. Up ahead, the higher reaches of Telegraph Hill were cut off by fog that leaned on the building tops. Red and yellow traffic lights blinked at intersections, and an occasional taxicab whizzed past. The reed-thin Southeast Asian kids pawing through plastic garbage sacks for aluminum cans stamped each can flat with a cheerful shout.

Ingrid realized she was ravenously hungry. But the photo session with Rosemary Tanner was important; it was nearly seven o'clock already. She hoped she wouldn't be late to Rosemary Tanner's office.

Rosemary Tanner was a brilliant woman. Her talents had been barely tapped while her husband was alive, when she had organized all his social activities and managed his alcoholism at the same time. At last he had totally collapsed, thoughtfully managing to have a fatal heart attack soon after. He had left Rosemary in charge of his substantial real estate holdings—a modern gold mine in a city of perpetually limited land mass with water boundaries on three sides, steep hills throughout, and the constant threat of earthquakes.

Tanner was such a success that her local newsletter column had been syndicated in a national magazine.

Out of what seemed like four billion photographers in all stages of professionalism in San Francisco, Ingrid was the only one who had thought of joining Rosemary Tanner's women's network to meet people who wanted pictures.

Her donation of her services to shoot luncheon guest speakers and newsletter mug shots paid off. Some of the women liked her work; Ingrid had done two portrait sittings and a catalogful of antique furniture for a store owner. A discarded newspaper clinging to a lamppost reminded her that even the gallery opening where she had met Jason Grapelli had been a photo job for a club member. A sharp pang of desire began to displace the more mundane sensation of hunger as she remembered the pressure of Jason's body against her own.

She had been strangely moved to hear how he rescued his art materials from the world of garbage and put them together. She knew what it felt like to live on handouts and to feel discarded. She responded instinctively to the urgency with which Jason performed every action, from talking about his artwork to making love. He was a handsome devil. But so selfish. Except in bed.

Ingrid turned right on Pacific. Rosemary Tanner's building was brick, a former warehouse. In the 1950s, when Rosemary's husband had bought the building, it had been a practical location for a company headquarters. Now these warehouses stored architects, decorators and trendy law firms.

The street door operated on a buzzer. Rosemary's secretary, a lithe Frenchman, verified Ingrid's identity. Behind him stretched a carpet of arctic-ice pale green. Etched and frosted glass dividers sliced the former main floor into small office areas. The original brick interior walls and wooden beams had been painted white. Steep carpeted ramps wove among the cubicles and created different levels. The toboggan teams would be coming through any moment.

Several crystalline cubicles hung from the walls like observation platforms and could be approached through an off-center staircase of polished-metal slabs. Ingrid hung on to a chrome handrail as she followed the Frenchman's admirable derrière to Rosemary Tanner's office. Hovering over the main floor, her office had a skylight an artist would have killed for, though tonight fog dimmed the city lights. A piece of convoluted sculpture rested on a stand near the center of the room.

The few walls were plain and white. Good. Ingrid could bounce her strobe off that white ceiling; maybe clip it to some handy piece of furniture. She missed her tripod for the second strobe, but it was too awkward to carry around all day through the financial district.

It took a moment to find Rosemary. The white leather executive chair was empty behind the chrome-and-glass executive desk.

Aha. On an evergreen sofa at the far wall sat Rosemary, coiled like a cobra. She had just come from a session with a really good hairstylist. Ingrid decided to take a color shot of her on the sofa.

"So Ingrid, we meet again."

"Hello, Rosemary. I'll try to finish up quickly here so you can get on to your dinner party. Let me take a light reading. This sofa is great—I'll try some color shots." Ingrid realized that she was chattering a bit, mostly in an effort to keep her energy from waning. She felt suddenly very cold, tired and broke.

Rosemary's pale-green, button-flat eyes did not move, but she gestured with an elegantly manicured hand. "Would you like a Campari and soda? That's what I'm drinking."

"Just soda, thanks. I don't drink liquor."

"Henri?" Rosemary raised her eyebrows. The Frenchman seemed to have lingered for that very purpose. He went to a cabinet, opened what appeared to be a small refrigerator in its antique wood base and poured Ingrid a cola over ice cubes in a cut-crystal glass.

"Thank you, Henri. I'll ring if I need anything more."

The Frenchman seemed amused by her manner. Ingrid envied his self-possession; he must have served an apprenticeship as a waiter.

"Beautiful old building here." Ingrid hated the things she found herself saying when she photographed people. But the pictures went more smoothly when she kept up a wall of soothing chatter. "Did you decorate it yourself? It's very interesting, this mixture of high tech and antique."

"Thank you, I think. Yes, I did put together the things in this building. Did you know that I was on the board of the heritage committee? You've heard of Preserve Our Past?"

"No." Didn't the lady do *anything* that didn't lend itself to abbreviation? "Tilt your head please, no, to the left. Chin down. But this building must be one of your projects."

"Well, it's post-earthquake but early century. Just young enough for people to think they'd like to tear it down. There are quite a few from that period around here."

"You must know the Bramwell Building then. I worked there today."

"Really." Rosemary suddenly leaned forward, blurring the picture Ingrid was trying to take. "Tell me about the murder there! You must have been right in the thick of it."

"Well, it was an accidental death or maybe a suicide— the police didn't seem too sure. I hadn't realized it was in the news yet." Ingrid had now exhausted the possibilities of the sofa. She wondered if Rosemary had already consumed too many glasses of Campari to walk.

"Oh, I didn't get it from the media, dear. I have my own sources. Of course I knew the Bramwells, and it seems I've known Atherton Flint forever."

"An old beau, perhaps?" Ingrid shamelessly tried to coax a flirtatious light into Rosemary's slightly hooded eyes.

"Hardly." Rosemary spoke sharply, but her expression was wistful, and interesting enough to cause Ingrid to take another shot, though she knew she would never be able to use it. The effect was too melancholy.

"Flinty never let himself care about anything—too distracting to the career." Rosemary broke off and put down her drink. "Still, the Bramwell Building is one of POP's victories, and we owe it all to Flinty, so I shall speak no evil of him. Of course, that foreign money got the building next door. I only hope it falls away from the Bramwell Building in the next earthquake."

"I'll drink to that." Ingrid sipped her soda and began to fear that these pictures would not prove usable. Rosemary's different expressions all had a carnivorous glint that would not do at all.

Ingrid was beginning to feel her sleep debt keenly. Right now, all she wanted to do was curl up on the rug and sleep.

Her martial arts training saved her. She took a balanced stance on the mirror-polished parquet floor and breathed deeply, mentally thanking Ito-*sensei* for his stern insistence that students work on the slippery floor as well as the mats.

"Let's try another location. You have some really fine artwork over there," Ingrid lied. She could scarcely see the paintings; the room was like a football field. The glacial far wall held several framed paintings, each lit by its own spotlight.

She hiked over to the nearest picture and planted herself in front of it. Within the elaborate frame was a watercolor with fragments of trash embedded in the shards of a smashed mirror. A scrawl of spray paint across the right corner read, "j g graffiti."

"Oh, I know this artist—Jason Grapelli... well I guess he calls himself graffiti."

Ingrid turned to face Rosemary and found the woman was staring at her, white with rage. "You *know* him, do you? *How* do you know him?"

Ingrid resisted a temptation to say, "Let me count the ways." Could Rosemary be jealous? It certainly looked like it. Ingrid shrugged. "I met him at Madeline Trumball's gallery opening. I've seen some of his work. I don't know if you've seen the kinds of things he's done lately. They're all done with mirrors."

"Not all. Some are done with other people's money."
She paused and seemed to collect herself. "But let's talk
about you. Where have you been all weekend anyway?"

Ingrid had hoped to bring Rosemary out of that fetal
posture and bring a little light into her face. Rosemary rose
smoothly from the sofa and headed for the rosewood desk,
away from the wall of artwork. Her platinum-blond hair
caught the light but didn't move, damped down by a thick
coat of lacquer.

Ingrid shrugged and followed her. *Fine,* she told Rosemary silently, *snarl if you must, but give me some expression that's slightly warmer than a black widow spider
picking her teeth, while waiting for the next gentleman
caller.*

Rosemary settled herself on one corner of her desk. She
hopped up and crossed her legs like a 1940s cheesecake
model, raising the hem of her green silk dress a few inches
above her knees.

"Let's hear some more about this Bramwell Building
murder, Ingrid."

Ingrid clipped her second strobe to the gooseneck of a
chrome floor lamp. Looking at Rosemary almost solely
through the lens, she framed her against the closed curtains behind the desk.

"Accident or suicide you mean."

Rosemary snorted skeptically. "They all say that."

"But wait a minute, Rosemary, she mentioned your
name to me. She said you had invited her to some of the
Professional Women's luncheons."

"Did she? Yes. We met when we were in the same business. She worked for another realtor—to use the word
loosely. The man is actually a slumlord. In fact she asked
me about you and I had to say you've taken some very fine
pictures for us. Where did *you* meet her? I've forgotten."

"We went to school together briefly."

"Ah, yes, well, I doubt if anyone who knew her would
be surprised if a boyfriend or ex-business associate had
shoved her out the window. Who was with her before she
died?"

Ingrid listened with half an ear. She had a few frames now that looked better. "All I know is that the receptionist said no one came out of the room after two P.M., and there are only two ways out of that office: past the receptionist or out the window."

Ingrid walked around to the other side. The Trans-America Pyramid loomed a few blocks away through the skylight, its nighttime necklace of lights only slightly dimmed by fog.

"What were you doing over at Bramwell, when you weren't discovering bodies—you didn't think I knew that, did you?" The subject's expression had livened up a great deal. Her eyes almost sparkled now. "I'm on a few boards of directors over there. This is a very small town, Ingrid, if you travel in certain circles. I might be able to help you."

Ingrid held her breath and snapped what looked like her best shot of the evening. A picture Rosemary's eager readers might interpret as a tough but kindly woman exec offering advice.

"Well, Rosemary"—Ingrid started packing her equipment away; she no longer cared about anything except getting home to bed—"I get the money to pay my rent from my honest toil as a word processor for temporary agencies. You know, as in computerized typing pool."

"And never be ashamed of it my dear. As you say, it is honest work. Don't worry, I won't tell the Professional Women."

"Thanks." There was irony in Ingrid's voice. The woman she trusted least in that organization now knew her secret.

"I'll make sure that you stay in our little network. But do let me know if you need an attorney or a bail bondsman. When you come with the pictures, we'll talk about people jumping out of windows. Death is an invaluable source of gossip, quite fascinating, so long as it happens to someone one doesn't know too well."

"You probably knew her better than I did. I hadn't even seen Miranda for fifteen years."

"Don't sell yourself short, dear. You may know more than you realize."

Ingrid shrugged, turned and saw that Henri was waiting in the doorway. He shrugged also, but with far more expressive body language.

In thirty seconds Ingrid and her equipment were on Pacific Avenue. In another hour she was home and in bed, alone. Asleep at last, but not for long.

NINE

SHE WAS AWAKENED at ten P.M. by an emergency call from the gallery owner whose opening she had photographed the weekend before. Madeline Trumbull was a flirtatious woman in her late sixties. Although she seemed totally disorganized, she managed to have dyed her hair a different shade every time Ingrid saw her. Perhaps her hairdresser kept track. Madeline had decided that several clients at a small dinner party would like to have their pictures taken with the artists whose work they were buying.

"Could you come over right away? I know it's late and on short notice, but the food is excellent and I'll pay double what I did last time for your pictures."

Ingrid had awakened feeling terrifically hungry. Her refrigerator contained only two eggs, a pint of questionable milk and half a twenty-roll brick of Vericolor-3. It seemed easier to climb into the Mustang and ease it up to Nob Hill than to go out and buy food for herself. Her camera bag was already packed, and she could just put on her black jumpsuit (she had removed the JOE'S SERVICE STATION logo), loop a string of turquoise beads around her neck and go. She looked presentable, she decided, although every muscle in her body protested. Getting too old for that party-all-night, work-all-day stuff, was the message.

The twenty guests at the dinner party were all of retirement age and heavy drinkers. She hoped they might be counted upon to pass out early, but she had underestimated their staying power.

Some of the guests were artists, although Ingrid could not imagine which, since they all looked like Chamber of Commerce material to her sleep-deprived eyes. All had clear-cut ideas on how to be photographed. Tonight Madeline had copper-penny-red hair—to match her dress—and she made it a point to interrupt with cheerfully manipulative suggestions whenever Ingrid was taking a picture.

One beaming old gentleman adopted Ingrid. He remained at her elbow offering a variety of food and drink and occasionally hugging her with a warmth that caused his wife, hovering nearby, to quiver with the effort of suppressing her rage. Ingrid made a few attempts to fend him off, but the room was too small and the food and drink too welcome.

It was nearly one o'clock when Ingrid shook Madeline's soft wrinkled hand and escaped into the night, promising to deliver the stately yet reasonably candid photographs soon to her hostess. She was sleepy enough to consider pulling over for a nap, but it seemed easier to keep driving.

An odd light loomed in the sky as she made the left turn from Pine Street onto Van Ness. The low ceiling of fog seemed to be lit with a pinkish glow, reminding her of the Los Angeles horizon, which is always pink at night through the smog.

Fire! The thought woke her up. She circled around to Octavia. The fire must be quite near her apartment building. And she already had color film with her. What an opportunity!

Ingrid had never sued for admission into the guild of photographers who specialize in pictures of accident and injury. But a fire within walking distance of her apartment!

Without taking her eyes from the road, she took out her camera and looped the strap around her neck with her right hand, gripping the steering wheel with her left. Ingrid had photographed a fire at night once before with black-and-white film. The pictures had been too murky. She had made some mistakes in exposure, and she hoped she had learned something.

Ingrid pondered possible exposure times as she parked the Mustang just short of the corner of Octavia and Oak. She fished her 200mm zoom lens from her shoulder bag to replace the 85mm she had been using for the party shots. It was dark enough to load film in the car. As she started walking toward the fire, she saw that the commotion was in the next block. Her own block.

A wave of uneasiness tempered her excitement.

Rounding the corner onto Oak Street, she saw it. She began to run.

It was her own building.

Flames shot out of the windows on one of the upper floors. All thoughts of photographs were driven out of her mind by the thought of losing everything in a fire. The sum total of her earthly possessions, brought down from Humboldt County in the trunk and backseat of the Mustang, was in the burning apartment.

She saw Mrs. Phelps standing solidly on the sidewalk near where the firemen had pushed the crowd back. The manager, like many in the crowd, wore a robe and slippers and clutched an armful of papers and framed photographs, obviously rescued from the fire.

"Mrs. Phelps, what happened?" Ingrid approached gently as the old woman gazed at the fire as if hypnotized.

Mrs. Phelps turned and looked at Ingrid for a moment. Then she dropped everything and flung herself upon Ingrid, arms windmilling in frantic attack. Ingrid held her off as much as possible, deflecting her blows with a circular side motion.

"You started this," Mrs. Phelps screamed. "It's all your fault. I warned you about that heater. If you're going to have guests, or leave the place alone, the least you could do is think about not killing other people while you're away!"

A tall, portly man with a large mustache put his arms around Mrs. Phelps and pulled her away gently. Ingrid thought she recognized him as the man across the hall—the daytime bartender at MacHarg's Bar.

"She's overwrought," the man explained gently. "They say the fire started in your room. You'd better find some other place to stay. No one will be able to sleep here tonight, or maybe ever again." Mrs. Phelps continued to glare at Ingrid but allowed herself to be walked over to a safe doorstep to sit down. Another tenant, an ebony-dark firmly upright woman in a house dress and slippers, gathered up Mrs. Phelps's small pile of possessions and pressed them back into her arms again.

Ingrid walked numbly to her car with too many questions throbbing in her head. Too much had happened in too short a space of time.

Her sweaty encounters with Jason. Seeing Miranda after all these years, then finding her body a few hours later. The man she had seen who looked like Vic driving the brown van—had it been her friend Spyder's van? Now this fire. If her sanity had been the least bit shaky, the whole mess might have congealed into a plot against her. Instead, she shelved all of it for lack of coherent data. Right now she only wanted to sleep. For a moment she even thought of calling Jason Grapelli in his Sea Cliff mansion.

Too soon for that, she decided. She would decide later where she stood with Jason. Rosemary's anger certainly made her curious. Usually the best way to get Ingrid to do something was to tell her not to.

Fortunately there was Carmen. Carmen didn't get home from work until three. Still, Ingrid could think of no one else in the city who would welcome her. She put her camera back in its case and stumbled back to the Mustang.

Ingrid was dozing in her car in front of Carmen's house where Anza Street dead-ends at Sutro Heights Park when Carmen tapped on the window to waken her and bring her in out of the cold.

Carmen's house faced Sutro Heights Park, with its thinning stand of eucalyptus and cypress trees and statues, the remains of Adolph Sutro's ruined pleasure gardens. Below the cliffs and across the Great Highway, the hoarse barking of sea lions on their offshore rocks sounded above the waves, like baritone seagulls or dogs in a distant echo chamber, punctuated by an occasional questing fog horn. Ingrid had not quite reached the westernmost edge of the continent. The Pacific Ocean was still two blocks away.

TEN

Tuesday, December 20

SAN FRANCISCO WEATHER comes in slices dealt out at random throughout the year, with the wind doing the cutting. By the next afternoon the wind from the ocean had scraped the clouds out of the hard blue sky, and the low winter sun heated Carmen's living room until it became a drowsy hothouse.

Ingrid and Carmen sat and drank red tea, insulated for the moment from the winds outside and from the sudden death and damage Ingrid had seen the day before. They talked about the fire and about suicide.

"Miranda told me she used pills the first time she tried to kill herself. I just don't understand how she could do it this time in such a painful way," Ingrid said.

"We don't know that she killed herself. It might have been an accident."

"There was a note, Carmen."

Carmen's husband, a policeman, had killed himself with his service revolver one night in the very room where they now sat. Archie O'Rourke had not left a note. When Ingrid asked Carmen why she stayed in such a place, Carmen simply replied that it was hers.

Carmen was about Ingrid's age, but several inches shorter, with a heart-shaped face, generous curves and a laugh as rich as a bakery shop. She dyed her long black hair red, and the thickness of it ensured that there were always two or three shades in transition. Her narrow, long nose detoured slightly, as if it had been broken. It had been, twice, by her late husband.

A few weeks after her husband's funeral Carmen had gathered her courage and had attended the support group for battered women where she met Ingrid. Before long the two had created their own private support network. For the past few years it had worked very well indeed.

Ingrid had taken up aikido and Carmen had begun to weave, first rag rugs and then yarn hangings of violently warring colors. Sometimes when the weather was good, she sold her work at a table in front of the Cliff House a few blocks away.

"Ingrid, please stay as long as you want. After a month I'll start to charge rent, of course. But look out, you can get hooked on the sea air." Carmen poured more herbal tea. Ingrid could see she was going to have to buy some coffee if Carmen would allow it, or hide it if she wouldn't. "I'm hooked on the park across the way for my silly old tom-cat—isn't that true, Mugwort?"

Mugwort the cat sat on Ingrid's lap, accepting Carmen's caresses while staring into Ingrid's eyes. Roughly the same shape and weight as a bowling ball, he was covered with long black hair and had a small fox-pointed head with a clownish ruff around his neck. He continued his sultry gaze, put one black paw between Ingrid's breasts and laid his head beside it.

"Faithless, but charming, isn't he?" Ingrid said.

"He's a total infidel, Ingrid. He'll sleep on the sofa with you when he feels like it. But he's got most of my neighbors feeding him, and sometimes they can persuade him to stay the night."

"Speaking of spending the night..." Ingrid said as they heard the sound of a key in the lock, and Spyder let himself into the apartment.

Ingrid had to take responsibility for introducing Carmen to Spyder, an old friend from Humboldt. She had not expected them to fall in love. Sypder was about five years younger than they were, but his incurable romanticism made him seem even younger than that. To Ingrid's surprise they had paired off quite naturally. Given the average duration of love affairs in San Francisco, Ingrid had decided to reserve judgment in hopes of retaining both friendships, when and if a breakup should occur.

Carmen greeted Spyder now with languorous affection similar to Mugwort's. During the first year of her friendship with Ingrid, Carmen had begun to play albums from the Berkeley Radical Feminist Collective School of Music. Her affair with Spyder had distracted her; now, in a slightly more domestic phase, she usually had Baroque chamber music or classical guitar on the stereo.

Spyder stood in the doorway, his bewildered grin reflecting his eternal surprise at Carmen's warm greeting. He was a tall, thin man with curly brown hair. All his limbs were elongated, as if he had been built an average size and stretched. He wore a corduroy jacket over his blue jeans in a grudging concession to business attire. Ingrid smiled, thinking first of Jason's polished charm and then, oddly, of her ex-husband, Victor.

Spyder had originally been Victor's friend back in Humboldt. Ingrid knew him as a fellow photographer and had gotten to know him again later when he called up to ask if she knew of a darkroom in San Francisco and they ended up taking the same photography courses at San Francisco State. Ingrid wanted to ask Spyder about the van, but she had to tread cautiously. Although Spyder seemed to say whatever came into his head, there were some things he refused to talk about at all.

However, Spyder was not often sullen. Indeed he was almost too tenderhearted at times. He pushed her to sell her pictures and held back his own. Spyder specialized in journalistic photographs of embarrassment in action. At State he had had a rare gift for catching professors scratching indelicate itches, or marching-band members who were out of step. He seemed to want to maintain an ironical distance from his subjects.

Spyder was carrying copies of both daily papers, the *Chronicle* and the *Examiner,* which he brandished at Ingrid behind Carmen's back. "Look, Ingrid, your apartment building is in the news." He opened up one of the papers and followed as Carmen led the way to the kitchen at the back of the house, carrying her cup and the teapot.

"I just came from your place, Ingrid. I drove over to see if you were all right, after I couldn't get you on the phone. It looked like the whole building was burned out. So I figured you'd be here. Are you okay? Did you—"

Ingrid held up a hand. "No, I did not get a picture of the fire, and yes, thank you. I'm fine. I was out when it happened, but the building manager literally attacked me when I got there, claiming it was started by my electric heater, which I don't think is possible because I *always* unplug it. Worse yet, Spyder, someone jumped out the window at the law firm where I was temping yesterday, and I didn't get a picture of *that* either."

"Too bad. Ben Resnick would have bought both pictures. You know how he is: The only things he hates more than losing a low-income apartment building like yours are those financial district high-rises—he'd like to see someone jump out of one."

Ben Resnick's weekly *Bay Area Gadfly* stood squarely against tearing down old buildings to put up crackerbox condos and downtown high-rises. The *Gadfly* was pro-poor people, pro-low income housing, pro-local beer and chocolate cookies.

She and Spyder were friendly rivals for a photo-stringer job that Resnick had dangled in front of them enticingly. Neither expected it to materialize in the next decade, but it gave them an excuse to keep showing and sometimes selling photos to Resnick.

They both sat at the kitchen table as Carmen dropped more dried red flowers into the black iron teapot. Spyder seized Mugwort and attempted to pet him. The cat freed himself, weaving just out of reach of Spyder's hands, and headed for the open window, tail lifted gleefully.

"Don't mess with him—he only flirts with women. There's more food in it for him that way." Carmen liked to chide Spyder, and he seemed to enjoy it. "So, you were saying, Spyder? You must have a secret, you look so smug."

"Well, there's no use hiding it any longer." Spyder's long-jawed face twisted in an uncertain smile and he shook his head before speaking. "It's your husband, Ingrid."

"My what? I have no husband. Haven't for three years—well two years technically." Ingrid tried to speak lightly, but a nagging memory shot through her like the thrill of pain from a sore tooth. "He's been driving your van, hasn't he? And he's following me—I *thought* I recognized him."

Spyder looked away and rubbed his jaw. "Yes, that's true, Ing. We kept in touch. After he got out of jail, all he wanted was to see you. Some people might find that kind of touching."

Ingrid stood and walked over to the kitchen doorway. She stood for several seconds, gripping the door frame, unable to respond. Had she been thinking of Victor with a certain nostalgic lust a few moments ago? Suddenly a powerful rush of confusion swept over her, and she didn't know what she felt.

"You could at least see him, Ingrid. He's still in love with you, you know. He even forgives you for your sordid weekend with that rich guy in Sea Cliff."

"Say, that's damn generous of him." Ingrid turned away from them and went to the open kitchen window, staring blankly out at the small backyard, knotting her fists against the unwelcome feeling of panic. Rage was followed by fear and a hint of the old longing she had felt when she had idolized Victor in the early days of her marriage. She seemed to be boiling over with contradictory emotions.

The teakettle whistled for several seconds before Carmen got up to take it off the burner. Ingrid's eyes met Carmen's; they were both marveling at how naive Spyder was, although he was only a few years younger than they were.

"Spyder, you're too idealistic," Carmen said, pouring hot water into the teapot. She passed Ingrid on the way to the cupboard for another cup and shrugged expressively. "Everyone deserves a second chance."

Ingrid paused a moment, considering how little she knew about Spyder from the days when they both had lived in Humboldt. He had lived out on the land with a girl his own age. The girl had left him not long after Ingrid had moved down to San Francisco. Then Spyder had turned up in the city, recovering from a broken heart. Perhaps his own unhappy experience had made him more romantic.

The telephone rang, and rather than talk to Spyder she fled from the room to answer it. In the background she heard Carmen, gently explaining that many of the women

she had met who had been beaten by their husbands concealed their present whereabouts for fear of more violence. She was telling him about women who had been
tracked down and killed by crazed ex-husbands.

Spyder's response was inaudible.

On the phone was Dana Ingersoll, Ingrid's counselor at
AdventureTemps, the agency that came up with most of her
office jobs. In continual high gear from nervous energy,
coffee and cigarettes, Dana was a verbal contract specialist
who fired out words at a machine-gun pace and always tried
to get a commitment before revealing the more horren-
dous details of an assignment.

"Hi, Dana, it's me. I'm glad you got the message with
my new number. I got burned out of my apartment, so I'll
have to earn some money soon."

"Drop by the office tomorrow—I'll have another job for
you. Also, we got a package from Bramwell, Stinson. You
really must be more careful—I guess you left something
over there and someone was nice enough to send it over by
messenger."

Ingrid agreed and wandered back to the kitchen.

Spyder offered to meet Ingrid downtown and take her in
his van to pick up any of her things that could be salvaged
from the burned-out apartment. Ingrid accepted gratefully. "I may need a bodyguard to protect me from Mrs.
Phelps."

"Ingrid, you can count on me anytime to fend off any
sixty-year-old lady who tries to trash you. Oh, I forgot. I
have something of yours in the van."

He went out to get it.

Ingrid and Carmen's eyes met again for a moment. "I
hope it's not my misplaced ex-husband," Ingrid said.

Carmen laughed. Ingrid looked at Carmen's coppery
hair, purple India-print dress and purple velvet jacket. Ingrid wondered for the hundredth time how her friend
earned enough to keep her household going. The occasional handwoven rug sale didn't bring in very much
money. Carmen had told her vaguely that she worked in a
restaurant in North Beach a few evenings a week till two
A.M., but she had asked Ingrid not to call her at work; in

fact, she had never told Ingrid *which* restaurant she worked
at. Ingrid wondered if Carmen worked as a topless waitress, but if Carmen wasn't ready to talk about it, Ingrid
could respect her privacy.

Spyder returned alone. He handed her a copy of the latest *Bay Area Gadfly*. "Look on page twelve."

"Hey. They used my Berkeley Flea Market picture. I sure
didn't expect that."

"Why not? It was a good picture. Look, he used one of
my financial district pics too. We'll have to wring a couple
of microscopic checks out of him for it."

"Oh, Spyder, I think I got a shot of the senior partner of
the law firm where I worked yesterday, taken in front of the
alley where the woman died, outside his building. I'll have
to see how it comes out when I develop it. The problem is,
should I give the film to the cops?"

Spyder raised his eyebrows. "Do they want it?"

"You know, I forgot to mention it when I talked to them.
Old habits die hard. I'll run it and take them a proof sheet."

"You won't give them the negs?"

"I hope I won't have to."

"Talk to Resnick. Maybe if they get interested in your
negatives and you refuse to give them up, he might get interested in you. He may buy some more of your pictures if
he sees you as the valiant gal photographer defying the
grand jury in the name of anti-high-rise press freedom. Just
don't try and take that stringer job away from me. I may
have to arm wrestle you for it."

ELEVEN

Wednesday, December 21

WHEN INGRID ROSE at five, the wind was sandblasting the trees in Sutro Heights Park. As she left the house, she could see the moon with the offshore clouds blowing across its face. The wind tumbled her hair and cut at her clothes as she crossed the Great Highway.

She descended the steps of the seawall and crossed the rain-packed sand to the firmest part at the water's edge. She had to take a moment even in the cold to watch the moon as it highlighted each wave, following its path to shore.

When she had run here before, there had been other runners, but today she met no one. The loneliness of the scene made her anxious after the violence she had witnessed the past few days. Climbing the stairs back up to the sidewalk, she saw a shadow coming down. It belonged to a woman of fifty or so with a towel around her neck; she was being dragged along double-time by a determined Doberman pinscher on a leash.

Ingrid smiled in relief and returned to the house for a shower. She barely squeezed into Carmen's kindly offered "conservative suit," a ruffled lavender cotton skirt and button jacket. It was inches too short, but at least it lacked Carmen's usual gold-thread embroidery. Ingrid shared milk and cornflakes with Mugwort, who emerged from a secret hiding place on top of a china cabinet when she opened the refrigerator. He lapped up the milk and carefully left each cornflake. Ingrid left him grooming his neck hair with long tongue swoops and walked out to join the small knot of scrubbed and office-suited workers holding umbrellas at the ready and glancing up at an occasional sprinkle as they stood on the spongy ground under the cypresses at the end of the 38 Geary line, waiting for the A Express.

SHE FOUND DANA INGERSOLL puffing a cigarette in the closet-sized lobby of her building, staring moodily at the elevator door a few feet from her eyes. Dana was forced to retreat to the lobby whenever she wanted a nicotine fix, which was often. Ingrid waited for her to take one last, deep puff and exhale in staccato bursts of chatter. Then they went up in the elevator.

Dana rolled her eyes to the ceiling at Ingrid's outfit but said only that Ingrid must have lost a great deal of her wardrobe in the fire. Ingrid nodded and smiled. Dana always dressed stylishly but with small flaws—a ripped seam or a button missing in a conspicuous place. Her shining, short black hair was as sleek as a painted doll's, with a line of gray roots peeking out along the partline.

Something about Dana made Ingrid want to join the personnel agency game of "finding the faults in this person." The object of the game was generally to point out the person's most obvious defects and help hide them—at least until the job was secured or the temporary assignment completed. This game opened up a whole universe of deficiencies in other people.

The agency occupied the fifth floor of the building. It was a large room with tables and desks of finely carved wood in the reception area. Beautiful throw rugs covered parts of the polished floor—they were out of the line of traffic, as if too valuable to be stepped on. A few applicants were seated on a worn rattan sofa-and-chair group; they cast envious glances at Ingrid as she was ushered into the back.

Dana's desk filled up her cubicle, crammed right next to an identical cubicle for another counselor. She rummaged in her desk and handed Ingrid a large, square envelope—thin as a wafer of cardboard with a *SUDDEN SERVICE COURIERS* label on it. Ingrid could not recall ever using that messenger service in her secretarial jobs, but there were dozens of courier services in the city. She surrendered her time sheet to Dana, who cocked her head to one side, pursing her lips for the next cigarette several minutes in advance.

"They want you back at Bramwell, Ingrid. They wouldn't say why, but I guess they'd have said if they were disputing your hours. You'll be able to take this back and get it signed properly at the same time. Put in a good word for us with the new Personnel head, will you?"

"If I do that for you, maybe next time you can find me some more word processing jobs and less of that secretarial babysitting junk."

"I'll do my best, Ingrid. You're so good as a secretary, and not everyone can do that. Those word processing center jobs are in short supply, you know. Everybody wants them."

Ingrid let that remark hang on the air for a moment. "So Bramwell's got a new Personnel head already? They do move fast."

"This woman's held the job before. Maybe you met her when you were over there. Her name is Nell Scott. We never got much work from her last time, but we're hoping this time will be better. BSF is a large firm. Miranda steered us a couple of assignments a week. Of course, she *was* a former employee."

"She *was?* As a counselor or a temp?"

"Oh, she was a counselor." Dana stared at the ceiling as if wishing to blow smoke at it.

Ingrid almost laughed but turned her expression into a confidential smile. "So, how was she?"

"Pretty hot at first." Dana tapped her coffeecup with a peach-colored fingernail—the polish was chipped. "She sort of ran out of steam later on. She had a habit of exaggerating and embroidering."

Ingrid raised her eyebrows in mock surprise. "And you didn't find that helpful?" Overzealous matchmaking was a common Personnel agency trait.

Dana laughed. "Well, okay, we try to present the jobs and the temps to each other in the most favorable light, of course. But Miranda forgot that we do want the businesses to use our temps again after the first time. She was great on the initial sale and hopeless on the day-to-day accounts. I was surprised to see her at Bramwell."

"Are you saying she had bad judgment or was unreliable in recommending people to companies?"

"Let's just say that the minute details of the project at hand never interested her for long. She was always planning something bigger down the road. She was quite impressive if you just let her talk and sometimes lie a bit to the clients. She had a knack for making up very plausible-sounding numbers that had nothing to do with anything in the real world."

"How long did she last?"

"Oh, we never had time to get rid of her. We sent her around to this real estate developer—Helmut Kubler. She said she knew him. We thought maybe she could work up some business for us with him. Sooo, we sent her to pay a call on him with Christmas gifts for his office manager. Sometimes a bottle of fourth-rate Scotch at Christmas can do a world of good to warm things up. Next thing we know, she goes to work for them."

"I see."

"A few years later we heard she'd moved on to Bramwell; it's the law firm that represents Kubler." Dana straightened up and put her coffee mug to one side. "Well, I've got an interview coming up, so I'll just give you one of our current rate cards and send you on your way." She slipped a printed circular into an envelope. "Just give this to Nell Scott, and I promise you'll get the next word processing job that comes through the door—if you happen to know the machine, of course."

Ingrid sat on the steps of the Pacific Coast Stock Exchange, deserted in midmorning, to open the Sudden Service envelope. It contained only a familiar-looking small sheet of buff paper with "Memo from Miranda" engraved on the top. It was an awfully big envelope for the small note inside. The message was scrawled in the same expansive handwriting she had seen on the note in Miranda's typewriter.

Did you like the fire?

A shiver ran down Ingrid's back. Miranda had already been dead by the time her apartment went up in flames.

Had she set that in motion somehow before she died? Ingrid continued reading.

I've told everyone that you're keeping my scrapbook for me. You'd be surprised how many people would kill to get my little golden book of memories. We should have done business today, Ingrid, but the fire seemed like a nice idea just to let you know I mean what I say. Meet with me Tuesday and run that little errand for me. When you've done that, I'll call off the dogs. I'll be in touch. As Ever, MF.

It certainly didn't read like a note from someone who was contemplating suicide. Except for the more explicit threat and the promise to "be in touch," it seemed similar to the note rolled into Miranda's typewriter. The part about meeting Ingrid Tuesday and then calling off the dogs didn't sit well with Ingrid. It was now Wednesday. How could Miranda call off the dogs, whatever they were, when she had been dead before Ingrid even received the message? Or was she just bluffing when she said people would kill to get whatever this scrapbook thing was that she was supposed to have given Ingrid?

As she approached the Bramwell Building Ingrid saw a bicycle messenger sitting on the curb a few feet away, staring at her. He had SUDDEN SERVICE DELIVERIES embroidered on his orange jumpsuit. He was a big, muscular bruiser with a shaven skull. His chin showed either the beginnings of a beard or a lack of interest in shaving below the ears. A crude tattoo ran down his scalp, bisecting what was once his hairline. A skull-and-crossbones flag flew from the basket of his heavy-duty bicycle. He might almost have been expecting her, so insolently did he stare at Ingrid.

Ingrid took out her camera, meaning to take his picture.

But he stood up at the same time as she did, flung himself on his bike and pedaled away rapidly. She took a few shots of him as he rode, talking into his two-way radio, perhaps on his way to make a pickup. He disappeared into the midmorning traffic, steering with one hand and weaving around slow-moving cars as if they were standing still. The fact that he had watched her made Ingrid wonder if he might be one of Miranda's dogs. Taking the picture gave her a feeling of control again.

THE CHRISTMAS TREE on the twelfth floor had been decorated, but the bright ornaments had done nothing to lift the receptionist's spirits. Pammy had abandoned the struggle to put up her hair. She whispered hello to Ingrid and lapsed into silence, holding the door open for her to pass into what was now Nell Scott's office.

Nell Scott was one of the generation of office females inescapably referred to as "gals" by the bosses whom they served so faithfully as secretaries. She had settled into Miranda's office with no visible qualms, perhaps since it had been her own once before. The dangerous window was firmly shut. Of course, it was cold and rainy outside. An electric forced-air heater, like the one accused of burning down Ingrid's Oak Street apartment, hummed away just to the right of Nell's desk.

Miranda's typewriter and the speaker attachment to her telephone were gone. The African violets drooped on their cart, which had been pushed over near the door next to a stack of cardboard cartons filled with random office furnishings. Next to the desk was a new worktable bearing several thick loose-leaf folders, a tape-transcription machine and a modern antique—a five-year-old magnetic card typewriter.

"Oh, you've got a Mag Two. I've used those." The mag card was an old friend to Ingrid, although the so-called "blind" machine had been driven into near extinction in the past few years, as machines with display screens invaded most offices.

Nell said nothing but nodded cautiously.

Ingrid noted the thick stack of cards in its hopper. "Looks like you've got a long project there. What's fun with those twenty- or thirty-page documents is to let them run and go out for a coffee break. It's like being in two places at the same time—the machine is working and you're not."

The yellow-haired woman angled her eyes at Ingrid as if expecting ridicule. "I'm running off the Bible," she volunteered.

"The Bible?"

"Our form manual. I've been editing it for the past year or so when the pressure of Mr. Flint's work permitted. I'll turn the final draft over to our proofreaders next week." She signed Ingrid's time sheet without even glancing at the hours but did not hand it back at once. "Sit down, Ingrid—I'd like to ask you something."

"If I answer your questions, will you answer mine?" Ingrid heard herself reply. When Nell raised her eyebrows, she said, "Just curiosity." After reading Miranda's memo, Ingrid had a sudden desire to uncover any possible members of this pack of dogs that was supposed to be snapping at her heels.

"All right. I'll go first." Nell crossed her speckled hands in front of her with the self-righteous candor of a Sunday-school teacher. "How well did you know Miranda Falk? I'm asking you because the address she gave us is a fake. No one seems to know where she was living or even any friend or relative to contact. This is a very sad matter, and the firm seems to be under a certain moral obligation here."

"What? No beneficiary on her life insurance policy?"

"Very clever. Actually she named a member of the firm as her beneficiary. A joke that was in rather poor taste."

"Did you try Valley School?"

"We've tried there, and of course the police have, too. But none of the addresses for relatives in their files are current, and she doesn't seem to have kept in touch with anyone at the school."

"And you have no other records to trace back through?"

"Uh, actually no." Nell Scott seemed quite embarrassed. "Either there never was a résumé and application or she took her records out of the files herself. She came to us at the recommendation of one of our senior partners. And, as you must know"—Nell essayed a dismal failure of a cheerful smile—"their word is law who sign our paychecks."

"Of course you asked the senior partner in question."

"Well, he's not in the office now, but when we asked him he became remarkably vague. Says he met her through a client." Nell's voice crackled with exasperation. "If I'd prolonged the conversation another minute, he would have started invoking attorney-client privilege."

"Mr. Flint Senior, I presume."

Nell flinched but did not answer. "Such a tragedy," she said, staring at the wall behind Ingrid. "When I think of that poor broken body lying down there..."

"Too bad you never got to see it."

"There's no need to be offensive." Nell touched a hairpin securing her fiercely bleached bun. "I guess you're right to say that after the scene I made Monday. I was overwrought. Just very upset, that's all."

"But now that you have your job back, you're all better."

"That's a very rude thing to say, young woman, and a very mistaken one. First, I do not have this job. I'm just filling in until they find a replacement and I can retire. Believe me, I'm counting the days. Perhaps you would care to try some of your Nancy Drew, girl detective, questions on our Office Administrator, Mr. Tobias."

"Not right now; another time perhaps. Look, Miss Scott, the evening after Miranda Falk died, someone tried to burn down my apartment. It might be a coincidence, or they might have been looking for this." She held out the Sudden Service Messenger envelope.

Nell leaned forward in spite of herself. "What is it?" Her attempt at a careless tone didn't quite come off.

"It was sent from this office by Miranda Monday just before she died. Someone knows I have it, and they've tried to get it, or destroy it and me." Ingrid was bluffing, but as soon as she spoke, she wondered if that might be true.

Nell's mouth curled down in contempt. "It does sound awfully coincidental to me," she said.

"I thought so too," Ingrid said, pulling the memo halfway out of the envelope, "until I saw this memo from Miranda. You know, it looks and sounds an awful lot like the note in her typewriter, the one they think might or might not be a suicide note."

"You mean she talks about suicide in her note to you?"

Ingrid slipped the memo back in the envelope and closed it.

"Well, what does she talk about?"

Ingrid said nothing.

"Well, girl detective, let me deduce something. You haven't rushed to the police with this note, and I must assume that whatever is in it is something you wouldn't like to have generally known. You didn't kill Miranda yourself, did you?"

"I might ask you the same question, Nell."

"Yes, well, I at least was not alone during the time she died. You can ask the janitor. The police certainly did. I was working in my little office in the basement all afternoon. Now, did you want to talk to our Office Administrator?"

"No thanks, office administrators usually know even less than personnel managers."

Nell just barely regained her composure. She was obviously not used to using emotion for effect. For her, any argument was with all swords drawn. Ingrid began to like her just a little bit.

"Well, ah, Ingrid, you certainly have a highly developed sense of curiosity." Nell cleared her throat in embarrassment. "Perhaps you are more suited to this assignment than I realized before you came out with your...uh...questions. I've been authorized to ask you to try to trace any mutual friends who might know her family. If you could reach some relatives, find someone to—"

"Take the body off your hands, so to speak."

Ingrid watched in awe as Nell reined in what looked like an uncontrollable spasm of anger. It still simmered. It must.

"You realize it's not our responsibility. The county has facilities for unclaimed bodies. But... our senior partner feels we should try to be absolutely sure her family is notified, wherever they may be. They must want to know. Of course we'll pay your time and any expenses. We'll even keep your agency out of it if you want to make a separate agreement."

"No, no, that would leave us both vulnerable to a lawsuit under the ninety-day slavery clause." Ingrid enjoyed playing the stiff-necked-citizen role. She realized she had forgotten to deliver the AdventureTemps leaflet. She pulled it out and put it on the desk in front of Nell without comment.

"AdventureTemps will charge their top hourly rate, I'm sure. I'll check around for you and send you a separate accounting of any expenses. I have to work somewhere this week, and I might as well do this."

Nell nodded and pushed the signed time card across the desk blotter.

"Just a few more questions."

Nell's lips clamped shut as if stapled by her teeth.

"Miranda took your job—twice. How did that happen, anyway?"

"Just an old man's foolish vanity," Nell said, staring past Ingrid's shoulder at the vacation schedule. "His health had been bothering him lately. He wanted a pretty girl out front to make a statement to the other men. He didn't realize he'd grabbed a young pit viper until she'd already bitten him."

"She wasn't all *that* young, you know. Could she have bitten him even before he hired her?"

Nell shrugged. "Some client recommended her as the sexy, fluttery sort of girl who would impress the other men. I don't think it occurred to him to wonder if she could do the work, which, alas, she could not. He brought her in as his secretary and promoted me to Personnel." She smiled rather grimly. "Not that it made much difference, just two jobs for me. I still spent most of my time on Mr. Flint's work—he records his daily instructions on microcassettes. Personnel Manager is hardly a very taxing job around here; I didn't mind two jobs. Then *she* demanded a management job."

"They had to give her yours?"

Nell shrugged. "There aren't many management jobs in a law firm. So they banished me to the basement with my Bible."

"Your what? Oh, right, the form manual. May I see one?"

"Certainly. Here's the original." Nell pushed a thick binder across the desk top at Ingrid. It was filled with examples of legal documents. "Stored here." She tapped the stack of mag cards in the machine's hopper. "Of course, that was hardly full-time either. I just continued to quote—help out—end quote Mr. Flint's secretary. The newest decorative female. Even less competent than Miranda, if such a thing is possible. Not that Mr. Flint cared, so long as his work got done as usual."

"Why did you put up with it? You could have protested, or quit?"

"Mr. Flint had made up his mind. He always has his reasons for everything. When you live a little longer in this world of work, you may find yourself doing some very unexpected jobs for the sake of fringe benefits—like not starving in your old age."

"Was Miranda his mistress?"

"She certainly tried to give that impression, but only Mr. Flint could tell us that. For various reasons I doubt it. You've met the man. I've worked for him for over twenty years, and I would never dare to ask him such a question. You seem to like asking impertinent questions. Ask him yourself."

"Is Mrs. Flint still living?"

"She died many years ago."

"And he never remarried?"

"No. He's a very private person. All I can say with certitude is that until two years ago his worst vice was compulsive legal research."

"You know Flint Senior as well as anyone here. Why should he be so worried all of a sudden about making a statement of virility?"

Nell Scott looked at Ingrid steadily. "I'm sure I don't know."

"By the way, Miranda said she was overhauling the staff. Had she been firing a lot of people lately?"

"What an odd question; of course not."

"Monday Miranda scheduled two termination interviews just as she was walking me up to Flint's office. She said something about 'we might whip this place into shape'—do you have any idea what that was all about?"

"Well, she would say something like that. Who was she supposed to have fired?"

"Max Leon, the word processing supervisor, and Frank Bates, the messenger."

Nell smiled indulgently. She liked Max Leon. "Max was quitting anyway. He's been saving up to open a restaurant in Noe Valley for years now. Everybody knows that. Frank Bates is a different matter. Even if she caught him drinking on the job, as she said, he's a hard worker. And his mother has been the Flints' cook for years and years. She's one of the best cooks in the Bay Area—she can make a hospital diet tray taste like cordon bleu. Several of Mr. Flint's friends have offered generous terms to lure her away, but so long as there's a job here for her son, she'll never leave. Frank will stay, so long as he doesn't do anything overtly criminal, and I doubt that he ever will."

"Did Frank know that his job was safe?"

"Frank knows it. If Miranda didn't know it, it's because she wasn't paying attention."

Thinking back to Frank Bates' face, taut with rage, Ingrid wondered if perhaps Miranda had been paying very close attention indeed. Perhaps she had meant to harass him into quitting on his own.

"It will be a great help for us if you can find someone responsible to take her belongings." Nell gestured vaguely at the office around her. "We can't have her things cluttering up our office forever."

"I see you've inherited her African violet collection."

"Oh, those nasty hairy things. They'll be dead soon, I expect. I can't be bothered to water them."

It was the first time Ingrid had ever worried about the fate of a member of the vegetable kingdom, but the look on Nell's face inspired sudden sympathy for the flowers. "I'll take them, if you don't want them."

"Sure, take them all. Take the cart too."

She didn't take the cart, but Ingrid left Nell Scott's office with a cardboard box full of flowerpots in her arms, a two-week visitor's pass tucked in her purse and her all-important signed time card.

Pammy saw the box as she passed the reception desk and called out, "Wait!" Ingrid waited, then watched in horror as the girl balanced yet another plant on top of the rest.

"I found this in the coffee room the day after Miss Falk died. She used to take them in where the running water is to repot them or something." Pammy gulped back a sigh. "I guess she never got the chance to finish."

Ingrid felt silly lugging her box of flowers through the corridors, past groups of lawyers with briefcases and secretaries bustling along with folders and envelopes. She detoured down to the basement before going up to the penthouse. She had a few questions for the janitor. She found him in Nell's basement office, just across from his own stronghold, where a rolltop desk piled with invoices was visible through the open door.

The janitor was a stocky, white-haired Irishman in dark-green coveralls, and his old-country brogue made Ingrid feel as if she had just stepped into a 1930s movie. Barry Fitzgerald must be just around the corner somewhere. As she set her box of flowers down and rubbed the soreness out of her arms, the janitor folded his arms over his broom as if glad for an opportunity to stop and talk.

"Oh, indeed she was here all afternoon. A very hard-working young woman, that Nell. I thought I'd be glad of a little company when she moved down here. My helpers do most of the work, and I'm with the stockroom and supplies most of the day. But no, she was always typing on that godawful machine of hers. Can't say I was sorry to see *that* thing go. Myself, I couldn't leave till the wholesaler called, and she was just banging away all afternoon at the boss's tapes and something she called the Bible." He shook his head. "A sacrilegious lady but a hard worker. She was so busy that day that it was midafternoon before I could talk her into taking a break for a bite of my own homemade coffee cake."

Ingrid thanked him kindly and narrowly escaped being plied with coffee cake.

Back upstairs, she found Tanya at her desk looking up at Tony Flint, who stood tapping a red pen on a stack of lawbooks. "This is what you get for trusting an index," he said, flickering a glance as dry as a snake's tongue at Ingrid as she approached with her box of flowers. "This thing is misindexed. Should have been in 'insurance.' It was under 'autos or damages or marriage.'"

Tanya's gaze glazed over slightly as she listened, but she smiled sympathetically. Tony included Ingrid in his gesture of frustration, picked up his books and stalked off. A moment later his door slammed at the far end of the hall.

At the desk next to Tanya's, a young Hispanic woman sat unstapling copies of a long document. She had not even pretended to listen to Tony Flint. She gave off a fever of youthful vitality like a perfume.

Ingrid greeted Tanya, who introduced her to Lucinda Aguilar. Lucinda promptly dropped her staple remover, reached into a huge purse under the kneehole of her desk and withdrew a large roll of pink toilet paper. She quickly unrolled a strip big enough to sneeze into. She sneezed into it.

"Whooo. Sorry you guys. I've still got this terrible cold. The last place I worked they gave out boxes of Kleenex. We ran out back at the house, and I don't get paid till practically Christmas Eve. Talk about cheap. Maybe Miranda really did get rid of the bonuses. That's what the grapevine says."

"Sounds awful. Are you sure you should be back at work?" Ingrid asked.

"Are you kidding, at this place? They don't give you sick pay without a doctor's excuse. I can't afford to be sick no more. Good thing the old guy is out of town. I just sit here and try not to sneeze on Tanya." She smiled cheerfully and sneezed again.

"Did you know Miranda?"

"Course I did. She's the one told me to take off Monday—then I come back and find out it's without pay. Ha! Thanks a lot. I shoulda got it in writing." Lucinda stood. She was even taller than Ingrid's five feet ten—of course the three-inch-spike heels helped.

"Who hired you, Lucinda? Miranda or Mr. Flint?"

"Oh, it was her all right. You know why she hired me? I think because I'm so tall. She liked to get the old guy off balance. He never complains, though. Okay, he bitches about mistakes in the work, but Tanya says he does that with everybody. If I get any calls, I'll be in the rest room."

Lucinda took her handbag and wandered off, leaving the roll of toilet paper on her desk.

Ingrid sat in Lucinda's chair. "Tanya, I've been meaning to ask you, how did Miranda get all those violets?"

"She sort of hinted that the old man bought them for her every time he went on a trip. He'd come back, and there would be another plant on her desk. Then she'd hint about how beautiful Washington was at cherry-blossom time, how it was snowing in New York or wherever Flint had gone, like she'd gone there too, and brought back another flower as a souvenir."

"Like notches on a gun handle."

"Then she had to get that big white cart to hold them all. She made it pretty hard not to guess what was going on."

"Sex and violets?"

"That's what we all thought. But I'm not so sure now. The old man never did anything like that before, and he's never tried anything with anyone else who works here, certainly not with Lucinda or me."

"A healthy kid like Lucinda? Cold or no cold—half an hour with her might kill a man his age. If he didn't blush to death first." Ingrid and Tanya laughed together at the thought.

Flint Junior stuck his gorgeous blond head out of his office as they laughed. He came out into the hallway and beckoned to her. Ingrid hesitated, but his expression was gentle and tentative.

"Miss Hunter, I owe you an apology. Could you come into my office for a moment so I can deliver it properly?"

Ingrid followed Tony into an office that was as cramped as any ordinary low-ranking associate's quarters. It had a nautical air, like a small ship's cabin containing quantities of brass. The walls were covered with framed photos of sailboats. Or many photos of the same sailboat—it was hard to tell; the images were not of the best quality. In none of the pictures could she read the vessel's name.

"I see you looking at my little gallery, Ingrid. That's my old sweetheart, the boat I took to South America. I lost her, alas, but I've got my eye on a new sloop. Who knows, if we get to know each other better, maybe I'll name the new boat after you. So, for starters please let me call you Ingrid. You call me Tony—Atherton Flint is a terrible name."

"Did you know everyone calls you Junior?"

"Not to my face. Ingrid, come here. Sit."

She sat on a chair of bentwood and leather, so close to the small desk that she could smell his after-shave lotion again. This time it was citrus with a faint metallic undertone.

"Sometime I'll show you my latest shots. This album has some nature shots I took in South America. I haven't been able to go back for a few years. What about you? Do you specialize in anything in particular?"

He was trying very hard to be charming, and she liked his taste in after-shave lotion. A very attractive man.

"Until a few years ago I mostly shot nature photographs," she said, turning the album pages slowly. His pictures seemed to lack even the most elementary sense of focus and composition. "Since I moved back here I've been working on urban ecology: packs of roving executives, herds of migrating commuters, seasonal swarms of tourists. As long as I'm stuck here, I might as well make the best of it and shoot a few pictures."

"Doesn't all the dirt disgust you?"

"Well, I've been shooting more black and white than color, what with all the concrete and glass. But the countryside has its own kind of pollution."

"Sometime I'd like to take you out on the Bay. In my new thirty-six footer. Promise you'll come."

"Sounds like fun," Ingrid said cautiously.

"Maybe you can teach me something."

Like how to focus a camera, she thought unkindly. But she gave him the number of her message machine before wondering if it was a mistake. She might not enjoy the man's company at all. He had a strong physical presence that seemed to flow from his extraordinary health and strength. As he ushered her out of his office, he joined Tanya and Lucinda and watched as she awkwardly picked up her box of violets.

It wasn't until Tony's door had closed solidly behind him that Ingrid realized that during his "apology" the words "I'm sorry" had never escaped his lips.

Flint Senior came down the hall as she turned to go; he did not meet her eyes or greet Lucinda.

Tanya advanced on him. "Mr. Flint, are you feeling..." He waved her aside. He seemed almost too exhausted to walk, but Ingrid recognized the workaholic mentality and realized there was no stopping a man on his way to his in-box.

He managed to unlock his double doors and get through them. Ingrid saw him stand for several seconds, staring at the hill of dirt, smashed pottery and broken flowers on his carpet. The pots had been stripped from their shelves, broken and upended in a ragged heap in the center of the thick Persian carpet. Slowly Flint Senior crumpled to the floor. There was an audible thud as his head hit the carpet.

Lucinda rushed in to kneel beside him. "He's still breathing. Call the paramedics," she said.

Tanya lifted the receiver. "You'd better get going, Ingrid," Tanya said as she dialed. "I'm going to have to report this to building security. I won't mention your name, but you'd better go now, okay?" She spoke briefly into the receiver, put it down and stared firmly at Ingrid.

"Who would have known where Lucinda kept the key to that room?" Ingrid asked her.

"Oh, anyone who saw her take it out and go in to put his mail on his desk." Tanya sighed distractedly. "Anyone could have come in early or stayed late to trash the place. Lucy hasn't touched that office since she came back to work this morning."

"Before I go, Tanya, in case no one mentioned it to you, Nell Scott told me Frank Bates is unfireable. Is he back?"

Tanya's brow furrowed, as if she didn't want to think about Frank Bates in such close conjunction with the recent vandalism. "I haven't seen him since Monday, but

Junior, uh, I was told . . . he wasn't going to be fired after all. Go on now, I've got to tell Junior his daddy's feeling ill.'' As she started to dial the phone again, she jerked her head at Ingrid. "Out!"

TWELVE

WHEN HE PICKED HER UP in front of the Bramwell Building, Spyder allowed Ingrid to load the violets into his van under protest. Only when Ingrid assured him that Carmen would be thrilled did he agree. Then they had to risk injury from outraged drivers on Montgomery Street as they leaned into the double-parked van, propping boxes of darkroom chemicals around the plants so no dirt could spill onto Spyder's immaculate shag rug.

At last they set off to the accompaniment of the loudest heavy metal rock Ingrid had ever heard. The doors where the speakers were concealed vibrated visibly.

Spyder insisted on detouring several blocks south of Market to see Ben Resnick.

The *Bay Area Gadfly* office was located on Brannan Street near where it meets the Embarcadero at Pier 34. The busy loading dock of the warehouse next door gaped open on one side at the *Gadfly*. The licorice factory on the other side shared its parking lot with a trio of pale-blue tanks on stilts as tall as the warehouse itself, labeled CORN SYRUP, LICORICE, and DYE.

At the *Gadfly*'s front desk sat a young woman, her long black hair wound up in a knot fastened only by a cleverly twisted in #2 lead pencil, which stood out sharply against the gleaming coils. Pencil thin herself, the woman wore faded overalls over a T-shirt. She might have just clambered down off a tractor but for the designer label on the denim and the "Filipino Power" button on one overall strap—signs of a junior sophisticate and City College student. She was the receptionist and sole office staff—the only person actually paid a salary by Resnick, who tried to get by on volunteer and free-lance help as much as possible.

She was taking a classified ad by phone, writing legibly with yet another #2 pencil for the typesetter. The ads brought in enough money to allow Resnick to distribute the paper for free.

"Let me just read that back to you, and see if I got all of it." The receptionist looked up from the phone and winked at Spyder and Ingrid.

"Okay, for the headline: *'Cinderella Where Are You?'* And the text: 'Single, white Prince Charming foot fancier seeks dream girl with size three or smaller feet for serious fun and possible marriage. Send foot tracing or footprint. I am for real. My kingdom is yours if you fit the glass slipper. No midgets please. Answer to *Bay Area Gadfly* Box 2X 237.' Yes, sir. What?" She threw back her head and laughed heartily. "No, sorry. I wear size sevens and I gotta boyfriend. Now what was your Visa card number?" As she wrote it down, she motioned Spyder and Ingrid upstairs.

Laughing, Spyder led Ingrid up the narrow stairway of the warehouse. Small cubicles with ancient typewriters housed the floating staff of volunteer writers and the lay-out artist, whom Ben had been promising to put on salary for two years now.

Ben's office was a tropical inferno, eternally overheated and filled with smoke from his small, fat cigars.

"Photographers!" a resonant voice bellowed as Ingrid and Spyder crossed the threshold. "Nothing but reporters without brains! Any fool with a camera can take a picture right, Spyder?" He waved them toward seats in the bat-tered folding chairs that lined the walls.

Ben Resnick returned his attention to the telephone cra-dled between his ear and shoulder. He was a short, slen-der, hawk-faced man, somewhere in the neighborhood of seventy years old. He wore a faded red baseball cap at all times, not so much to conceal his baldness as to cover the age spots on his head. He put the phone down at last and pointed at Ingrid. His deep voice filled the room; it could be heard on the stairs, and even occasionally on the street below in hot weather when the windows were open.

"Hey, kid, you're the one who used to sell the *Gadfly* on the streets, back when we had to charge for it, huh?"

When Ingrid had run away from home to come to San Francisco in the summer of 1968, the *Gadfly* had sold for about twenty cents. Resnick had marketed it the same way a dozen other counterculture weeklies were sold: The vendors paid fifteen cents and sold the papers for twenty-five cents or whatever they could get away with.

Ingrid had been fifteen and she hadn't known Resnick in those days. Later she learned that he was a blacklisted newpaperman who had moved back to his native San Francisco from New York. He had acquired a certain clout within the local bohemian and leftist circles by virtue of his age and his persecution.

When Ingrid returned to San Francisco nearly two decades later, the *Gadfly* was still buzzing. Resnick had developed new survival tactics for an age when people jogged for fitness rather than marching for justice. The *Gadfly* now caroled the consumer delights of the Bay Area, while continuing to sting the power establishment.

"Tell him what you got, Ingrid."

"I caught a picture of Atherton Flint Senior in front of the high-rise under construction next to the Bramwell Building."

"Show it to me. I'm interested. The old fox has been in both camps on the high-rise story. Let's see."

Ingrid cursed herself for coming unprepared but put a brave face on it. "Actually I don't have it on me. I just dropped by with Spyder."

"To get our checks," Spyder put in, "for our pics in the last issue."

"Also to see if you have any photo needs just now," Ingrid said helpfully. "I'll check that Flint shot out on the proof sheet and drop it by." She had no way of knowing what she had on film. He might discount everything she said from now on if the photo turned out blurred or unrecognizable.

"Sure, honey," Ben said easily enough. "Show me whatever you did get."

"Just one slight problem."

"Such as?"

"I keep thinking I should show it to the police, but I'm afraid they'll want the negatives. I have to go in and sign a statement."

Ingrid explained that Miranda had died a few feet away from the spot where the photo was taken. Ben smiled a slow dreamy smile when Ingrid had finished, and asked, "Did you tell them about the film yet?"

Ingrid shook her head.

"Better and better. Just let me see it first. And tell me any hard information you get on Flint. Just the facts, ma'am. I'll do a little checking on my own. There might be a story in it. Don't worry about the cops. I've got all the best lawyers—used to get wholesale rates, but now I just get a discount."

It was the second time in two days that someone had mentioned finding a lawyer for Ingrid. The idea passed over her like a chilling breeze.

"Do you ever think how ironic it is, Ben, that all these expensive ads that pay the bills are aimed at the people who work in those monster high-rises? The same people who are turning this city into the kind of place no one wants to live in—except maybe your advertisers."

Spyder gripped Ingrid's shoulders convulsively, preparing to wrestle her out the door. He could be very sarcastic himself, but would never dare to challenge a possible buyer of photographs.

But Ben Resnick chuckled in amusement. "Those kids like to read about the old San Francisco, but they wouldn't have wanted to work on the docks or the warehouses. They need a city that can support them in the style they prefer, even if they kill the place in the process. But what the hell, the damn thing's not smothered in concrete yet—compared to other places. And so long as it isn't, I'm going to use the money from all these ads to try to wake up a few people to the folly of this mindless greed, and where it's going to get us if it continues. We could have rational growth—if we think with our heads instead of our wallets."

He leaned forward and blew smoke at both of them. "I spent years as a kid in New York, working on newspapers in the forties and fifties. I like going back there on visits, like any tourist, but I'd be skinned alive if I ever thought this city would turn into a reasonable facsimile.''

"Well, if it doesn't, Ben, it will be your good efforts that turned the tide," said Spyder, gently edging Ingrid toward the door through the rolling clouds of smoke, clearly hoping to ease her out before she could ask any more undiplomatic questions.

But Ben held up a slender hand. "You kids will be interested in my latest project for the bed-and-breakfast set." Spyder reversed his steps abruptly, pulling Ingrid back toward Ben. She shook free, taking out a notebook to write down any pertinent details.

"It's an entertainment and services supplement. I've already sold the ads.''

"You're a pretty good salesman for an old red guard," Ingrid teased.

"Honey, radicals are the best salesmen on the block— they have to be. I could use a few shots for the first issue— The Zen of Commuting. Shots of BMWs caught in traffic on one of the bridges, stuff like that. We're shooting for a February publication date, so next week would be nice. If you get some hot stuff on Flint, call me anytime, day or night—I live above the shop. Now scoot." He waved them away. "We'll talk next week."

"About those checks..." Spyder began, but Ben was already back on the phone.

Spyder drove through the gutted but sunny fields south of Market, fenced in chain link and prowled only by the homeless. Once a neighborhood of low-rent hotels, small grocery stores and cheap restaurants, its buildings had been leveled but nothing had gone up in their place. Now weeds grew in the pits where the foundations had been rooted out. Flaps were cut in the rusty chain link fences so that the more courageous street people could sneak through and camp out under the one-story-tall overhang of the sidewalk edges.

Spyder turned the music down to mild earthquake level as a prelude to serious conversation. "Ingrid, I honestly doubt that anything's left of your stuff. That place was gutted.''

"Thanks, Spyder, that's real comforting.''

"Just warning you what to expect. Besides, looting is a very popular indoor-outdoor sport in your neighborhood.''

"That's not what you said that day at S.F. State when you suggested the building. You said it was a safe neighborhood.''

"Well, it was much better than that Ellis Street dump you were in when you first came down from Humboldt. All I said was it wasn't too dangerous. There's a difference. Besides, I said it was cheaper, and it was, wasn't it?''

Ingrid conceded the point.

Spyder crossed Market at Seventh and turned onto MacAllister. "Do you think I can persuade Carmen to let me move in with her?''

"Don't hold your breath.''

"Do you think it would help if I asked her to marry me?'' He stopped at the traffic light at Van Ness and waited a moment after it turned, for the inevitable red-light runner to whiz past in traditional San Franciscan contempt for all laws.

"No.'' Ingrid cast about for a safer subject.

"You think she might suspect my motives.''

"Just warning you what to expect.''

Spyder parked on Gough, a block away from the building. It didn't look so bad from the front. The flames had licked soot around the edges of the windows, and an official red-framed notice sealed the door. An odd assortment of charred, water-soaked furniture stood in the alley behind the building, reeking of smoke. The metal steps up to the back door had been broken sideways and hung away from the building. Another sticker sealed the back door, which had been boarded up and nailed shut: OFF LIMITS. Ingrid dragged a damp kitchen chair over and stood on it to stare into the broken window of her former studio apartment. The walls looked like charcoal. The basement yawned where the floor had been. Nothing she had owned could have survived such intense heat.

Ingrid climbed back down from the chair and stood staring numbly at the damp, acrid-smelling mattress near her as tears began to run down her face. Spyder stood next to her, waiting and saying nothing. After a few moments he reached out and hugged her fiercely. "Come on, it's okay, you're going to be all right," he said. "Let's go, Ingrid. You need a drink." She followed limply.

MacHarg's on Gough near Market was the closest. Ingrid had never been there. She was half afraid she would run into Mrs. Phelps, but the dimly lit bar was deserted except for the bartender who recognized Ingrid.

"Hey, it's the girl next door. Guess we all got moved out, like it or not."

It was the first time she could remember seeing the bartender in daylight. From the street the bar's interior had looked like an eternal twilight. As her eyes adjusted, she saw he was a red-haired, red-bearded man of medium height, full bellied like the caricature of an overstuffed innkeeper. He had taken great pains to wax his mustache ends up into little points. Although she found that fashion repellent, Ingrid wanted to take his picture—but she was too drained to give in to the impulse.

The bartender found encouragement in her expression. He leaned forward and touched her wet face, making her flinch. Spyder moved protectively close to her.

"Okay, bud, that will be one beer and..." Spyder looked questioningly at Ingrid.

"One cola—any kind."

"You said Bud?" The bartender moved back to the tap behind him. "We got Bud. Here you go." He set a glass in front of Spyder, then put a bottle and glass in front of Ingrid and poured expertly. He looked at the money in Spyder's hand, clearly going through some sort of moral struggle. "On the house for both of you on account of the lady's being a neighbor."

"Very kind of you. Thanks," Ingrid managed, wiping her face clumsily with the sleeve of Carmen's India cotton suit.

"I take it you've just seen our former abode. Quite a shocker, isn't it?"

"Sure is. Looks like my stuff burned out completely."

"Did anyone get hurt?" Spyder asked.

"No, somehow everyone got out that back door. No one had to be rescued. Still, the vacancy rate's been up lately; not every apartment was full."

Spyder retreated slightly down the bar. His eyes held a speculative gleam that Ingrid guessed had to do with finding a way to shoot in the bar using available light.

"Did anyone save any of their stuff?" Ingrid wanted to know.

"Oh, sure. The people in the front of the building on the top floor got a lot of their stuff out. But it started in the back, in your room, they say. The first floor in back was totally gutted."

"Do they really think my heater started it?"

"Mrs. Phelps swears that's what happened."

"Where is she, anyway?"

He laughed and shrugged. "No telling about our Eugenia. She may have a rich relative or two. You should see her when she goes on a bender. She wears all these pearls. You'd swear they were real. I kidded her once that she must be Princess Anastasia, heir to the Russian throne. She pulled herself up and said, 'Don't be ridiculous, that was thirty years before my time.'"

Ingrid smiled and drank her cola. "Who owns the place, anyway?"

"It's that little realty company down at the corner of Market. Looks like an investment company from the window. Don't see them buying or selling out in the open, but they must own a lot of property around here. I've got their card back in the office, if you want to come help me look." He leered cheerfully, twirling his mustache points, but made no move toward the office.

"No, thanks, I can find it myself."

"Suit yourself. Anyway, they're the ones to sue if you don't have renter's insurance."

"No risk of that. I don't have anything that cost anything in the first place."

He sighed and mopped the bar. "That's the way I live myself. Easier that way, ain't it, buddy?" He winked at

Spyder this time and went back to the other end of the bar. He kept flickering his eyes over Ingrid as if searching for hidden weapons.

Ingrid sipped her Coke again and found she had lost all taste for it. "Look, Spyder, let's go. I've had just about enough for one day."

"If you don't want the rest of that Coke, I'll take it." Ingrid handed it to him, and he downed it in one gulp.

They left, escorted by the bartender, who rushed around the bar to follow them. "Come on back anytime, folks."

Ingrid was trying to ignore him when she saw a sign a block up on the far side of Market. She had walked past it several times a week for three years and never noticed the Kubler Realty Office. She turned back into the bar and collided awkwardly with Spyder, nearly knocking him into the bartender, who was just behind them.

"Hey, watch it, Ing," Spyder protested.

The bartender seemed a little stunned, perhaps wondering if she were going to ask for his phone number.

"That realty company across the street—Kubler—is that the one that owns our old building?"

"Oh, yeah, that's the one."

"What was that all about?" Spyder asked as he and Ingrid climbed into the van.

"Just some people I want to talk to, sometime when my brain is working again." She would visit Kubler later without Spyder. She might get more questions answered on her own.

THIRTEEN

Thursday, December 22

INGRID HUNG the last strip of film by one metal clip to the line in her darkroom and fastened another clip to the hanging end to keep it from tangling with the other strips nearby. She opened the door slightly to get some fresh air. The sound of bodies hitting the mats in the aikido class next door rose in volume slightly.

She stretched luxuriously, her fingertips almost reaching the ceiling of the former laundry room. Her muscles ached in virtuous post-exertion protest; Ingrid had worked out with her classmates in the color belt class just before running the film. She hated to admit that Miranda's threats had made her nervous, but she did feel safer with all these martial arts students around. And she was relieved that at last she had developed the rolls of exposed film that had been piling up at the bottom of her camera bag for weeks now. Negatives that now hung drying in rows like straightened strips of image-catching flypaper.

On the counter in her darkroom, across from the sink, Ingrid's enlarger squatted like a giant microscope. The thing had cost her a month's take-home pay. In an hour and a half she could use it to print a proof sheet and clearly see what she had captured on film. Then she could begin the work that took the longest time—teasing the best possible prints out of the most promising shots. Ingrid's long hours in the darkroom had made Spyder and her fellow classmates at State nickname her "cavewoman." She couldn't do anything more to any of the negatives until they had dried awhile, but she had made a few guesses as she wiped the excess water from the strips.

The Flint picture had registered in one but not all of the frames—a white-haired man in an overcoat walking past a building site, that was all she could make out.

The black-and-white film on Rosemary Tanner showed promise. She would drop the color film off at the custom lab later. That was a gamble, because Tanner hadn't asked for any color shots, so Ingrid might have to absorb the lab charges herself.

Ingrid scribbled the time on her log and sat on the stool next to her enlarger. On a shelf under the counter was her message machine, hooked up to the wall telephone. She decided to put in a few hours' work for Nell Scott, trying to find some relatives or friends of Miranda Falk alias Mary Valkevich.

With a start Ingrid realized that all her old address books, high school yearbooks and records of any kind had burned in the apartment fire. Involuntarily she jumped to her feet as if there were something she could do. But her things were gone and Miranda was dead.

Ingrid pushed the door open farther to get more air and climbed back onto her stool, hooking her feet on the rungs under it.

Why would Miranda's firestarter destroy Ingrid's records? She forced herself to think clearly, but no reason presented itself. She shook her head. Maybe it was a coincidence. Besides, she still had her photo files.

Her print archives and photo logs were stored in a battered old file cabinet just outside the darkroom door. She quickly tracked down the envelope with proof sheets from the Tri-colleges Shakespeare Festival. Her first credited assignment from that summer after her first year of college.

There was more there than she had remembered. In a file of tear sheets from publications with her pictures from high school and college newspapers, Ingrid found some publicity stills she had taken that had been printed by the local papers—without a photo credit, but they were her own shots nonetheless. The caption under each photo helped her put names to the faces.

Then she looked at the rows of head shots for the festival program. There was her own face. A self-portrait taken with a timer.

Victor Nagel's picture was there, of course. He had played guitar for the Festival lawn show. Handsome dog he was in those days. She still remembered taking it, a few minutes after meeting him. She didn't believe Spyder's suggestion that Vic wanted to get back together with her. But what could he want from her now?

Could Miranda have known Vic back then? Possible, but not likely. Miranda might have met him or even smoked some of his product, judging from the gossip she had produced for Ingrid's luncheon entertainment. But Miranda had been so intent on gaining power that a self-styled outsider could have held no allure. Ingrid couldn't see how Miranda might have fit Victor into her program.

She pulled the stool a little closer to the wall phone and began to call information for the telephone numbers of everyone she could put a name to who might have known Miranda.

None of them still lived in that small suburb of Los Angeles. Almost two decades is a very long time, after all, to live in one place in California.

At last she found someone whose parents still lived in the Valley and didn't mind giving out a number to an old friend. Mitzi had moved only a few miles down the freeway to Santa Monica. Although it was a weekday, Mitzi was home and answered on the first ring. At least one small child was wailing in the background.

"Oh, yes, Ingrid. I remember that summer. Though to be honest, I don't remember you *very* well."

Ingrid looked at Mitzi's picture from *The Taming of the Shrew:* pure vanilla ice cream. "Let's see, I'm looking at a picture of you now that I took when you played Bianca. It was printed in the *Valley Gazette* as publicity for *The Shrew.*"

Mitzi warmed up to that one immediately. In Los Angeles, a city where surface appearances are both a science and a religion, no female resident can forget having her

picture taken for publication. Unless, of course, she makes
a career of it.

"Oh, yes, I remember now. Bobby, you put that right
down this minute. Excuse me, what were you saying?"

Ingrid wondered what Mitzi looked like now. Possibly
the same but slightly more leathery from assiduous tan-
ning, fine lines around the eyes. She was sure that Mitzi was
wondering the same thing about her.

"It's about Miranda Falk—well, I guess back then her
name was Mary Valkevich."

"Oh?" Mitzi was familiar with the name. The tempera-
ture of her voice dropped abruptly. "She played Miranda
in *The Tempest* the year after that. Perhaps that's where she
picked up the name." Mitzi's tone implied that Miranda
might have picked up many other things in addition to the
name. "What about her?"

Ingrid explained about Miranda's death and her assignment to find a next of kin.

"Oh. Just a minute." Mitzi put the receiver down and
demonstrated that her powers of vocal projection had not
eroded with the years as she screeched for several seconds
at Bobby and Kenny, banishing them to another room.
When she returned to the phone, she was thoughtful.

"I don't know about this. What did you say your name
was, Ingrid? Did you know about that soap opera part she
landed? We all watched her in the dorm. She was never a
student at college, only part of the summer festival. But
still, she was the only person we had ever known who was
on TV. Even if she was a bitch, it was exciting. But she
dropped out of the soap opera. It even got into a Hollywood gossip column—we pinned it on the bulletin board at
the dorm—about her going off with a mysterious man.
That didn't last long. She showed up back in the Valley with
her new nose when the tryouts for the next summers' festival came up. She auditioned with the rest of us slobs, and
one director, for reasons then unknown, gave her Miranda
in *The Tempest*. Something about a 'quality of sensuous
innocence.' Then when the summer was over, she ran off
with that very same director. I think they were supposed to
be going to India. You remember Nick Burnet.''

Ingrid did, vaguely.

"Well, I never expected either of them to stay in India. There are too many people there already, aren't there? Anyway that was the last I ever heard of Mary or Nick." Her piqued tone suggested that she might have expected better of Nick.

"Oh, I hadn't realized that you and Nick—"

Mitzi laughed with a sound like glass cracking. "One of those schoolgirl crush things. We had a little affair—it was the sexual revolution, remember? Nick was married, so I never expected anything to come of it. But then Mary waltzed off with him and I got stuck consoling the abandoned wife. Oh, well, that's all ancient history. I married my first husband shortly after I graduated. Then when that didn't work out I married my divorce lawyer. Go for the gold, that's my motto now."

"Thanks a lot, Mitzi, you've been so helpful. I hope you have a championship season."

Ingrid laughed after she set down the phone. Then she called Kubler Realty.

The woman who answered paused before replying to Ingrid's question. Miranda's name seemed to produce a moment of silent meditation in a lot of people. "Yes, I know her. What about her?" She referred to Miranda in the present tense, Ingrid noted.

Ingrid asked if they could meet and talk. The woman at the other end of the line hesitated again.

"I'll be here all afternoon. But I'm going out of town for the holidays. So today is really the only time."

Ingrid glanced over at her film but decided it would keep. "I'll be right over. Don't go away."

WHEN SHE ARRIVED at the Market Street office of Kubler Realty half an hour later, the place looked deserted. Ingrid parked almost in front of the plate-glass window, behind a jeep with two bumper stickers: "God Rides a Harley" and "Support Solidarity Polish Workers Union."

As Ingrid studied the bumper stickers, she saw a woman on the other side of the window watching coolly. Ingrid smiled, took a deep breath and entered the storefront realty office.

FOURTEEN

"IS THAT YOUR CAR? Very interesting bumper stickers," Ingrid said, then paused at the woman's total lack of enthusiasm. "My name is Ingrid Hunter. I called earlier."

The woman placed her arms on the counter of a security window just inside the door and stared sullenly at Ingrid. Her pale-blond hair was cut very short in a modishly asymmetrical fashion. Her cheeks seemed to be pink from exercise and sunshine rather than makeup. She wore a red silk blouse and tailored black wool pantsuit with the pants tucked into gleaming black-leather boots. Absentmindedly she raised her hand to trace the knot of the small red-and-black-striped bowtie at her throat. Ingrid couldn't help but stare for a moment at the pair of interlocking female symbols tattooed on the woman's left wrist. The right wrist displayed an anchor. The inspection was not lost on the woman, who winked, an almost imperceptible gesture, and shot her cuffs down over the tattooed skin with the expertise of an Edwardian dandy.

Ingrid shrugged blithely, implying that different strokes for different folks were fine with her. She waited. There were no customers or other employees in sight. A seamless gate jumped open when the woman pressed a buzzer under the counter.

Behind her was a cozy group of sofa and chairs in soft, squashy imitation leather. A duck decoy rested on a knick-knack table below an etching of a pair of water spaniels. There were tasteful watercolors of skyscrapers behind glass on the other walls. Something that looked like a general's terrain map hung on one wall; it was marked with small gold pins. Did they indicate property owned by Kubler? Ingrid wondered.

"It's about Miranda Falk."

"Yeah? What about her?" The woman slid off what looked like a red plush bar stool set up behind the security window. She ambled over to Ingrid and glared up at her with the self-assurance of a small hawk.

"Did you come for Miranda's things, or what? Why didn't she call herself?"

"Miranda is dead."

A look of disbelief passed over the woman's face. She looked away, shook her head slowly and wandered over to a chair. She sat down heavily. "I thought she'd just run away," she said softly, as if to herself.

Her face suddenly looked naked and drained of all hope, and Ingrid realized all at once that the woman was perhaps ten years older than herself and Miranda.

She shook her head again, then looked up at Ingrid and past her. "I told myself, if she runs, she runs. I never expected her to stay, really."

Ingrid nodded sympathetically. Here at least was one person who mourned Miranda's death.

"Sit down." It was a command rather than an invitation. Ingrid sat. The woman slowly collected herself from the toes on up. She went over to a Pyrex coffeepot sitting on its hot plate and poured two cups of coffee. "Cream and sugar?"

"Sugar, thanks. I'll get it."

She set the coffee in front of Ingrid, then sat in the nearest chair and gripped her own bone china cup. Ingrid noticed that her hand trembled as if it were a great effort not to throw the cup against the wall.

"Tell me about . . . how she died."

The coffee was almost too strong to drink, even for Ingrid. The telling took half an hour.

"And the law firm wants you to find some relative of hers to make funeral arrangements?"

"Or a friend. I keep drawing blanks. No one I can reach from L.A. knows anything about her. Or her relatives. She didn't seem to have any strings."

"This is true." The woman pondered a few moments. "Oh, my name is Wanda Sikorski." She had a strong, firm handshake. Ingrid remembered the name. She had seen it before on the prescription in Miranda's purse. "I knew Miranda when she worked here, and she came to me when she was in trouble."

"What kind of trouble?"

"Well, not pregnant, I didn't mean *that*. She needed a place to stay. I didn't expect her to stay very long, but I kept hoping. She said she didn't know if she was gay or not. Maybe I could help her. Well, we just explored those possibilities for a while."

"And?"

Wanda shrugged. "I don't think she was gay. At least not any more gay than she was straight. If you know what I mean."

"I'm not sure I do."

"Well, from day one when she worked here, I knew she was a pathological liar. But that's an occupational hazard in sales; I don't see it as a drawback if a woman is pretty enough. I just didn't take anything she said too seriously. Also she was ambitious. I'm sure she'd lie down for you as soon as look at you if it meant enough extra sales. But I just don't think Miranda knew what she wanted. She'd been faking so long, she didn't know how to find it anymore—if she ever had. Poor baby was lost way down inside there. I would have liked to put on my miner's lamp and go exploring, maybe help her find it." She smiled a little too brightly, and Ingrid sensed that she was close to tears.

"Too late. Maybe she did run after all. I hadn't seen her since Friday. When did you say, again, that she . . . ?"

"Monday."

"Monday. Okay. Monday."

"If you two were close, maybe you knew her well enough to make some kind of funeral arrangements. I know the law firm she was working for will pay for it."

"Oh, no you don't, honey. No way. I have enough trouble keeping track of my own social life. Miranda and I had a nice little bread-and-butter affair going, but we were nowhere near making commitments. Come on, you don't agree to bury every man you sleep with, do you?"

"Much as I would often like to. No. Would anyone else at Kubler have been close to her? I can ask the other people, if you'd rather not."

"There aren't that many other people. The owner is overseas now, so that would be rather an expensive call, not that I'd give you his number. But I'll tell everyone that she's dead." Her vermillion lips twisted slightly. "That should interest them."

"And the police haven't called you yet?"

"No. Why should they?" Her expression was wary.

"Your name was on a codeine prescription in her purse."

"Oh." Her eyes grew more distant; then she smiled. "She must have stolen it when she stayed at my place. My doctor gives it to me for back pain. Look, no one can tie her to anyone personally at Kubler. She worked strictly on a day-to-day cash-commission basis. As for our relationship, we could just as easily have met in a bar—can't even say how often we got together. My memory is becoming very hazy."

"Here's my card," Ingrid said, standing up, "if you or anyone else should want to contact me. You can also call Nell Scott over at Bramwell, Stinson & Flint. She's handling it for them."

Ingrid turned to go, but Wanda held up her hand, palm flat. "Wait. Do you want to look at her things? They're over at my place—or should I say the place where Kubler lets me stay when I'm in the city. Come on, we'll lock this up. It's getting close to quitting time anyway."

Ingrid sensed that Wanda wanted a little time to compose herself. She went around the office shutting off lights and machinery.

"What kind of property does Kubler deal in, business or residential?"

"Both." Wanda locked the street door behind them.

"Shall I take my car?"

"Oh, no, Mustang Sally, you better leave it. I'll run you back here. It's not far, and there's not much parking space over there this time of day."

They climbed into the jeep and Wanda made an abrupt left turn across several lanes of oncoming traffic and up onto the first block of Haight. Ingrid was grateful that the serious rush hour had not yet begun.

As they roared up the initial hill of Haight, Ingrid remembered her first day in San Francisco as a runaway in 1968. Walking from the Greyhound Bus Terminal at Seventh down Market to Haight, and up the roller-coaster hills to Masonic, where the circus started. Some of today's street people seemed awfully familiar—less charming in their craziness as they aged, looking as though they hadn't changed their Army surplus clothes in the intervening twenty years. The permanent carnival atmosphere had proved to be alarmingly transient.

Wanda turned right at Stanyan and right again a few seconds later. A sign on the front of the building identified PARK VUE CONDOMINIUM UNITS—ACROSS THE STREET FROM GOLDEN GATE PARK. The underground parking garage was built to hold perhaps twenty cars. They went up in a carpeted elevator, getting off at the third and top floor. Wanda opened a door marked 301. On a tripod next to the door a cardboard sign read MANAGER'S OFFICE.

The room inside seemed to be a living room, although a phony antique secretary desk just inside the foyer had a few official papers on it and a sign-in book headed GUESTS. The plump, cotton-floral-print sofa looked totally virginal, but the stubbled and sparkly ceiling displayed some alarming bulges.

"The boss lets me camp out here until he finds a buyer," Wanda explained, "and they don't seem to be moving, so that may be another year—who knows." She took off her shoes and motioned to Ingrid to do likewise. "Here are some disposable slippers. They save the carpet, if you don't mind."

Ingrid preferred, in fact. She took in the view of the park, a dark mass of trees stretching on endlessly across the street. Only cellophane wrapping was lacking to proclaim the newness of the place. Yet it had a stamped-out quality, like factory-line bread aimed at the lowest common denominator.

Ingrid followed Wanda into the back bedroom.

"Here are Miranda's things." She hauled out two large
suitcases and a cardboard box. "I already looked through
them, when I was packing them back up for her. I thought
she'd found another sugar. Some man. I expected him to
come and pick them up. I really didn't think I'd see her
again, anyway." Wanda was crying now. "Excuse me." She
fled from the room and Ingrid heard a door slam down the
hall.

The suitcases and cardboard box stood forlornly outside the sliding louvered doors of the closet. They reminded Ingrid of the pile of boxes in her own apartment—
now burned to cinders. She slid the frail white doors shut
in irritation. Now she knew what the whole place reminded her of—a ship's cabin. Not built for comfort or
prolonged habitation. The most efficient cramming of
minimal furnishings into the smallest space. No wonder
these condo units weren't selling. They might set sail at any
moment.

Miranda's suitcases were fine leather, dyed just-cut-your-
finger red. They were not locked. Ingrid would have expected to discover black underwear, perhaps a few vibra-
tors, scented oils and possibly a few whips and chains. But
she was disappointed.

Several suits of the pinstriped wool and beige linen variety. The dress-for-success outfits no personnel director
would be caught dead without. A little heavy on the an-
gora and suede, but no hot colors or kinky cuts. Even the
baby-doll nightgowns were childishly subdued. Although
they were short, they might have fit a serious-minded
twelve-year-old. The white cotton underpants were embroidered with strawberries.

Ingrid paused at a stack of souvenir magazines from the
Island Paradise Club neatly tied with nylon string. They
showed an assortment of sun-kissed, overfed Americans.
The average age was fifty-five, Ingrid noted. Hadn't Miranda said something about retiring soon? One of the
magazines had several pages taped together. Ingrid set the
stack aside.

She glanced through the small pile of personal records:
an expired passport for Mary Valkevich with stamps from

several different countries, including India, as Mitzi had suggested. An autograph book that dated back to high school. Ingrid had not seen one of those in years. Several minor celebrities had joined the reluctant classmates who had signed. Well-thumbed copies of the *Kama Sutra* and *Ana Aranga*. A hardbound set of works of Helen Gurley Brown. A bank book from a Bahamian branch of a Swiss bank with twice-yearly deposits of $5,000 to $10,000 each and occasional withdrawals of like amounts. The entire account was closed and all funds had been withdrawn three years earlier. No pictures or scrapbooks. Neither the kind people would kill for nor the more innocent actor's memories. Miranda must have put her brief acting career far behind her. Or maybe she kept her scrapbooks somewhere else.

In a corner of one box Ingrid found several letters, held together by a golden silk ribbon. She would have liked to slip all the papers into her purse but decided that Wanda would probably inspect the boxes to make sure nothing was missing.

The letters were all from men. The one on top was post-marked Hawaii, ten years earlier. The writer said Miranda's visit had given him a new appreciation of his wife. He was enclosing a little something for Miranda's education; how much he did not say. No greetings from the wife were enclosed. He hoped to repay his obligation to Miranda by giving her the number (business card enclosed) she had wanted of his old buddy in Frisco. The business card he mentioned was not with the letter. The letter was signed with an indecipherable scrawl.

Ingrid blinked in surprise as she read the postscript, in the same handwriting but somehow disconnected from the letter. "Don't try to bleed me anymore. You've got all you're going to get from me no matter what you have in that damned scrapbook." The scrapbook again. The envelope yielded no return address.

Almost none of the letters in the small stack had return addresses. None was from a relative or a woman. Some mentioned money. A few were vaguely romantic or flirtatious but none had any of the explicit sexual references that often make the letter writer squirm and wish the letter back in later years when the flame has died.

The last letter was written in an all-too-familiar handwriting. The post mark was also a familiar one in extreme Northern California. Ingrid stood up and crammed the letter into her purse. She retied the gold ribbon and dropped the rest of the packet casually on the top of the pile of belongings in the box.

There was no sign of anything that could be remotely considered a "scrapbook" or "files." Not so much as a folder of souvenirs.

The door opened abruptly and Wanda strode in. Ingrid jumped a little guiltily. As she had expected, Wanda pointedly inspected the contents of the boxes, but seemed to find nothing amiss.

"Are you just about finished?" She didn't wait for a reply. "I'd let you take this, but let's wait till you turn up a relative and we'll ship it to them. I'd rather just keep it here till then if you've no objection."

"No. But the police might be interested. I'll ask them when I go in to sign my statement. You won't mind talking to them, of course, if they decide they need more information."

Wanda shrugged carelessly.

"One thing I would like to ask is if I could borrow these Island Paradise Club magazines," Ingrid said. "I don't know if there's anything in them that might help, but I'm curious."

Wanda glanced at the magazines as if at a free coupon for an item she didn't care to purchase. "Keep 'em. Dunno why she saved those. They're old issues. I'd trash 'em myself. They have all the newest issues at the office—Kubler owns the damn thing."

"Where is it, anyway?"

"One of the Bahamas."

"Did Miranda talk a lot about getting some money together and going off to live on some island paradise? It sounds like Kubler's already done that." Ingrid waved a magazine at Wanda, who had her coat on and was tapping at the door frame with her car keys.

"Sure she did. So do I. Kubler thought he wanted something like that too, but then he had to turn it into a business. Maybe when you get what you want, you don't want it anymore, right?"

"You don't have any reason to suspect that Miranda was closer to her goal than an ordinary office worker might be?"

"No, honey, any money she ever had she spent as soon as she got it. She was just a working stiff like the rest of us. Are you finished or what?"

Wanda whipped the jeep down the now-darkening hills of Haight Street in silence.

"Do you know if Miranda ever went to the Island Paradise Club?" Ingrid asked.

"Sure. The boss gives us all a paid office-party vacation out there every year—all in a group so he can keep an eye on us. One of the few perks of the job."

"Even the contract commission sales people like Miranda?"

Wanda shot Ingrid a nasty look and said nothing.

As they neared Market Street, Ingrid remembered to ask, "Say, does Kubler handle the apartment on Oak Street that burned down on Monday?"

"Yes, we do. Why?"

Ingrid explained that she was a tenant and asked about the security deposit refund. It seemed to relax Wanda to discuss mundane business matters.

"Try next Monday. You'll want to talk to our bookkeeper."

"What will they be doing with the building?"

"I think they've been meaning to tear it down for years. This will just speed things up. This neighborhood is hot right now. What with the new opera house and all the building restrictions downtown." For the first time since Ingrid had met her, Wanda seemed to warm to a subject.

As they got out of the jeep on Market Street, they noticed a familiar figure locking the door of Kubler Realty. Wanda called out to her, in an unselfconscious Brando imitation, "Hey, Stella! Stella!"

The woman waved cheerfully at Wanda but almost dropped her purse when she saw Ingrid. Before Ingrid could call out to her, Stella sprinted with amazing speed to an orange VW Rabbit parked at the curb and clambered in.

"Wait!" Ingrid ran toward the car, but Stella cast her a terrified look and gunned the engine. She put the car in gear and tore off down Market Street. She snagged on a raft of rush-hour traffic a block away. But a moment later the right-turn lane opened up and the Rabbit was lost to view.

Wanda and Ingrid stood staring after the car for a moment. "Who was that, anyway?" Ingrid asked.

"That's our bookkeeper, Stella Anderson. Boy, people really take a shine to you right off, don't they? You don't even know her name and already she's running away from you. What did you do to her?"

"I don't know. But I'd like to talk to her. Could you give her my card?" Ingrid dug a pen out of her purse and wrote Carmen's number on the card. She underlined her own message-machine number and added, "Please call—I want to help." For some reason it seemed appropriate.

Wanda took the card and studied Ingrid's note carefully. "Okay. I'll put it on her desk before I go. She'll be in tomorrow morning unless you've frightened her into calling in sick. She does that sometimes. Anyway I won't give you her number. We'll let her decide whether to call you or not. She's a consenting adult, right?"

"You too. Please call me if you remember anything that might help."

"Okay." And with that Wanda slammed the glass door of Kubler Realty in Ingrid's face.

FIFTEEN

BACK AT THE DARKROOM there was a message on her machine that Jason Grapelli had called. Ingrid wondered whether she should call him back. She didn't seem to have the emotional armor to enjoy one-night stands, or even compulsively casual love affairs. Still... To get Jason's number she had to shift through the contents of her camera bag. Before she could find her wallet with its small address book inside, her hand encountered the letter she had taken from Miranda's box. It was from her ex-husband, Victor.

Just seeing the letter gave Ingrid a sinking feeling at the pit of her stomach. She thought she had written Victor off the night she'd found him on their living room sofa with another woman. She had left him a few hours later. But the idea that he might have been in touch with Miranda gave her a dizzying, sick feeling that was very close to jealousy—or fear.

As she started to open the letter, the telephone rang and Ingrid jumped as if someone had tapped her on the shoulder. She stuffed the letter back into her bag as she answered. It was Jason calling again. Very persistent. He wanted to show her his latest "work in progress." In spite of herself Ingrid felt flattered.

"I'll have to finish up in the darkroom first," she told him, determined to give herself a little space to cool off. "I can be there in about two hours." This fulfilled both her idea of not rushing over the moment he called and her plan of making a print as a gift for him.

Ingrid had decided to give prints as Christmas presents this year to everyone on her gift list. Most of the prints were on their way, and she would be able to process the rest tomorrow. In Jason's case, she realized that she wasn't so much giving him a gift as "proving herself" to be a serious artist behind the camera. She scolded herself for caring about his opinion. But there it was. She wanted his approval.

Besides, she was proud of the shot. She had taken it that Sunday as he hung his collages on the café walls. The photo captured his bantam-rooster toughness: it was black and white, taken from the rear from about the shoulder blades up. His head was turned in full profile to ask the café owner a question, his arms raised to put a picture to the wall. He had noticed her taking the picture and a moment later had swooped down from his stance on the step stool to place an expert kiss on her lips.

She finished the print. While waiting for it to dry, she printed proof sheets for the rest of the film. She hurried through them and put on some makeup. She had to postpone looking at the pictures carefully. She slipped the picture of Jason into an envelope and stowed it in her purse alongside the stiff cardboard Sudden Service envelope that held Miranda's memo.

It was just after seven P.M. when she left the darkroom. Ito was warming up for his evening class. Sometimes Ingrid came and went through the *dojo*, skirting the mat area but stopping to bow in polite quasi-Japanese fashion at the picture of the original *sensei* and the incomprehensible calligraphy that surrounded it. When there was a class, she went down to the end of the hall and through the side door, passing Yoshiko's kitchen with its small sewing-room annex, where Ingrid often saw her sewing with a few other Japanese ladies. They always waved her in and she always smiled, accepted a cup of tea and a cookie and left soon after. The talk was all Japanese and all the sewing made her nervous.

Hiromasu Ito, the aikido master, was Ingrid's height, tall for a first-generation *issei*, born in Japan. His English was none too strong, but he was a terrifically good-natured man who looked at least twenty years younger than his reputed age of sixty.

His son Mas, American-born *nisei*, four inches taller and seemingly a foot wider than his father, was working out with him and getting the worst of it. He was the only one of Ito's three sons to have followed him into martial arts.

They concluded their sequence, bowed to the picture of the school's founder at one end of the mat and stepped off the mat as if leaving a separate room.

"Coming in tomorrow, Inga?"

"Looks like she's got a hot date, dad," Mas observed, pointing out Ingrid's sudden bloom of makeup, the gauze dress and the high heels she kept at the studio in case of sudden evening engagements. She was mildly nervous about the night, but she had decided that even if danger lurked out there, she could probably get from Ito's to the Mustang and from the car to the safe harbor of Jason's place before it could catch up to her. Even in high heels.

"Well, we'll see how it goes, Mr. Ito. Maybe I'll get so tired that I'll have to miss class tomorrow, maybe not." She winked at Yoshiko, who was just coming out of the kitchen. She laughed and slapped Ingrid so hard on the back that she reeled. Ingrid bowed involuntarily in reply to their bows when she said good night. The Itos peppered their speech with conversational bows as punctuation. It was catching.

It didn't take long to drive from Arguello to Twenty-fifth, but finding a parking place near Jason's house was not so easy. Someone seemed to be having a holiday party. She negotiated the U-turn in the cul-de-sac at the end of Twenty-fifth. After she recrossed El Camino Del Mar, she noticed another car idling along behind her. Was someone else looking for a parking place? It was a large black car—a Cadillac or a Continental, something with a grille. She disliked how close that grille kept coming to her rear bumper. At Lake Street a parking place presented itself. She stopped and waved the black car around her. It didn't pass, but it wasn't blocking her so she slid the Mustang into the place, barely fitting between two driveways.

The black car drove slowly by as she finished parking. A Continental, she noted as she leaped out, preparing to walk to Jason's as fast as possible. The Continental's closeness made her nervous. As she locked the door, the Continental backed up so abruptly that she almost walked into its tail light. Ingrid gasped in shock. It had almost run her over.

The driver seemed unrepentant, even unsurprised. The car now backed up even farther, blocking the driver's side door to her Mustang completely, and Ingrid realized with a sinking feeling that it had effectively caged the Mustang into the parking space. Even before the driver got the door open, she turned and ran. She heard the car door slam and footsteps pursuing her.

Instinctively she continued down Lake Street rather than turning back onto Twenty-fifth Avenue. A mistake. Lake Street was flatter than Twenty-fifth Avenue. She could run better on Lake Street, but so could he. He was gaining on her.

Ingrid cursed her high heels, running in the stiff-legged gait they allowed. She should have run back toward California. There was more traffic there, and at least she could have run out into the stream of cars or into the market at the corner.

In front of one of the houses on Lake the sidewalk had been torn up. Taking up a parking space next to the curb was a portable trash bin with five-foot-tall sides and an interior the size of a small mobile home. YOU-FILL, WE-HAUL was printed in white on its red metal side. Ingrid stumbled over a loose chunk of concrete and fell against the side of the trash bin, twisting her ankle. Damn those shoes. She narrowly avoided going down headlong. She glanced back. He was only a few yards away. She stumbled through the rubble of the torn-up sidewalk and began to yell for help.

She recognized the muscular man with the shaven head. Tonight he wasn't wearing the messenger uniform.

A light went on in an upstairs window. Then the man was on her, pinning her with a thud to the side of the dumpster. Her attacker was breathing heavily. He stared intently at her just as he had done on the steps of the Pacific Stock Exchange. She noticed that he had a snake tattooed on his skull.

"What's wrong?" she managed to pant. "Didn't you get paid for that delivery?"

"I'll take that," he growled, yanking her camera bag off her shoulder.

She surrendered it silently. She was beginning to find her footing. He had her in a difficult grip, pinning her against the metal. She concentrated on his breathing, which was just slightly labored. "You got to learn not to butt in where you're not wanted, lady. Okay. You gonna tell me where that scrapbook is? Come on, you can show me."

"I don't know. I haven't got anything like that."

"Let's go." He pulled her away from the trash bin. Ingrid followed him for an instant, then levered his fingers into a *Yawara-Tori*. She squeezed his already clenched fingers with all her might, and as his body arched away from the pain, she reached up to lock his elbow into a come-along. She saw her error instantly, but Ito was not there to stop the action. The man's elbow was still bent and he careened back and around, knocking the two of them apart. Her camera bag fell from his grip onto the sidewalk, its contents spilling every which way.

He turned back to her with a power she had not expected and carried her with him, up against the side wall of the trash bin. But she had thrown his timing off enough to be able to duck the blow he aimed at her eye. It glanced off her cheekbone as she flinched away from it. His fist hit the metal with a loud clang. He let out a bellow of pain and fell back, holding his hand.

Ingrid scurried away. She stooped to grab her wallet, which had fallen out of her camera bag onto the gutter.

"Hey! You! Get away from that trash bin!" Both Ingrid and her attacker paused as an irate homeowner came charging down his driveway toward them. "I'm gonna call the cops. I paid good money to rent that. Nobody's gonna dump anything there but me. Get out of there!"

Ingrid's attacker shoved her mightily, snatched up her camera bag and ran. As Ingrid staggered back, trying to keep her balance, her shoulder blade caught the corner of the metal bin and down she fell backward into the street. A sudden darkness and a shooting pain overwhelmed her as her head hit something hard and flat. Vaguely, she heard a car engine starting somewhere in the distance before everything went black.

SIXTEEN

INGRID LOOKED UP at a surrounding rim of faces peering down at her in the dimness. She took no interest in them at all for a moment, then she had the idea that she should sit up.

"You okay, lady?" Someone was coming down to her level. "You want us to call the paramedics?"

"No." Ingrid sat up abruptly. That cost money. A wave of dizziness washed over her.

The formerly irate householder now offered her his hand to help her up. "Can you do it?"

"Sure." Her own voice sounded strange. She noticed that she was still clutching her wallet tightly.

As she leaned against the red side of the trash trailer, she saw that the homeowner had been joined by several neighbors.

"Were you hurt very badly?" a woman asked Ingrid. Then, without giving her time to answer, "Was that your boyfriend?"

"What? No, it was a mugger. You didn't happen to notice his license plate, did you?"

Several of the neighbors shook their heads in disbelief. "In this neighborhood?" an older man said. "A burglary sure, but a mugging?"

Ingrid left them debating the matter and turned to limp back to her car. Then she realized that the keys to her car were in her camera bag. Her spare key was at Carmen's.

She checked her wallet hopefully, but the only key there was the key to Carmen's door and the mysterious key she had picked up at the restaurant with its blue Dymo label: 10-12. Fortunately, there was also change for the bus.

She reversed direction and headed toward the nearest bus stop, taking inventory of which muscles had been strained. She felt bruised in several areas but had no broken bones.

She also had a tremendous headache. But no dizziness, although she'd been knocked out. She stopped and leaned against a lamppost at the corner of Clement. Well, maybe a little dizziness.

And a few hallucinations?

She could have sworn she saw Tony Flint Junior and an unidentified young woman getting out of a red Porsche on Clement Street. She shook her head slowly and painfully and looked again. It was them all right.

So Tony Flint still wore his three-piece suit on a date. Maybe he slept in it. She decided not to ask the woman, who wore the classic female-lawyer outfit: frock coat and straight skirt, complete with the sort of string tie Mark Twain used to wear.

"Lawyers, lawyers, lawyers. Why is it when you need a cop, all you can find is a lawyer?" Actually she didn't want to talk to the police; the possibility of getting her cameras back was balanced against the questions they might want to ask her. She hated to admit it, but she had to agree with the neighbors who had come to her rescue. This was no random purse snatching—the man had wanted to kidnap her. He had wanted Miranda's scrapbook. He had said so.

Tony Flint had stopped in the middle of the sidewalk and was staring at Ingrid. He said something to his female companion and walked over to Ingrid. "Are you okay?" His kindly air told Ingrid how battered she must look.

She explained how she had just been assaulted and had her purse snatched. He responded with outraged concern and did not mention her martial-arts demonstration with Claude in the Bramwell Lobby. Ingrid was grateful to him for that.

"Let me introduce my, ahem, colleague Josephine Lewis. We were going out for a drink before dinner. We have to meet a client later this evening. Perhaps we could drop you someplace—the police station seems like a good idea. You'll want to report this. Were there witnesses?"

"I don't think so," Ingrid said a little unsteadily. "Let me think about it. I'm not so sure I want to make a report just now. It would take a lot of time and make a terrible dent in my evening."

"Ingrid, you are clearly the worse for wear. Let's get you a drink," Tony said smoothly. "There's a nice little café in the next block on Clement."

Josephine Lewis was a short woman with long, brown, silky hair, dark-lashed blue eyes and a pretty, dimpled face. She seemed worried, but she said nothing. Ingrid could tell Josephine wouldn't want to give up her sole possession of Tony without a struggle, especially to a slightly rumpled street-crime victim.

Josephine's hostility stirred a chord of resistance in Ingrid; she already felt stung, realizing just how close she had come to being kidnapped.

"Look, you people are already on your way somewhere. I've got to at least call and say I'll be late. I don't drink alcohol, but a soda would be very nice. Someplace where there's a public phone." It was all she could do not to laugh out loud at the look of chagrin on Josephine's face.

"Are you sure you don't need medical care, dear?" The lady lawyer put a pink-nailed hand on Ingrid's arm. Ingrid looked at it until she took it away.

The café on Clement had a glass panel to protect its semi-outdoor tables. They sat near the glass, watching the sidewalk. She asked them to order her an orange soda and went to call Jason, thankful that she'd been able to salvage her wallet with its change purse and address book. Her possessions were sustaining heavy losses lately.

Ingrid began to explain why she couldn't come over after all. Before she could finish Jason broke in.

"Ingrid, stop babbling. I can tell you're upset. Let's just forget it tonight. You're in no condition to appreciate my work, and I guess you've already managed to lose whatever photo you were going to show me."

Managed to lose? Ingrid bit back an angry reply. It was most annoying to have someone tell you not to come before you could say you weren't coming anyhow. If he was agreeing, why did it feel like he was arguing? And if he was arguing, why not just stop seeing him?

Ingrid realized with a jolt that she had a certain horrifying talent for picking Mr. Wrong from a roomful of strangers. Still, she didn't feel like letting go of Jason yet. He was passionately involved and inventive in bed, and she greatly admired his artwork. It was all too confusing to think about tonight.

"Okay, Jason. See you next year."

"Oh, right, that's next week, isn't it?"

She touched her cheek. It hurt. More than anything she wanted a hot shower and then to go to bed. A brandy sounded good too. But Ingrid's prejudice against alcohol was stronger than her self-pity. So far.

She looked at her face in the mirror of the café's rest room. The bruise on her cheek didn't show yet. Her sweater was now deeply stained with grease, dirt and who knew what else. She took it off. It was warm in the café. The light gauze dress had been ripped only a little along the neck when the man had grabbed it. Ingrid decided it just gave her a slightly lower neckline. She pulled herself together with several deep breaths.

Back at the table the lawyers were talking shop.

Josie acknowledged Ingrid's return to the table with a shrug and a display of teeth that a shark would have envied.

Ingrid lowered herself delicately into the chair, wincing a little as the sore places touched the wood. Her orange soda had arrived. She sipped it and concentrated on Josephine and Tony to take her mind off her hurts.

"So, Josephine, you work at BSF too? I've never seen you there. Your office must be on a different floor from this guy's."

Tony beamed at her like a fight promoter sensing a newsworthy spat at the weigh-in. "Josephine is in Probate. Isn't that right, monkey pie?" He tugged at her string tie, as if beginning to disrobe her in the café.

Ingrid took a moment to admire Tony's deeply tanned blondness. If he ever stopped shaving for a few days, the stubble would glint like bits of gold in a miner's pan on that ocean-going bronze skin.

Too well-bred to suggest that Ingrid was ruining her evening, Josephine chose this moment to jump in. "Ingrid, I hear you're making some sort of inquiries for Nell Scott. What's that all about?''

"Just trying to find out who might have known Miranda well enough to be notified of her death. You know, set up your basic funeral for her and all.''

Tony leaned forward and Ingrid moved back instinctively, a little rattled. But he stayed his hand before touching her. "Ingrid, did it ever occur to you that Nell Scott was hoping *you* might set up some sort of funeral/memorial service for your old friend?''

"Oh, I'm sure you'd all like the corpse taken off your hands. But why me and not your father? He had a closer relationship to her than I did.''

"You think so? I wonder what gives you that impression; maybe your sources are more informed than mine.'' Tony stared at Ingrid intently, as if puzzled but intrigued. Josephine looked disgusted. Tony leaned forward again. "But you two did go to school together; wouldn't you say you were old friends? Miranda seemed to think so.''

"Tony, if she talked to you about that sort of thing, you must have known her fairly well yourself.''

Tony smiled slowly, still gazing at Ingrid. "Not my type at all, but she served my father's purposes. She seemed useful at first. But that was just an illusion.'' He stopped as if lost in memory for a moment, then shook himself slightly and continued, "We were business acquaintances. She was a very dynamic, aggressive person. You could call her a self-starter.'' He paused. "Stand still for a minute around Miranda and you'd have high-heel prints going up one side and down the other.'' No one laughed.

Ingrid had to turn away from Tony Flint, who had begun to stare at her as if mesmerized. Maybe it was the almost-transparent cotton dress she had worn for her hot date with Jason. Ingrid was annoyed to find that she was beginning to respond physically to his attention. "What about you?'' She turned to Josephine. "Did you know Miranda?''

"No.''

There was a moment of silence before Ingrid forced herself to meet Tony's china-blue eyes. "Is your father feeling

better? He was quite ill yesterday when he saw what someone had done to his plants.''

Tony looked at his watch. ''Right about now, I would say
he's finished his legal research for the day. For years his
routine would be to get home at about 8 P.M. Lately he
works in his own library after dinner for a few hours. He
spends the evenings and weekends with his African violets.
He should be in his greenhouse by now.''

''He didn't have to go to the hospital? It looked like he'd
had a heart attack or something, and then I saw a—'' Ingrid stopped herself before mentioning the hypodermic in
the wastebasket in Flint Senior's private bathroom.

''You saw a syringe in his wastebasket?''

She nodded. At least he was kind enough not to chastise
her for her snooping.

''My father is a diabetic, Ingrid. Since he was a child. His
doctor keeps an eye on his insulin dosage, but sometimes a
sudden shock like seeing his plants all wrecked like that can
have a bad effect on him. I saw him this morning, unfortunately. He was feeling well enough to lecture me for a
good three quarters of an hour.''

Tony and Josephine laughed.

Ingrid raised her eyebrows. ''You don't usually see your
father?''

''Not if I can avoid it. I've got a place on the slopes of
Nob Hill. I've all but completed the paperwork on a thirty-
six-foot sloop. When that's done, I'll live on board. Dad
still lives in the family house over in St. Francis Wood.
Since he's been away from the office lately, things have
gone quite smoothly. In fact Jo and I were just remarking
on how remarkably congenial the atmosphere has been the
past few days.'' They laughed again.

Ingrid felt suddenly queasy; she needed to get out into the
fresh air immediately. ''You people are going downtown. I
believe I'll just catch a bus home.''

Tony protested that she should come with them to dinner, and Josephine glared at Ingrid as if daring her to accept. She felt quite dizzy. Eating was even lower on her list
of pastimes than arm wrestling Josephine for Tony's fa-
vors.

At the very least, Tony insisted, they could drop her off at the police station, or at home if she preferred.

Ingrid refused firmly and left them at the café. She limped down to the nearest bus stop, at Twenty-fifth Avenue and Geary. She felt shaky, but somehow she didn't want them to know where she lived.

She felt a deep anger building and knew she had to get to the bottom of the whole thing now. As Ingrid waited for the 38 Geary bus, she scanned the horizon for homicidal bicycle messengers.

SEVENTEEN

Saturday, December 24

INGRID WOKE UP on Carmen's sofa with a sudden jolt. A dream about falling. She was falling through the floor of her burning apartment. No. It was an earthquake, maybe 8.5 on the Richter scale.

She had spent most of Friday considering the possibility that she might have a mild concussion, then falling asleep again before resolving the matter. Several times she woke up and decided firmly to have an aspirin but only once made it over to the bathroom medicine cabinet, and immediately limped back to the sofa.

In the late afternoon, Carmen forced a bowl of chicken soup on her and went off to work. Ingrid sat up for awhile but could not bring her mind to focus on her predicament. At last she turned on the television and let it talk to itself. Mugwort joined her on the sofa and sometime after two A.M. Carmen must have come in and turned off the television. Now she awoke with the definite conviction that it must be Saturday noon at least.

She sat up and instantly regretted it. She might have a mild concussion. She lay back down again to think about that. The sudden throb of pain was not intense, but returned each time she tried to sit up or change her position. A very bad headache, she decided, and severe stiffness and soreness in several major muscle groups. Her head had hit the side of the trash bin and then had struck the broken pavement when she went down.

As Ingrid was drifting off to sleep again, Carmen emerged from her bedroom, trailed by an insistent Mugwort, who capered around her legs meowing for his breakfast.

"Where did I put the chestnuts? Morning, Ingrid. Okay. Here they are. Now what about *The Joy of Cooking?* Could I have left it in the yarn room? Stay out of there, you vicious beast—I'll feed you in a minute. You know you're not allowed in the yarn room."

Not only Saturday but the day before Christmas.

Ingrid decided to get up. Although it was only mid-morning, Christmas Eve had set in. All the previous evening Carmen had been anxious about preparing the chestnut stuffing to go in and around her mother's turkey.

Carmen's mother lived in Fremont, over an hour's drive away. Carmen was convinced that the chestnut stuffing assignment was a way of punishing youngest daughter for living so far away. It was supposed to be the easiest part of the whole meal, and Carmen was a good cook. But somehow it ended up taking most of the day.

Carmen expounded her strategy for revenge this year, which primarily consisted of bring Spyder. Spyder was bringing his cameras. Ingrid envisioned him embarrassing Carmen's female relatives with candid shots of them gorging on turkey, while alienating the male relatives with a medley of leftist slogans. Ingrid hated to miss Spyder's performance, but she pleaded her injuries and a deep-seated need to be alone.

By early afternoon Ingrid's headache had faded to an acceptable throbbing, and she decided she could handle printing the rest of her film. Maybe Jason would call. Ingrid pushed the thought aside but then reconsidered. Perhaps she was too bruised to go looking for a new man immediately. Perhaps she just wanted to waste her time on horizontal aerobics. She told herself she must be healing rapidly if she found the thought of vigorous sex appealing. Anyway, she had to go pick up her car.

By five P.M. she was sitting at the counter in her dark-room, peering at her proof sheets through a circular magnifying loupe. Sorting out technical problems always helped Ingrid cope with holidays. There was the danger of drunken phone calls from her mother and the need to plan a safe topic for a call to her father. She postponed all these painful thoughts and turned her attention to timing exposures in the darkroom.

The Itos were Buddhists. Although they closed the school on Christian holidays in deference to American customs, Ingrid noted that they hadn't yet picked up the American tradition of yearly visits with the relatives who had become intimate strangers, with familiar quarrels and traditional wounds to renew.

Holiday housecleaning seemed to be the Japanese custom. Or was it just practical to clean since the *dojo* was closed? She asked Mas about this as he wandered into the darkroom, where she was using the overhead light to inspect her proof sheets.

"It's for New Year's—kind of like spring cleaning here. New Year's is real big in Japan," he answered, showing more interest in her enlarger than in the subject at hand.

Ingrid's shot of Flint Senior had been blurred. There was a very light frame next to it that might have been the first one she squeezed off after she switched from the telephoto lens. She would have to enlarge that quite a bit.

Automatically she reached for the big magnifying glass she kept in her camera bag.

"Damn."

"What's wrong?" Mas was squinting through her enlarger at nothing.

"Oh, I keep forgetting my camera bag was stolen when I was mugged yesterday."

"Mugged?" He stared at her face more closely and seemed to see her bruised cheek for the first time. "Wow! You sure walked into that one."

She explained what had happened the night before. "He got my cameras and most of my lenses. But he didn't get any exposed film. I'd left it all here."

"Do you think he wanted your film?"

"If he wanted my film, he might come here. Maybe we should tell Ito-sensei."

Mas nodded gravely. "I'll tell my father. We'll keep an eye out." He clearly relished the prospect. "What do you think he did want?"

"I'm not sure."

Mas shook his head thoughtfully. "At least he didn't get your wallet," he offered in consolation. "You watch out, Ingrid. Sounds like you were pretty quick with the counter, but maybe you need more than two classes a week, neh? It's a jungle out there." He went reluctantly back to the mop and pail he'd left outside the door.

"Right," she called after him.

She turned back to her proof sheets, then halted in mid turn. The letter from Victor had been in her camera bag, as had Miranda's memo to her. Someone wanted Miranda's scrapbook, and Ingrid had no idea where to even begin looking for that. Wanda might have even taken it out of Miranda's belongings already.

Ingrid's eyes lit on Miranda's magazines. They sat in a tidy pile on the floor, waiting for her to take them to Carmen's. They didn't look very valuable.

She shrugged, winced at the pain that created and returned to printing the very light frame of the ghost of Flint Senior. It was two stops overexposed. With Tri-X it was worth trying, though.

In fact she was able to coax a print out of it.

When the image came up, it showed Flint Senior walking across the alley with the metal frame of the new building hardly visible in the background. No blurring there. He was carrying a briefcase. But the background had gotten lost.

She tried another print, giving the background details more time to darken, just out of curiosity. Then she saw the silhouette of a figure standing in the alley under the fire escape, looking out. It was a tall, heavyset woman, looking almost into the camera's lens, perhaps waiting for Flint to pass. Stella Anderson, Kubler Realty's bookkeeper. She certainly seemed to have hated Miranda. But what was she doing standing in the alley below her office window? Ingrid hung the print to dry.

The Rosemary Tanner film gave her something to work with. Tanner might not have been a platinum blonde in her youth, but she managed to carry it off well these days. The olive skin fit well with the candy-floss hair. There was one very close shot that treated her wrinkles and jowls very

kindly, but the hair looked dirty. Ingrid shielded the hair
from the enlarger's beam with paper dodging tool stuck on
a piece of wire. She moved the shade between the enlarger's light source and the image's hair, giving the rest of the
print a few more seconds of exposure to bring the woman's features out. Not bad. Too much of the Florida so-
cialite look perhaps—peroxide and suntan. But it made
Rosemary look healthy, wealthy and wise. She probably
was the first two, anyway. Ingrid hung her up to dry.

It was evening when she finished. As she went out the
door, she picked up the stack of magazines. Then she
stopped and studied them more closely, noting again the
issue with the taped-together pages. She untied the nylon
string, cautiously cut the tape with her scissors and shook
the magazine gently above the counter. A computer diskette fell out. A floppy diskette. The right size for BSF's
machines. She put it in a folder with the prints and proof
sheets she planned to take downtown soon. She brought the
magazines back to Carmen's, along with a few prints,
wrapped in improbably shaped packages, she had made for
Carmen and Spyder as Christmas presents.

The Mustang had weathered the night safely. She hopped
in and nervously drove away. No sign of the black Continental either along the way or behind her. Ingrid decided to
install a new ignition, trunk and door locks when Auto
World opened again after the holidays, in case the mugger
tracked her car down to try the keys he'd found in her
shoulder bag. She was relieved that she hadn't lost the key
to Carmen's house. That would have made her really nervous.

She stopped to buy some groceries and brandy for Carmen. The brandy was particularly well received. The
chestnut stuffing was safely in its bowl in the refrigerator.
Carmen sat staring at her fingernails, which seemed to have
become permanently stained by chestnut pulp.

Ingrid settled down contentedly with the Island Paradise
Club magazines. Spyder looked over her shoulder for a
moment, then took one and began thumbing through it,
exclaiming over pictures of orange-sherbet sunsets and en-
vying the photographers who had been paid to wander

through such a lush resort. It had begun to rain outside, making the fireplace a natural magnet for Mugwort, who turned on his back with his rump pressed against the screen and dozed with all four feet in the air.

When Carmen wasn't looking, Ingrid slipped her presents under the live silver spruce. Each year, Carmen adopted a new tree to decorate, and planted it in her large backyard. The place was starting to look like an annex to Golden Gate Park.

Like many San Francisco houses, Carmen's place had no real front yard, merely a strip of ground-hugging succulents between the front walk and the sloping driveway, which dropped abruptly from the sidewalk to a garage sunken below street level. The front bay window loomed over the driveway; there was just enough room to park a car there. Spyder's van always stuck slightly into the street, preventing anyone from blocking Carmen's driveway. She liked that.

"Carmen, whatever happened to those African violets I brought home? Were they totally lost?" Ingrid asked.

Carmen looked up from the black-nailed hand that held her brandy. "Oh, they were a little parched is all. They're in the back by the kitchen window. They like the indirect sunlight. Oh, I forgot. I found something when I repotted one of them. I've been meaning to show it to you. Here, I'll go get it."

Carmen brought back a folded newspaper with a Ziploc bag resting on it. There were bits of potting soil around the edges.

"It's a little dirty, Ing. This thing was at the bottom of the pot. It was cutting water from the saucer underneath, so that plant was drier than the rest. Look."

Ingrid held up the bag. It held an ordinary house key. She unsealed the top and took it out. Turning the key over and over in her hand, she thought for a moment, then went to the hall closet where her jacket hung, its pocket bulging with her wallet. She found the blue-labeled key. She held the two keys together and up to the light. The teeth did not match.

Different keys. The one Carmen had unearthed had no label.

She showed Carmen.

"So. You know what they are." It was not a question.

"Well, I know this one fell on the table while a woman was returning it to Miranda the day she died."

Spyder put down his magazine and came to look.

"What's it the key to?" Carmen asked.

"I don't know." Ingrid took the keys and the plastic bag and weighed them in her hand. "One way or another, both of these came from Miranda. I think the guy who took my purse wanted these keys. Maybe *he* knows."

Spyder pinned Ingrid with one of his sharpest looks. "Ingrid, I think you really ought to talk to Victor. He might know more about all this."

Ingrid turned away and stood staring at the fireplace for several moments.

"Yeah, but would he tell us?" she asked Mugwort, so softly that no one else could hear. The cat opened one of his eyelids a fraction of an inch, showing the inner eyelid, and closed it again, too zonked on hearth heat to take any heed.

"Come on, Ingrid," Spyder said. "I mean it."

Ingrid stretched and yawned, unwilling to look away from the fireplace. "Do you think Vic and Miranda were in touch with each other?"

It was Spyder's turn to be reluctant.

Carmen was staring at the two of them in irritation. "Come on, you guys, level with each other and with me."

Spyder joined Ingrid at the fireplace. She turned to look away, toward the window and the park beyond. Ingrid saw their reflections staring back from the night-shrouded glass. The only shield against the darkness was the white lace shawl Carmen had hung in the window, its V-shaped fringe just brushing the sill. Somewhere out there lurked the "dogs" Miranda had set on Ingrid, waiting to attack. Or could one of them be inside with her now?

Ingrid stood beside Spyder for a moment. For the first time she wondered if the man who had attacked her might be a friend of Spyder's. What did she really know about

Spyder, anyway? He had been Victor's friend in Humboldt, not hers.

Carmen abandoned any effort of talking to Ingrid or Spyder. She snapped on the television.

Ingrid went to sit with her. "Carmen, I'm sorry, I'm worried about putting you in danger by staying here. I mean, whatever all this means, I have to at least try to find out. I don't know who these people are, but it looks like my ex-husband is involved. Spyder, you say Victor is a very romantic person. I don't agree. And I don't want Carmen to become a target just because I'm staying here or because you're going with her."

Both Carmen and Spyder stared at Ingrid in surprise, as if physical danger were the last thing they could have imagined.

Ingrid stopped in confusion, afraid to risk explaining about Miranda's memo.

"Okay, confess, Ingrid," Spyder demanded. "You killed Miranda, didn't you? To keep her from hassling you."

Ingrid threw the nearest Island Paradise Club magazine at him. He caught it handily.

"A clear admission of guilt. I can see I'm going to have to buy a ticket to Island Paradise Club and take pictures of braless bronzed bimbos, instead of all these paranoid big-city gals." With that, he stretched out in the armchair near the fireplace and buried his nose in the magazine.

Ingrid looked to Carmen for help, but she was tuning in to *Miracle on 34th Street*.

"Okay, Spyder, I give up. If Carmen has no objection, do you think you could set up a meeting with Victor?"

"Just keep him away from my house," Carmen said flatly. "I don't want him to even know where it is."

Spyder looked up casually. "He said he'd meet me tomorrow at Stanyan and Geary when Carmen and I head out toward the freeway on our way to Fremont. Is that all right with you?" He glanced at Carmen out of the corner of one eye.

Carmen shrugged and looked at Ingrid.

"Stanyan and Geary is fine," Ingrid said. "We can walk around, maybe get some coffee if anything is open."

No one could concentrate on the familiar *Miracle on 34th Street*. Spyder smoked moodily. Carmen nursed a final brandy but drank very little of it. Ingrid took her next installment of aspirin for her dozens of strained muscles with a festive snifter of cranberry juice. At midnight they exchanged presents:

Highly flashy sweaters Carmen had created for Ingrid and Spyder.

A battered camera bag for Ingrid from Spyder. "To replace the one you lost—it's used, but it looks like it should last," Spyder said gruffly. Ingrid smiled and gingerly slung it over her shoulder. It seemed bizarrely empty without the familiar drag of her cameras and lenses. Carmen asked to look at it and Ingrid guessed that she was planning to design another strap for it like the one she had made with Ingrid's name woven into it, which had been attached to one of the stolen cameras.

Ingrid offered her mat-mounted prints sheepishly. Spyder laughed at the picture she had taken of him. He was lying on the ground near a meter maid, shooting her picture from a very low angle while she put a ticket on his van. The laugh helped to lighten up everyone's mood.

Carmen turned her eyes away in embarrassment from the first of the two pictures Ingrid gave her, suddenly shy at seeing her own likeness. But she did like the second picture of a black street musician playing his guitar on Montgomery Street, with the morning light glinting off his white shirt front, guitar and one of the dimes in his instrument case.

Eventually Spyder drew Carmen back to the bedroom. "Men are all alike," he growled as he went. "They only want one thing."

Do they? Ingrid wondered, preparing to sleep on the sofa. She awoke much later during the night to find Spyder standing not far from the sofa, bent over the camera bag, where she had conspicuously stowed most of her remaining belongings.

"Do you want the bag back, Spyder?" she asked. He started violently.

"Damn it, Ingrid, you scared the hell out of me."

"If you want those keys, they're not in there. But I'll talk to Vic tomorrow, will that do?"

"I guess it will have to."

EIGHTEEN

Sunday, December 25

CARMEN PROPOSED THAT they have breakfast with Victor before trusting Ingrid alone with him. "You just want to get a look at Vic," Ingrid teased.

"You bet I do."

They drew up to Geary and Stanyan. The chestnut stuffing and presents were crowded into two large shopping bags in the back of Spyder's van, his speakers blasting rock and roll as usual. Ingrid wore dark sunglasses to hide her bruised cheek.

Victor lounged against the wall of Pier 1 Imports. He seemed thinner and older, but then he would be forty now. He still had those hawk-sharp eyes that were brown enough to be black. He had indeed grown a beard. A little white streak along the chin at the center made him look as if he had a dimple in his chin. He had never even considered a beard before.

"A smuggler has to blend in," he always said. "It goes with the territory."

Maybe he hadn't returned to his former business. She could not think of anything to say to him in the back of Spyder's van. It was like meeting a stranger. Luckily the music made conversation both unnecessary and impossible.

The twenty-four-hour coffee shop on Geary was almost deserted. The subdued but cheerful lighting and the slick orange-and-brown plastic decor took away some of the strangeness.

Ingrid could feel Carmen relax slightly, seeing that Victor appeared calm and rational, with no fire of violence burning in those coal-dark eyes. Ingrid was a little relieved

herself. He was as handsome as ever, and the waitress fluttered a little when she took their order.

The black hair on his hands made them look more sim-
ian than Ingrid remembered. She had rehearsed a meeting
with him on countless occasions. But meeting him now, she
felt oddly tranquil, with no immediate urge to either kiss or
kill him. Had the old mad tie that had bound her to him finally been broken?

"So are you on parole now or what?" she said.

"Yes. But not for long. I'll be free again. Miranda gave
me a good reference getting out of the joint. That helped."

"So you did know Miranda." Ingrid spoke lightly,
watching Vic intently. "Were you surprised by her death?"

Vic took a drink of orange juice and reflected a moment. "No. She tried it before, you know."

"Tried?"

"Suicide. When she was a teenager."

"And you think this time she succeeded."

"Ingrid, Ingrid," he said, the hand with its tarantula-
black hair covering hers, "you've gotten so gray. Have you
been pining away for someone?"

Ingrid laughed a little skittishly and moved her hand, not
quite ready to risk skin contact. She was a little irritated to
see that he was more worried about her gray hairs than she
was, as if she were still his possession, slightly tarnished
from lack of adequate polishing.

"No, Victor, it runs in families. Remember my gray-
haired Aunt Kristin? Well, she's been that way since she was
thirty."

"I lost my lease when I was in prison," Victor said. "All
my money all went to the lawyer. If you'd stuck by me instead of divorcing me when times got rough, we both could
be up there now."

"No, Vic. I left you before you got busted. Remember?"

"Yes. I remember that."

Everyone finished soon after that. The waitress brought
the check, which Victor paid without argument from anyone. Spyder and Carmen waved, and the van tooled off toward the freeway.

Victor and Ingrid walked along the broad sidewalk of Geary Boulevard, both shyly silent.

There wasn't much traffic. A few families, shyly clumsy in Sunday best, carrying foil-wrapped containers to relatives' houses, reminded Ingrid that she would have to call her parents later in the day.

"How well did you know Miranda, Vic?"

"There's one thing I want to hear from you first."

"What's that?"

"Why did you leave me?"

"I've been thinking about that a lot for the past three years."

"So have I. Only I was in prison."

"Don't expect me to feel guilty or sorry for you about that. You took a gamble on an illegal business and lost. We're none of us innocent victims. I just don't believe that now."

Vic reached out and gripped her hand and held it very hard. It hurt. Ingrid looked down and saw that her fingers were turning white in his grip. A veil seemed to lift from Victor's eyes, and they filled with a bitter light as he spoke. "Ingrid, what can I think? One day you leave me, a few months later I get busted. What's the connection? There must be some connection."

Ingrid moved with him as he pulled her and felt for the moment when he would be off balance. When it came, she shoved him in the direction he'd been pulling her, and Victor stumbled backward along the clean gray width of sidewalk. She moved aside but did not run.

He caught his balance before falling but glared at her with pure hatred in his eyes. Ingrid felt cold all over. She knew that if Victor could have reached out and killed her without suffering any consequences, he would have done so instantly.

He moved close but this time did not touch her. "Well?"

"I'm sorry you think I turned you in, Vic. It's not true. I never told anyone about what you did for a living. If anyone else knew about your business, it's because you told them."

"Okay." He did not seem convinced, but let it go. "So why did you leave?"

"Well, there *was* that woman I found you in bed with the night I left. But even before that, I guess I stopped believing that noble-outlaw stuff. Not that I respect the drug laws. I think they're hypocritical, the same way Prohibition was hypocritical. But I can't see patting yourself on the back for breaking them. It's like congratulating yourself for cheating on your wife. And I wish I'd known your views on *that* subject before we got married."

"It wouldn't have made any difference to you back then, Ingrid. You were hooked on me, I could tell."

"Maybe," Ingrid said, wondering if that was true. "But I couldn't go on, knowing you were sleeping with someone else. Let's see—I also got fed up with your hitting me. These are all the reasons I can think of at the moment. If I think of any more, I'll let you know."

"No. No. That's enough."

They walked on in silence again for another block.

"Okay, Vic, now you tell me about Miranda. Had you been seeing her already when we met?"

"Yes."

"And you kept seeing her all along while we were married?"

"Well, it was mostly business, but... Remember what she was like before she got her nose fixed?"

Ingrid had to laugh because the question caught her off guard. "Yes."

"What was she like when you knew her?"

Ingrid thought a moment. "Unsure of herself. She wanted to be popular. She'd do anything to make people like her. If that didn't work, she'd do anything to make them hate her. Just so long as someone would pay attention and care about her. But it was never enough, no matter what she did. You're the second person I've met who knew her and liked her."

"You know, I did like her. I think it was because she was such a sex maniac." Ingrid saw that he was watching her for some sort of reaction. She realized that she was supposed to be jealous and discovered with some pleasure that she felt nothing remotely close to that emotion.

His eyes met hers. "I mean, you were pretty wild for the Valley, with all your silly little patented teen-queen moves— but you were too beautiful. You never had that quality of hook-nosed desperation like Miranda—Mary, she was back then. Of course, she dumped me for two or three other guys. Guys who could help her with her so-called acting career. She wrote me one of her little 'sorry to have to cut you up into little pieces, but here goes' notes, She was a little bitch, but hot." Victor sighed, with a certain moist nostalgia. "She would do anything. Anything. Anywhere."

"Sounds like she was training for a profession."

"Oh, no. Strictly amateur. Well, maybe practicing up for the casting couch. She didn't want money so much as . . . well, if she'd had a little encouragement, she would have wanted to be loved. Too bad. I don't think she had it in her to love anyone back, for one thing."

"I found a letter from you in her things," Ingrid said carefully.

"Oh, yeah?" Vic's eyes were wary. "What was the date on it, what did it say?"

"I didn't have a chance to read it. Someone stole my bag." She saw Vic relax visibly. "It wouldn't happen to be a friend of yours who stole it by any chance?" He didn't respond at all. After several seconds she asked, "So you two kept in touch—business and pleasure?"

"I'd see her from time to time, just an occasional screw, nothing serious. I let her know that you came first with me. If you called, I had to go."

"How touching." Ingrid had thought herself immune to emotion, but now she felt a hot anger. She was angry with herself for having been so blind to him while they were married. The whole marriage now seemed to have happened to a different person.

"I'm sure that Miranda must have been particularly pleased by the way you held me over her head that way," she said.

Victor shrugged. "If you could have seen the guys she was hanging out with when I ran into her in Thailand.

Walking scum. With all the human emotion of a sea slug. Guys who would not only kill their own grandmothers to get an edge on a dope deal—they'd stash the hash in the corpse and smuggle it across the border. Good stuff, though. That's how Miranda and I got back together.''

''You never told me any of this at the time. Were you ashamed?''

''I guess I knew you wouldn't stand for it, and I felt guilty getting it on with one of your old school friends, even if I had known her first. I'd never have met you if she hadn't invited me to come to that festival to play the guitar in the lawn show and do a little backstage business. She got a percentage, of course. Once I saw you, I just forgot Miranda. She had other fish to fry, but we kept doing business. She was very organized about her dealing. She'd never touch the actual stuff. She had some hopes of making it in show business—that's why she changed her name, why she was so careful in her drug deals. She'd sell someone a key and an address. The key would be to a locker in the Greyhound station or at some local college. Hell, once she even gave me a key to a locker at the YMCA. She was efficient, but she was greedy. She kept spending her own profits from the business.''

Ingrid recalled the times just after each harvest when Vic had spent the fifty or sixty thousand dollars profit he boasted of and they had had to fall back on her five-dollar-an-hour clerical pay. But she said nothing, and Vic went on.

''When she was broke from time to time, she'd start moving drugs I wouldn't touch with gloves on. You know how I am, Ingrid. A purist. Acid, grass and hash. Never touch those white powders that get you so much attention from the *federales*. Kind of a moral thing with me too—doing well by doing good.''

Ingrid nodded. Vic's views on amphetamines, cocaine and heroin were well known; she'd heard his stock speech on the subject dozens of times.

''Anyway,'' he continued. ''My bet is that Miranda didn't die very rich.'' He cast an odd glance at her, as if he wanted to ask a question but couldn't think how to begin.

"That's just as well, because no one can seem to find a next of kin. That's what the law firm hired me to find out."

Vic snorted, "Hired *you?* Why?"

"Because, Victor, no one will admit to knowing her but me. Anyway, I can't seem to find any blood relatives. They're looking for someone who might like to claim the body."

Victor was thoughtful. "You want to talk to Mrs. Phelps."

"MRS. PHELPS!"

"You must know her. She used to manage your building. Just shut up a minute, Ingrid. Let's go in and sit down in this coffee shop. There's something we need to get straight."

The coffee shop had a painting of a rose on the window blind; it was called the Rose Garden. The floor was black and white, like a huge chessboard. At each table three pink paper roses nodded from a milk-white glass vase. The chairs were wrought-iron, painted white.

"If it's about that bicycle messenger in the black car who gave me this"—Ingrid raised her sunglasses—"I want my cameras back."

"I don't know what you're talking about, but that looks terrible." Victor examined her eye and pushed the dark glasses back down gently. "Here, I don't want anyone thinking I did that to you."

"You've done worse."

"Yeah, but not recently."

"So what is all this about Mrs. Phelps?"

The waitress, an impossibly slender, almond-eyed woman with a clipped Thai accent, took their order for coffee and brought it immediately.

"There's not much to tell, except that she let me into your apartment."

"MRS. PHELPS!"

"Ingrid, will you stop that noise. The waitress will kick us out."

"I doubt it. This is not the best day for business."

"Think about how you got your apartment, Ingrid. Who recommended it—Spyder, right?"

"How did you know?"

"Because I asked him to when he visited me in prison. Then I got a message to Mrs. Phelps if she kept an eye on you, there might be something in it for her. Spyder watched out for you too. I told him how much I still love you, and he thought we might get back together again."

Ingrid pushed Victor's talk of love aside. Could they possibly have been two other people when they fell in love and married? She tried to concentrate on what had happened to Miranda, and ensuring her own personal survival. "What has Mrs. Phelps got to do with Miranda?" Ingrid asked.

"She's the closest thing Miranda had to family. Looked after her for years during the time when her mother was away. Miranda found the old lady that job managing the apartment building. They didn't get along that well, but Mrs. Phelps would know where the family is and how to get in touch with them. She let me into your place the other night."

"You were in my apartment? Why?"

Vic hesitated, "Miranda told me you had her scrapbook. She had some papers of mine. She said her whole file was at your apartment. You were supposed to be microfilming them."

"That's ridiculous. I don't have the equipment to do that."

"She said you didn't tell her that until you got the file, and then you wouldn't return it."

"I never even heard it existed until after she died."

"Don't be naive, Ingrid—she must have had her famous scrapbook even in high school."

"She never mentioned it to me. What is it?"

Vic sighed and ran his fingers through his dark hair. "You're not kidding me? You really don't know what you've got there? What did she do, give it to you all wrapped up without telling you what it was? If you had looked, you would have guessed what it was."

"I'm telling you, she didn't give me anything. She sent me a note telling me she had *told* everybody I had her scrapbook and I was in deep trouble until I did her errand for her, whatever that was.''

Victor smiled bitterly. "So you maintain you never saw it, eh? That won't help you when they start trying to persuade you to tell them where it is. If you don't know, Ingrid, you'd better find out."

"She told you to set the fire, didn't she, Victor?"

"Yes. How did you know?"

"The memo I got from her was sent the afternoon before the apartment burned. She asked how I liked the fire. She was dead before you even set that fire, so she must have put you up to it."

Vic nodded. "Except I didn't know she was dead till the next morning. It was a pretty nasty shock, considering that I hadn't found the scrapbook at your place."

"You burned my apartment house down, Vic."

"I'm sorry, Ingrid."

"You could have killed someone!"

"No, Ingrid, I made sure no one got hurt. After your apartment was going good, I knocked on Mrs. Phelps' door and told her to evacuate everyone. I had to do it, Ingrid. Miranda said she was leaving the country the next day, and if I set that fire it would force you to cooperate with her or else destroy the scrapbook. Those things are dangerous, Ingrid. You'd be better off cooperating even if I had to frighten you into it."

"Except that I never saw any scrapbooks or files."

"You still say that? I should tell you, Ingrid, that scrapbook sounds harmless but it's deadly. Just tell me where you hid it. How about your friend Carmen's? I know you have a darkroom, how about there?"

"I told you I don't have it. Stay away from Carmen and my darkroom or I'll report you to the police."

Victor laughed, but it came out as a sigh. "As if that would do any good."

"Please believe me, Vic, I never got anything but a memo from Miranda. What kind of papers did she have on you, anyway?"

Vic picked up his coffee cup and examined its contents. He set it down untasted. "The real estate documentation for my dope farming operation. She helped me put the operation together, and she promised she'd take my name out of it and destroy all the documents. But my name went out on the papers and she kept records of who got what and when. Names, dates and addresses. If anyone put the cops onto them, those people would turn on me in a hot minute, especially if they thought it would help them with the D.A.''

Ingrid looked at him with narrowed eyes for several moments. "Victor. What was this errand she kept talking about me running for her?"

"I'm not the only person who wants the file, Ingrid. You've got it, so let's see it."

"I didn't know it existed until you just told me."

"Well you'd better get it. She must have told you where it is, or how to find it."

"That wasn't the idea, Vic. She never wanted me to have it. She just wanted people to think I had it. She said if I did what she wanted, she'd 'call off the dogs.' Are you the dogs?"

"Maybe one of them. There are others, Ingrid, and they'll have your pretty hide in slices. I mean that literally. I don't want to see you get hurt. Women have been tortured to death in this very city for less than what you are doing at this very moment."

Ingrid moved her chair back several inches. "You're sure you didn't hire a muscular bald man in a black Continental to rough me up and steal my camera bag to get at this so-called evidence? Or maybe to steal the key?"

Vic leaned toward her. "Have you got the key with you now?"

"I don't know what it's the key to. I got it by accident."

Victor stood over her and pinned her to her seat with one black-haired hand.

"You don't know what you're dealing with, Ingrid. My advice is to give me this key and any other information you have and leave town immediately."

"I can't do that."

"You may think you can forget about the whole thing, but there are people out there who want to be safe, and who won't be till they have that scrapbook."

He released his grip and walked out, leaving, Ingrid noticed, the check for their two coffees. Why not? He had bought breakfast, after all. And his own coffee was untouched.

NINETEEN

As SHE LEFT the coffee shop, Ingrid saw Victor across the street, speaking urgently into a pay phone. Who are you talking to, Victor? She said the words softly. She wanted to be alone. But Victor didn't even notice her; clearly he was wrapped up in his own plans. Could he be the dog that Miranda would have called off if Ingrid cooperated with her? She hoped he wasn't calling any canine reinforcements. She badly needed a rest. She was glad to see that he was still on the phone when the Geary bus pulled up to take her out to Point Lobos.

She picked up Carmen's Sunday paper from the doorstep and unlocked the door cautiously. A slow survey of the front room revealed only Mugwort, who yawned a lazy hello and watched her for several moments from his sunlit corner, to see if she would open the refrigerator. When she didn't, he dozed off. Feeling foolish, she nonetheless checked each room, closet and window and rattled the doors to make sure all the chains and bolts were secure.

She decided to make her calls immediately in view of possible holiday tie-ups. But the lines were miraculously clear when she called her father in Redondo Beach.

"Hi, honey, I got your photos of the Monterey cypresses. Most interesting."

"Thanks, Dad. Since you got me that zoom lens, I can get closer than before." She didn't mention that her cameras had been stolen. She had mended her adolescent feud with her father a few years earlier by sending him a truce offering of an album of photos she had taken of endangered species in Humboldt. He had accepted, and they could at last talk cordially as long as their conversation never strayed far from the wonders of the endangered Torrey Pine and Nevin Barberry.

Although he taught science at a local high school, Ingrid's father was both an amateur photographer and a botanist with a fondness for all wildlife, especially trees. They could talk easily about technical aspects of the pictures and peculiarities of nature. All in all the most pleasant dialog they had had since she had been able to ask his advice about her high school botany homework.

"Can I ask a favor, Dad? Do you still have the pics you took at my high school graduation? I ran into an old classmate, and I'd like to take another look at the pictures if you wouldn't mind sending me any extra prints—or you can send me the negatives and I'll get them printed up here and send them back to you."

"Oh, no, no, no, I'd love to." She could tell her father was pleased to be asked. It was the sort of archival project he enjoyed—although he would have preferred printing a picture of a rare or interesting tree. His print files went back to the days of Ingrid's mother's pregnancy. He was still in Alcoholics Anonymous, and he described their latest activities before they said good-bye.

Then she called Ventura to talk to her mother, who was also a schoolteacher, and her sister, Tracy, who was seven years younger. This was not too bad. Her mother was drunk but not too emotional yet, and Tracy was in love, which made extensive conversation just now impossible.

"He'll be coming over for dinner tonight, Ingrid. It looks serious," her mother said of the boyfriend as Tracy went off to complete her makeup.

Ingrid's mother had already found a frame for her photo gift—a color portrait Ingrid had taken on her last visit to L.A. of her mother's German shepherd, Mozart. Yes, Tracy had also received her portfolio of pictures.

"But I don't know if she's really going to pursue this modeling thing after all. The man she's seeing is very serious, and that takes up a lot of her time."

The boyfriend would solve all her sister's problems.

Her mother was an opera fan, and Ingrid could hear *Amahl and the Night Visitors* playing in the background. Ingrid explained about her apartment fire, minimizing the damage to her possessions.

"Do you think you could send some of my old clothes that are stored in the basement?"

"How about those old school uniforms," her mother suggested. "You tried them last summer and they still fit."

Ingrid laughed; why not?

They talked for half an hour. She billed both calls to her phone at the studio. She did not, however, give her mother Carmen's phone number, in fear of a later call when Tracy would have gone out and more vodka would have erased the memory of the first call. Instead she told her as gently and clearly as possible that she would be going out soon, and would have to talk to her again in another week or so. Her mother was not an angry drunk—just anxious, forgetful and pleading for some permanent reassurance Ingrid could never seem to give.

After she hung up, Ingrid sat for several moments, gazing blankly into space. She thought of the possible attackers who might be massing in the bushes across the way and decided not to go out after all. She went to the sofa and picked up the madly purring Mugwort, walked over to the window and looked out at the gap in the trees where the Pacific Ocean curved around to the south. She stared unseeing at the ocean and let the tears course slowly down her face, warm as blood. Mugwort licked them off with his sandpapery tongue as they reached her chin.

TWENTY

Monday, December 26

MONDAY WAS A HOLIDAY. But Ben Resnick was in and alone in his office, except for someone down the hall who was hammering away at a heavy-keyed manual typewriter. Resnick was light-years away from automating his office. As she entered, he was lighting his cigar with a burning brand from the wood stove beside his desk. He threw the stick back in, closed the door and pushed aside stacks of old books and newspapers to make a space for Ingrid's proof sheets.

"Honey, I like 'em." Why was it that she never minded when Ben called her "honey" or "sweetie"? She wouldn't tolerate that sort of thing from anyone else. "Do your own printing?"

"Yes, I fixed up a darkroom in an old laundry room."

"Good. I'll keep that in mind—maybe you can do some print work for us. Pays a little more."

"Sure."

"So, here we have Mr. Atherton Flint crossing Taft Alley—and here is an unknown female person standing in the alley. What's all this about?"

"I don't know—maybe you can help me figure it out."

Ingrid found herself telling him the events of the past week. It took a while. He didn't ask too many questions. None of it seemed to surprise him, even Vic's dope farming. When she volunteered the details of Miranda's threat, he rocked back in his chair and held up one hand to stop her.

"What did she want you to do, exactly?" he asked in an unusually soft tone of voice.

"We were interrupted before she could tell me. Then she died. Something about an errand. Maybe she just wanted me to work for free."

"No. She'd never have taken you to lunch. Don't tell me about economy measures. I'll *never* take you to lunch. That's a promise."

"Thanks."

For a moment the silence was broken only by the clatter of typewriter keys in the background. Ingrid suddenly felt worn out from all the talking.

"Do you think someone could have pushed her out that window?" he asked.

"People would have lined up to do it. But no one could have gotten into her office till the receptionist went to the rest room. She said when she came back to her desk, she saw that the light on Miranda's private phoneline was lit, but someone immediately closed the inner office door so the receptionist couldn't make out what was going on in there."

"So it looks as if she was alone in there. Did the receptionist actually see her closing the door? Anyone can close a door from inside."

"Yes, but after that receptionist was outside the door, no one could get in or out, except by the route Miranda took—twelve stories down."

"The other thing is the keys and this scrapbook."

"My ex-husband told me Miranda commissioned him to burn down my apartment to destroy the scrapbook or scare me into handing it over. It must have contained blackmail information."

"You do have those keys."

"Yes, but I don't know what they unlock or where it is."

"You can bet that they don't know, either, dolly. Otherwise, they could just pick the lock. Don't look so shocked. In certain circles it's the preferred mode of entry. Anyway, they must think you know more than you do."

"That must be why the guy who took my camera bag tried to drag me off to his car."

"They want to get you alone to persuade you to take them there."

Ben lit up another cigar and leaned back, gazing at the ceiling. He looked over at Ingrid a moment later as if suddenly remembering she was there.

"Can I see those two keys you found?"

Ingrid dug the keys out of her wallet and handed them over. "And"—Ingrid hesitated—"Spyder looked awfully strange when I mentioned the keys. He insisted that I talk to Victor. Vic wanted the keys, but all he said was that people would kill to get them."

Ben looked at her mournfully. "Too bad you let him know you had the keys. You say they fell out of the envelope with the cash from Kubler's bookkeeper?"

"One of them came from a flowerpot in Miranda's office, the other one from Kubler's bookkeeper. I can't figure out how Kubler is involved in this. I never heard of him till last week."

"Another example of your pathetic ignorance of political matters, kiddo. He's one of the biggest absentee slumlords in the city. Gets cheap properties in neighborhoods like the one where you lived that are up for urban renewal. Gouges the low-rent tenants for a few years till he can kick them out and tear the building down. Puts up whatever's hot—condos or office suites. Sells the lot to the highest bidder. He doesn't spend much time in this country, let alone this city, so he doesn't much care what happens to it."

Resnick was lost in his favorite subject. "They say they create jobs with these new monsters, but they never train any of the people they kick out. They say they'll replace the low-cost housing they rip out, but their idea of affordable housing is a bargain-rate condo. Greed, that's what's at the heart of it. But don't get me started."

"Okay. But getting back to the envelope—the bookkeeper was pretty disgusted by the whole thing, but she was complaining about being used by Miranda, not by Kubler."

"Something personal between the two ladies, maybe." Resnick thumbed through her prints again, dropping ash on them from the cigar clenched in his teeth. He dealt out the print of Flint Senior with Stella standing in the fatal alley behind him. "There's a freight entrance down here," he said, tapping the photo. "See where the stairs go down from street level just off the alley, to the lady's left? Probably leads into the basement for large deliveries."

"So?"

"Maybe someone got in and out of the building through that delivery door. They'd bypass the security guard that way. You say you saw the basement. Is that where the stairwell ends up? Usually it is."

"Yes. I took the elevator down but I did see a stairwell door."

"So someone could have come in the freight entrance and taken the stairs or the elevator anywhere in the building. And could have walked out through the front door. I take it people have to sign in but not necessarily *out* as long as the security guard is on duty."

"It's true. They don't worry about people leaving, just coming in. If someone let her in, Stella could have pushed Miranda out that window—she looked mad enough to do anything."

Ben turned his magnifying glass to another frame on the proof sheet. "You said this bicycle messenger is the guy who mugged you?"

"I'm pretty sure of that. There can't be that many people with snakes tattooed on their shaved scalps. But all you can see in the picture is the back end of the bike."

"Come on, Ingrid, you can see his bicycle tag number—those things are like license plates on cars. Shall I ask Spyder to run it down for you? He worked as a messenger for a few days doing a story on those guys. He knows all of them."

"No. Don't ask Spyder." Ingrid spoke too quickly; the fact that he had connections with bicycle messengers unsettled her. Perhaps Spyder had sent the man to steal her bag and had given her another bag as a Christmas present and a secret apology. No. It was impossible. Spyder wouldn't have taken her cameras—he knew how vital they were to her. Still.

Ben looked at her sharply. "You don't trust him."

Ingrid sighed. "Especially after you tell me he knows all those messengers. He could have hired the guy to get that key from me and make it look like a mugging."

"You think he would have hired someone to kidnap you?"

"No. I don't think so—I just don't know anymore. I could have sworn Spyder wouldn't hurt a fly."

"Not even a fly?"

Ingrid was forced to smile. "Well, maybe a fly."

"Okay." Resnick considered for a moment before speaking. "Let me get my latest Pulitzer Prize candidate here to ask the Sudden Service dispatcher."

Without warning Resnick dropped the magnifying glass and bellowed, "Van Horn!" The clatter of typewriting ceased and a short, wiry young man entered the office. To Ingrid he looked like a high school freshman, but she knew that most of Resnick's volunteers were college students. Resnick explained the information they were looking for and showed him the proof sheet. Van Horn scribbled all the while on a dime-store notepad.

He didn't inspire confidence at first, but as Van Horn wandered out, tapping his spiral notebook thoughtfully against his upper lip, she changed her mind. If Resnick—who looked equally unimpressive until he opened his mouth—could be such a powerhouse, maybe rabbity little Van Horn could win the Pulitzer Prize.

"Keep me posted, Ingrid," Resnick said. "I'll sniff around, maybe talk to a few cops I know. Watch yourself, don't take any risks or walk down any dark alleys, okay? Give me a call when you know more, or if you get in any trouble. Speaking of trouble, have you made your statement to the cops yet? Go ahead and give them all these extra proof sheets. Not that they'll use them, but they like to stay informed."

Ingrid was persuaded. She stopped by the Hall of Justice, signed a statement and even left a proof sheet with the homicide detective she had spoken with before. This time he actually wore his brown suit coat. He told her guardedly that the case was not closed, but suicide seemed very likely; the handwriting expert had found the note to be written by Miranda herself. Ingrid didn't mention her own memo from Miranda. She was unnerved by the way the man looked at her: the same way Mugwort looked at Carmen when she opened a can of mackerel. The memo was gone now, anyway, and it offered no information. She was afraid to get into the matter of her apartment fire and Victor's involvement in the whole matter. More than ever she wanted to straighten out the entire tangle.

She found a pay phone on Bryant Street.

Wanda answered at Kubler Realty, complaining that she was disgusted to be back in the office before the holiday weekend was properly over.

"I'm with a client, so make it quick. Stella's not in today. If she doesn't want to call you, that's her business. I gave her the number."

"Actually, it's not about her. It's rather important. I need to reach Mrs. Phelps."

"*MRS. PHELPS!*" Now Wanda was doing it.

"Someone who knew Miranda well told me that Mrs. Phelps might be able to reach Miranda's relatives. If she can help, why shouldn't she?"

"Funny you should mention that, because Miranda was the one who recommended the old lady for the job. Of course, she didn't mention the drinking problem. After the Oak Street fire, we had to tell Mrs. Phelps we couldn't use her anymore."

Ingrid noted that Mrs. Phelps' dismissal happened to coincide with Miranda's death. But she said nothing.

"I don't know where she is just now, but we have had one or two phone calls. Mostly the drunken, pleading kind," Wanda continued. "Here, let me look in my wastebasket—I've probably thrown out two or three messages since the last time the janitor came to empty it out." She put the telephone down, and Ingrid could hear her talking to someone else as she looked, but her words were indistinct. "Here we are. She left an address in case we might want to contact her, poor old bag. Let's see, she's over on Eddy Street in the heart of the Tenderloin. The Paradise Hotel." She read off the address. "Hey! That's one of ours. Well, they say if you stay on the staff of a mental hospital long enough you end up staying there as a patient." Wanda joined whoever was with her in a laugh.

Ingrid thanked her quickly and hung up.

TWENTY-ONE

THE DESK CLERK at the Paradise Hotel was a burly Samoan who sat in a cage of bullet-proof glass. Ingrid shuddered. If *he* was afraid, what must the tenants be like? A trio of grimy vending machines near the staircase offered an oasis for a small knot of young black men who leaned on the machines and against the wall and chatted easily. One of them was cleaning his nails with a hunting knife. She told herself that the presence of such easily burglarized machines in the lobby should make it a fairly safe place; still, all her senses vibrated to an inaudible chord of violence in the lobby.

Ingrid leaned close to the grille to make herself heard and asked if Mrs. Phelps was in number 200. The desk clerk shrugged. "You know the number. Go up and look. You'll have to take the stairs over there. Elevator's broken."

The men by the machines were tranquil enough as she passed them. But when they turned with a surprising degree of unity and followed her up the stairway, Ingrid did not feel good about it.

She climbed the stairs with alacrity, trying to remember everything she had learned from Ito about facing knives and groups. *Run away* was the thought that kept coming back to her.

As she turned off the stairwell onto the second-floor landing, the group made as if to follow her and then turned back onto the stairs with a roar of laughter.

"Awright, dude," one man called, apparently to the man with the hunting knife. "You scared that white bitch near to death."

After half a minute and several knocks, Mrs. Phelps opened her door, then turned back into the room wordlessly, leaving Ingrid to close the door. Mrs. Phelps sank down on the edge of the bed and looked up wearily but without ill feelings. Her angry outburst on the night of the fire was clearly forgotten. Perhaps she didn't completely recognize Ingrid.

"Hello, Mrs. Phelps. How are you feeling?"

"Not bad," she muttered. There was a long pause. Mrs. Phelps used it to drain a mug that rested on the bedside table. She sighed and meditated on the wall, then seemed to remember Ingrid's presence. "What do you want?"

Ingrid looked at the gallon jug of gin on the floor beside the bed. Half empty. "It's about Miranda Falk—you probably knew her as Mary Valkevich at first."

"Dead," moaned Mrs. Phelps, leaning dangerously to one side. "Can't help it."

"Do you know any way to get in touch with her family?" Ingrid tried to speak very clearly. From long experience she knew that Mrs. Phelps would be passing out soon.

"Lost it in the fire. Everything. Old address books. Nothing left. Kid's dead too. Took care of her when she was young. Greedy little kid. Never had enough. Couldn't give her enough. Parents worse. Just didn't give a damn." The thought moved her to reach down and fill her mug unsteadily from the jug on the floor.

"Are her parents still alive?"

"Don't know the father. Mother died in the asylum down in L.A. My letters came back. There's an aunt in Florida. Pompano Beach. Used to write my checks. Name of Elaine Greenberg. Husband's a dentist. That's all I know."

Ingrid was worried about Mrs. Phelps. She didn't expect a positive answer but it was worth a try. "What about you, Mrs. Phelps, do you have any relatives? Any children, someone who could take care of you?"

The old woman suddenly looked very candidly at Ingrid, as if seeing her for the first time. "Don't worry about Mrs. Phelps. She never had any children," she said. "I had a son once. But they took him away. Not Mrs. Phelps. She's dead, you know." Mrs. Phelps slid backward onto the bed. After a few moments she began to snore.

No more information would come from that source today. Ingrid hesitated a moment. Then she levered the woman's lumpy legs up onto the bed. She wore ankle socks only, no shoes. Her head and shoulders had landed on a big, squashy, black purse, but she seemed comfortable enough and unlikely to fall on the floor.

While Mrs. Phelps snored peacefully, Ingrid searched the place. She found very little of interest.

A pile of dirty laundry and a collection of recent newspapers. Mrs. Phelps had bought both the morning and evening dailies every day since the fire. A stack of torn-out pages held different versions of Miranda's death. The first story ran to five paragraphs on the third page of the first section. The stories crept backward, shrinking until the most recent, a one-sentence item on page seven of the second section echoing what the homicide detective had just told Ingrid: Since the handwriting in the note had been confirmed as Miranda's, suicide was considered the most likely cause of death, and no relatives had yet been found.

Mrs. Phelps had been interested enough to tear out these articles but had not come forward. Why? Ingrid scowled. Perhaps she had tried, but kept stopping off at liquor stores along the way.

Ingrid cast about for something else to search. A board creaked under her feet and she jumped. She was even more nervous than she had been in the lobby and on the staircase. She just wasn't cut out for this sort of work.

"Oh, hell," she said, and wrestled the purse out from under Mrs. Phelps's head. The woman did not stir.

The purse contained no wallet or address books—Mrs. Phelps hadn't been lying about that. There was a surprisingly large wad of money tucked in a plain white envelope, soft and grimy from handling. Aside from antacid mints and spare change, the only other thing in the purse was a blue velvet bag.

Ingrid opened it and gasped as a gleaming rope of pearls fell out. It must have been five feet long. The famous pearls that had made Mrs. Phelps the princess of MacHarg's Bar. No wedding ring. A broken Timex watch. A couple of shiny paste clip earrings. No other jewelry. The pearls looked real enough to Ingrid, a graduated loop of just faintly irregular, luminescent globes. The largest was surprisingly large. Ingrid vaguely remembered an old-fashioned method of testing whether saltwater pearls were genuine by rubbing them on the teeth. But she had forgotten what the real pearls were supposed to feel like. These were almost hypnotically beautiful. If fakes, they were expensive fakes.

She looped them back into their bag, then stowed the bag in the purse and the purse under the pillow next to Mrs. Phelps' head.

The bedside table was rimmed with unwashed dishes on a field of crumpled Kleenex. A framed picture was barely visible behind the Kleenex box. This must have been the frame that Mrs. Phelps had been clutching the night of the fire.

Ingrid reached out to touch it but snatched her hand away as a cockroach darted out of a bowl on the tabletop and scuttled into the dresser drawer. Ingrid paused, took a deep breath and eased the drawer open. She was relieved to find it empty, except for the cockroach, who was mercifully lying low.

She picked up the picture, which showed the Valley School graduation: pampered middle-class teenagers on the front lawn of the school under lazy oak trees that framed the small meadow. The property had been the *hacienda* of an old *rancho* in California's early Spanish days. A millionaire had modernized it and willed it to Valley School. The picture seemed oddly exotic in Mrs. Phelps' Tenderloin hotel room.

The school had considered itself above imposing a group graduation portrait. Each parent took his own, or hired a professional photographer. This picture showed Miranda, or Mary Valkevich, standing with her arm around Mrs. Phelps, who looked a little tipsy even then. Neither of them was smiling. Mrs. Phelps seemed anxious; perhaps she didn't like having her picture taken. Or perhaps they had handed the camera to an impatient stranger.

Ingrid had had enough. She decided to check her darkroom for any phone messages and then go back to Carmen's house to face the mountain of Christmas leftovers brought back from Fremont.

She stacked Mrs. Phelps' dishes in a small sink in the corner across the room. She held them cautiously, but no other cockroaches revealed themselves. Then she cleared off the crumpled tissues from the bedside table and left Mrs. Phelps a note, folded up against the picture, thanking her for the name of Mary's aunt and saying she would look up the address in the phone book. Ingrid wanted to say something more, but could not think of anything that would be acceptable.

What the hell. She couldn't expect it to help, but it was worth a try. She wrote: "Please try AA; there's also a group called Women for Sobriety." Ingrid wrote down the local numbers, which she still had in her address book. She paused a moment, made a face at the hopelessness of it and wrote, "They can work for people who give them a try. I've seen people quit drinking and feel good again. Don't give up on yourself."

In the lobby another group of tenants was clustered around the vending machines—this time some very old Asian men, taking turns sitting on the rusty kitchen chair next to the machines. They didn't even look up as she went past.

TWENTY-TWO

THERE WERE A PAGE and a half of Greenbergs in the Fort Lauderdale telephone book, and two dentists named Greenberg in Pompano Beach.

She ended up calling both and asking for the Elaine Greenberg who was Mary Valkevich's aunt. The second woman she talked to reluctantly agreed that she might be able to help.

"Mrs. Phelps gave me your name. I knew Mary in high school. I don't know if you were very close to her..." Ingrid began.

"If you want her address, there's nothing I can do about it. I haven't heard from the little tramp in ten years. Is she in some sort of trouble?"

"She's dead."

There was a long pause. "And?"

"The employer asked me to see if I could find some family. You're the only person I could turn up." The pause stretched on until Ingrid feared the woman would hang up. She floundered in the cold silence and then began to lie. "Actually, some money may be involved for the next of kin. Of course, her insurance policy from work will cover all the expenses, and there are her personal effects, money, clothes, jewelry."

Bingo. Ingrid could feel the interest rising at the other end of the line. "Whom should I contact?" the woman asked.

Ingrid smiled and gave her Nell Scott's name and phone number. She suggested calling collect as the closest relative of Mary Valkevich, also known as Miranda Falk.

TWENTY-THREE

Tuesday, December 27

RAIN AND HIGH WINDS were lashing the financial district. Ingrid came in out of the rain and dripped water all over the Bramwell Building's elevator. She stepped out on the twelfth floor, where workmen in white coveralls were dismantling the Christmas tree for Bramwell, Stinson & Flint. Ornaments were stripped and stored in frail paper boxes as the men towed the corpse, dripping needles and tinsel, toward the service elevator. Going into Personnel, Ingrid met Pammy coming out of the office, crying.

"Are you all right, Pammy?"

"I just got fired," she muttered, angrily wiping her eyes with her knuckles, then looking at the mascara on her hand. "Miss Scott said someone caught me using cocaine. There's just one person who could have told her—that snotty Josephine Lewis. Just because she's a lawyer, she acts like she doesn't put on her pantyhose one leg at a time like the rest of us."

Ingrid glanced toward the elevators, where the workmen were now loading the tree. She took Pammy over to the far wall and spoke to her in a low voice, trying for soothing tones. "Let's sort all this out. Here's a fresh Kleenex. How did Josephine find out?"

"She saw us."

"Did she accuse anyone else, or just you?"

This was too much for Pammy, who started sniffling again. "She'd never accuse *him*. She thinks she can trap him and get in good with his father if she protects him. He's not interested in her. She's old. She must be pushing thirty."

Pammy could mean only one person. "Have you been seeing Tony Flint outside of work or just here?"

Pammy smiled suddenly. She shook her hair back from her shoulders. "Isn't he awesome? We haven't had a real date yet. He's trying to protect me like I'm this real innocent kid. Okay, I'm too young for him to take me to a bar or anything yet. But I grew up in Marin County. I've probably had more cocaine than he has. He had some good quality stuff, though. Pure, you know, not stepped on hardly at all. He knows who he wants for company when he steps out in the stairwell. And it ain't her."

"Isn't it a little, uh, conspicuous here in the office?"

"No. He said it was the best place. He said he practically grew up in the building."

"When was all this?"

"Oh, it was last M—uh, yester—Oh, I'm not sure when it was. It doesn't matter."

Ingrid didn't know how to ask, so she tried to say it as quickly as possible. "It was the day Miranda died, wasn't it?"

"Oh, no. I don't really think it could have been that day, because I was at my desk the whole time, except when I was at lunch and a couple minutes when I went to the john." Her face suddenly puckered as if she had seen a possibility that hadn't occurred to her before. "I'd have to check with—with my appointment book if I needed to know for sure."

"You didn't sort of duck into the hallway with Tony Flint and just say you went off to the rest room?"

"I'm pretty sure I was at my desk the whole time, but like I said I could check." Pammy's suddenly steadfast gaze and open expression could be read as an attack of guile. Was Ingrid witnessing the sudden solidification of an alibi? If so, it came hard on the heels of Ingrid's own encounter with Flint Junior and Josephine Lewis, together for an evening. That man was going to be very busy if he had to keep both of these hungry females happy.

Ingrid wished Pammy luck and supplied Dana's number at AdventureTemps. She knew what it felt like to walk out of a job crying and run into a rainstorm.

Ingrid passed Josephine Lewis on the way out of Nell Scott's office and matched her curt nod with an equally brief incline of the head.

Pammy's theory that Josephine was the jealous informant seemed to be correct. No personnel director could afford to ignore a lawyer's accusation of drug abuse on the premises. Lawyers occupied the upper realms of privilege, forever closed to even the highest managers.

Nell Scott confirmed that Mrs. Greenberg had called and agreed to take charge of her niece's remains, "and anything else she could worm out of us."

"I'm sure it wasn't much. I'll arrange to have the friend she was staying with ship her clothes and other personal effects. You'll get a bill for my time from Adventure-Temps, and I'll send you an itemized statement of expenses."

Nell was so elated to see the whole thing settled that she jumped at Ingrid's hint that she'd be glad to help out in Word Processing whenever needed. Nell invited her to fill in the evening shift in Word Processing that very night. Ingrid agreed, pleased that she had brought along the diskette she had found hidden among Miranda's magazines. She had planned to ask Tanya for a few minutes of machine time, just to satisfy her curiosity about the information stored on the diskette, but the Word Processing Center at night was even more private.

It wasn't even noon when Ingrid left BSF, so she decided to brave the wind and rain and deliver her proof sheets and prints. She called for an appointment with Rosemary Tanner and was surprised to find that Rosemary could squeeze her in.

"JUST ONE MOMENT, please," the Frenchman told her as she folded her dripping jacket and firmly gripped the railing of the metal staircase and they climbed up to Rosemary's icicle office. They halted outside the door, and he gestured with hypnotic grace to a small red light set in a panel next to the door. "You see that button there—it says she's on the telephone," he said. "But..." The light went out. "Voilà, she is free now."

"Ingrid, dear." Enthroned behind her rosewood desk, Rosemary was wearing an apricot-colored silk suit. She looked like a point of flame in an Antarctic noon. She waved her hand with considerably less grace than Henri but more expansively. She gestured to the straight-backed chair next to her. "Do your worst, dear. Put them on the desk and let me look. Don't say a word."

Ingrid dried her wet hands on a Kleenex and dealt out the test print she had so carefully doctored, her black-and-white proof sheets and the stack of color shots with the best ones on top. The color pictures were not so good, but she decided to let Rosemary see them anyway. Who could tell—to Rosemary, these might be good pictures. After all, the developing had cost her some money.

Rosemary flipped through the pictures with an odd lack of interest. People usually could not keep their eyes away. Even when they found their own photos disappointing, which was usually the case, they kept looking back again as if hoping that the next glance would change things for the better.

But Rosemary didn't seem to be really seeing the pictures. At last she pushed them aside and spoke.

"Before I look at these, I want you to promise me something."

"What?"

"Promise me you'll stay away from Jason Grapelli. I don't want you to see him again."

"That's really none of your business." This meeting was not turning out at all the way Ingrid had expected.

Rosemary scattered the pictures with a rude shove halfway across the gleaming, naked surface of the desk. Ingrid hurried to rescue her prints. She was gathering them up to go when Rosemary stopped her with another imperious gesture.

"Leave the pictures. The black-and-white one is good—you've donated it to our organization and we will accept it for my column in the newsletter. The rest, we'll see. Now, tell me what you've uncovered about your old friend Miranda Falk. Find any relatives yet?"

"How did you know I was looking for relatives?"

"Oh, I have a few sources around town. Well?"

"It's all settled. Her aunt agreed to claim the body."

"That's all."

"That's all I found out."

"How boring. Anyway, remember what I've said about Jason Grapelli. Before I consider buying any photographs, I'll want to hear your answer on that. Think about it. You don't want me for an enemy. We'll talk at the luncheon meeting of the Network day after tomorrow. You're photographing that, aren't you?"

Ingrid nodded, not trusting herself to speak.

Rosemary rang for the Frenchman, and Ingrid left without another word.

TRUDGING UP NOB HILL, shielding her shoulder bag with its envelopes of prints from the gusts of rain, Ingrid couldn't puzzle it out. She stepped over the corpses of several wind-stripped umbrellas, their ribs sticking out at crazy angles, and turned in at the awning in front of Madeline Trumbull's gallery.

No art patrons had braved the storm so far. Madeline was alone and clearly waking up with a cup of coffee. She offered Ingrid a cup, and they sat down to look at the prints. Madeline sipped her coffee a little unsteadily, but she seemed to gain strength with each drop. Her hair was invisible in a turban. Ingrid wondered if she was in the process of redying it or if Madeline might actually be bald. The rest of her makeup was in place, and her social mask gradually emerged as she surfaced from a deep well of sleepiness. Ingrid decided a little gossip might help both of them.

"Madeline, I just came from Rosemary Tanner's office, and she reacted very strangely to something that came up." Madeline leaned forward in interest. "It was about an artist—you know, the one who signs himself 'j g graffiti'? He was at the opening I photographed for you." She slipped the prints from that day out of their envelope and selected one with Jason's picture. Madeline shook her head but involuntarily licked her lips. "When I saw one of his works in Rosemary's office and mentioned that I'd met the artist, she threw a temper tantrum. Told me to keep my paws off him.''

"I don't recall him, dear." Madeline put a hand to her temple and brought it away. The gossip was perking her up, though. Ingrid could tell. "So many people come to my parties . . . but . . . Rosemary is a little strange about young artists, well, about young men."

"You mean like Henri."

"Ah, yes. But aside from Henri, she likes to have the occasional protégé. Whoever this Jason character is, he might be, uh, under her protection." Now that her appetite was whetted, Madeline seemed to wake up completely. "Did you, uh, get involved with this young man?''

"I might have."

"But Rosemary stopped you. Typical, really. So sad, that she has to try to control people that way." Madeline sounded wistful, as if the idea of keeping an attractive young man out of circulation distressed her. But the chat had put her in such a good mood that she paid double what she'd promised for a hearty order of prints and said she was sure she would order more in a few days when she had conferred with her guests and artists.

Ingrid still had a few hours to kill, so she ducked out of the rain to the Muni Metro and took a rail car to the McAllister Street office where the building inspectors kept their records. She had taken a temporary typing job there a few months back. The records clerk showed her where to look up the ownership of the Twenty-fifth Avenue house in Sea Cliff where she had spent that Sunday night. It was owned outright by Rosemary Tanner.

TWENTY-FOUR

THE WORD PROCESSING Center at Bramwell, Stinson & Flint seemed deserted when Ingrid arrived at a little after 5:00. But when she closed the door, a man peeked around a six-foot-tall sound screen at the far end of the room and came out to meet her. Ingrid recognized the gypsy earring and gleaming white smile of Max Leon. He held a camel-hair topcoat in one hand and a wooden hanger in the other.

"Well, here's a familiar face," he said cheerfully. "You must be Ingrid. My, but you're wet. You can hang up your jacket back here; there's a rack with . . . well unfortunately all we've got left is wire coat hangers. I brought this wooden one from home."

"Oh, hi, you're Max, aren't you? I thought you were fired," she blurted out, before realizing how rude she sounded.

Max smiled even more broadly, casting small, laughing glances at her as he adjusted his coat carefully on the hanger. He slipped a metal flask out of the pocket and poured a stiff jolt of whiskey into a large plastic cup of steaming coffee. Then he sat down, gestured her to a chair, leaned back, sipped and sighed contentedly.

"The Irish whiskey makes it perfect," he remarked. "I get mine from this little shop over on Battery. Can't stand that instant crap they offer here. True, it's free, but I wouldn't drink it if they paid me. Now let's see, what's your problem? Oh, fired? Yes. I was. But that was the old regime. Miss Nelly Scott loves me dearly. The office manager won't let her rehire me; they're so stuffy about people who've been fired. Not that I would come back anyway, but she asks me in as a free-lance temp to help out whenever they're in a pinch, and that happens quite often. My restaurant venture is going slowly, so I can afford to sock away a little more cash." He was positively beaming.

"No work yet, but we're the only staff in here tonight, so when they start besieging us we'll be hopping. Just amuse yourself till the six o'clock rush descends. I'm going to look up a few old friends on the switchboard."

He disappeared, and Ingrid turned on a machine, fed in a program and inserted Miranda's diskette into the empty right-hand slot. The machine accepted it with a chattering sound as if a group of squirrels were playing roller derby inside the disk drive. The diskette name "M" popped up on the display. She wondered if it had been input in this very office.

She called up the table of contents. Only one document on it, labeled "10," but it was short; 98% of the memory was still available on the diskette.

Ingrid looked into document 10. The first page contained an address with no name on Third Street that seemed to be in the Hunter's Point district of town, not a place Ingrid would go after dark. Under the address were two words, "hall closet" and a date—January 2. She tried page 2. Another address. On impulse she tried page 12. This time the address was Randolph Street; that would be over near S.F. State. Then the words "kitchen cabinet above sink" and another date, December 28.

She went through each page and found the dates were in sequence and seemed to be always the first or last day of the month. The document ended on page 13. That address was on Fulton in the Western Addition, a few blocks from Ingrid's burned-out apartment. The date was December 31 and the notation was "upstairs fireplace." Ingrid ended the document, printed it out and stashed the pages and the diskette in her camera bag.

A few moments later Max returned and settled back into his chair to contemplate the dregs of his coffee.

"Say, Max, did Miranda ever come around here to use the machines?"

"Who, Miss Management of the year? Not while I was around."

"But she was Flint's secretary for a while. That desk has a word processor, so she must have learned how to use the machine at least a little."

"Oh, I think she knew how to start it up and maybe input a document, more or less. She could have come in after midnight—the night staff doesn't go much past one A.M. unless there's a really big rush project happening."

"You didn't welcome her, I gather."

"I was watchful but always cordial, until she started sending me the little regretful notes: 'Sorry, buddy, looks like you're on the endangered species list—Nothing personal, Love, Miranda.' Wait a minute." He tapped the cup against his teeth. "I'd forgotten till you just mentioned it, but I did see her coming into the building one night after midnight. There's no security guard after six P.M. You can get in if you have a key, but you're supposed to sign in, too. No one does it unless they're looking for overtime or comptime credit. I saw her walk in without signing the sign-in sheet one night when I was working overtime. I was a little high, so I asked why she wasn't signing for credit. Did she have a hot date on the thirteenth floor? That's what I call the so-called Penthouse level. I always joke around with everyone. It's an article of faith with me. But she wasn't amused. Come to think of it, she started gathering her evidence and writing those little regretful notes not too long after that." He leaned back in his chair until Ingrid thought it would tip over. "Maybe to her it was no joke."

"I take it you didn't tell that to the police."

Max's eyes flashed. "Sweetie, you can rest assured that I'll talk to anyone in the city before I talk to the cops. I just try to stay out of their way."

Ingrid nodded. "Understood. Do you think Miranda could have had a date with Flint Junior?"

"Oh, no, not Junior. He's not so easily won over." He paused and judiciously added more liquid from his flask to his cup as he looked her over, then lifted his cup to sip. "Are you, ahem, dating Junior?"

"No. Are you?"

Max choked on his coffee and exploded into laughter, narrowly avoiding spraying his clothes. He pulled a clean linen handkerchief from his pocket and dabbed at his mustache. "Don't say that sort of thing to someone who's just taking a drink, okay?" he said at last. "No. Junior's not my type. Strange kid. I poured one too many brandies into Nell once and she told me she used to worry herself sick about him. Something about his pets. They kept ending up dead. Finally they decided he couldn't be trusted with small animals. Josephine Lewis does all his work around here. Granted he's a hunk, but they'd never have hired him if he wasn't *the* son. Still I must say, he wasn't won over by Miranda. Well, maybe recently," Max admitted, leaning forward conspiratorially although they were alone in the room.

"When Miranda started as the old man's secretary, I'm sure she made herself a list of who was important. Then she set out to seduce the ones who counted. This one she bought tickets to the opera, or a packet of nose candy, or a man." He tilted his head to one side reminiscently. "A few weeks ago I even saw a very young girl come out of old Flint's office wearing a Girl Scout uniform—well, she wasn't wearing it exactly; she was putting it back on. Do you know if they make Girl Scout panties, or is it just the outside part of the uniform that they issue? I never realized what kind of hard sell they had to go through to get those cookie-selling badges."

"What did Miranda get you?"

"Oh, I never really counted. The lawyers like to have someone in charge to gripe to. No clout—just a few dollars more a month as an aspirin allowance." He waved a dismissive hand.

"You said Flint Junior wasn't easily won over, but he seems like such a charmer."

"All the more reason he couldn't be tempted; he knew all the games. She must have used some special tactics on him." He leaned over the chair as he spoke. "You know I can't imagine what possessed old Flinty to bring her in to begin with. You might know something about that. You know more than you're saying, don't you?"

Max didn't seem to expect a reply; he began talking again almost immediately.

"Must have been an awfully big favor to someone. She wasn't qualified for a secretarial job. He set her up like someone's mistress. No real work. Eyes and ears and other assorted orifices of the boss kind of thing. Nell Scott took care of Flinty's in-box before Miranda got to work every day. It was almost as if they didn't want her to know what was going on. As if she were spying on them as well as the rest of us."

"That would be consistent with her early life." Ingrid told Max about Miranda's role in the high school pot scandal.

He nodded. "Yep. That's her. Always coming up with some cute, money-saving plan like eliminating the Christmas bonuses, or firing all the people in the Xerox room and having the secretaries make all the copies. As if the legal secretaries would stand for any of that. They'd bring in their castration knives on the tray with the morning coffee. Their bosses would get the message real quick and vote it down in the management committee. The partners have the final say there. Looked as though Miss Management had been getting some leverage on old Flinty, though. He didn't take Nell back as his secretary after Miranda took over Personnel. Instead he accepted Miranda's advice on a very attractive but totally incompetent young lady.... I can't think *where* she gets them—Post and Mason at two A.M.? True, he likes them very young, but much younger than that—I mean, there *are* child labor laws in this country."

"I take it he was the customer for the Girl Scout cookies?"

"Oh my, we are the sharp one, aren't we? Well, I don't know who else would be using the senior partner's office for a jamboree. And that little girl I saw leaving the old man's office that night was too high to walk straight, and too spaced out to even stuff her panties in her pocket. I have no idea how she got down to the first floor, but Miranda didn't chaperone her. I made it a point to follow, discreetly, of course. I wanted to make sure someone called her a cab and gave her a voucher in case old Flint had passed out and Miranda had forgotten that little detail. The last I saw of her, she was getting into Tony Flint's red Porsche. First time I ever saw Flinty share anything with Junior."

He finished his coffee and meditated a moment on the empty cup. "The old man's in trouble. They never brought this sort of thing into the office before, or if they did, it was done very carefully, behind closed doors. You can't fool Word Processing. For as long as anyone can remember, he's been putting out more work than anyone—footnotes with hundreds of citations. Lately, he just hands out the occasional memo. Something's wrong. That man never could pass a lawbook without opening it up and jotting down a few cases."

"Could he be ill? I saw him collapse the other day. His son told me he's diabetic."

Max raised his eyebrows. "You *are* easy to talk to. Must be those pretty blue eyes—almost turquoise, aren't they? Yes, it's true, he's never taken very good care of his condition. Always missing meals. Nell is simply rabid on the subject—she's a real office wife, you know." Max smiled affectionately. "She's always dropping in to check if he's had his insulin shot or shouldn't he eat something soon. Very bad for him in a way. He's totally turned himself over to her. He should marry her, but she's forty years too old to be his type. I'm surprised he hasn't gone blind, or worse."

They looked up as a lawyer came through the door, coatless and looking rushed, clutching several pages of long yellow paper.

"Excuse me."

After he had date stamped and registered the document, the lawyer left and Max handed it to Ingrid to type. "Sorry, Max, could I ask you just two more questions?" He nodded. "First, how did Nell react to all this stuff Miranda put her through?"

"Poor Nell just carries on, holding it all together. A man like Flint, half his work gets done by his loyal legal secretary. Next question."

"Why did Miranda try to fire Franklin Bates?"

Max smiled. "Rumor has it she was tampering with the company pouch. We have a direct courier to one of our multinational clients, and to a few of their subsidiaries including a South American oil company. Frank Bates saw her taking something out of that pouch and mentioned it to the wrong person. It took her a few weeks to get it all smoothed over, and one of the ways she fixed it was to catch Frank drinking on the job—which wouldn't be all that difficult if you knew where to look." He shook his flask, now empty, and stored it away regretfully.

"You never heard what Miranda took out of the pouch?"

"That's three questions, and I'm afraid your guess is as good as mine. Information to sell to another client? Something she could use as leverage against someone here in the office?" He shrugged. "I don't think very highly of her, or anything she could possibly have done. But then, I'm hardly an objective witness, am I? I wouldn't have minded pushing her out that window myself, but I was busy at the time—the gang in Word Processing took me over to Sutter's Mill for a farewell drink or six. Ask anybody."

TWENTY-FIVE

WHEN NO MORE WORK had come in by nine thirty, Max made a telephone survey and found that all the lawyers had gone home to check for storm damage. Ingrid's cab driver informed her that the high winds were felling old trees in Golden Gate Park. Here and there blocks of darkened streetlamps testified to power outages. But before Ingrid had a chance to try turning on the lights at Carmen's the telephone rang. She jumped.

"Hi. It's me. I tried to sleep but couldn't. I've been thinking about you." Ingrid cursed silently when she heard Jason's voice and wished she hadn't given him Carmen's number. She wished she could sit still for a while and puzzle over her next move. She considered putting Jason Grapelli off for another evening, but the warning from Rosemary had aroused her curiosity. She refused to acknowledge any passionate urgency in his voice—well, maybe a small flame. Besides, if she *was* always picking the wrong man, perhaps it would be informative to take one more look at the most recent specimen.

Victor's threats gnawed at her. She had no intention of going on a suicide mission to try either one of her two keys on any of the addresses she had gotten from the diskette marked "M." But maybe, she told herself, Jason would have some information that would supply the missing puzzle pieces. And the sooner she knew what she was up against, the sooner she could deal with it and be safe again.

The wind whipped the power lines against their poles in sudden gusts, and a bead curtain of rain flowed over the Mustang's windshield. There were no power failures on Jason's block. He opened the door and pulled her inside in a steamy embrace.

Ingrid broke away. "Is Rosemary home tonight?"

Jason didn't even blink in surprise, but he released her and took her hand. "I'm here alone tonight," he said. "Come on. I'd like to throw a big party to celebrate my latest work, but the two of us can probably have more fun together. Let's talk Christmas presents." He led Ingrid past the small front bedroom where they had stayed last time, into the living room, at the rear of the house facing the Golden Gate. It was lit only by the lights on a huge Christmas tree decorated with antique, primitive-looking ornaments. The night lights on the Golden Gate Bridge glimmered just beyond Baker Beach. It was a cozy room, despite speakers the size of walk-in closets and stacked black boxes of stereo and video gear. Waist-high vases filled with a small forest of pampas grass framed the window and invited the eye outdoors. She could imagine sinking into the deep wine-colored sofa near the picture window and staring out at the bridge.

"Want a drink?" Jason stood near her but did not touch her.

"If you have a soft drink, please."

"Oh, right. You don't drink." He lit a green lamp next to an antique armoire. From a refrigeration unit built into the base of the cabinet he brought out a beer for himself and a cola for her. "You said you had a gift for me, or did you forget it?"

"Oh! Here." She handed him the picture in its protective envelope. "It's just something I took the day we…uh, the day you hung your pictures in that café."

He took the photo out and examined it under the lamp for a moment, then tossed it onto the nearest table.

"You're a photographer, Ingrid. Do you know anything at all about real art? The kind that demands All and gives back Nothing in return?"

There it was. Ingrid knew that she had been looking for Jason's approval of her photography. She could see in a sudden flash that he wasn't going to give it to her and that even his praise would not have convinced her to believe in herself. No one could give her that, she realized. Least of all Jason, whose specialty was obviously taking rather than giving.

Instinctively, Ingrid batted the question back at him. "It's not *that* bad for you, Jason—you do sell some pictures, don't you? I saw them on Rosemary Tanner's wall. Or was it something else you sold her?"

He smiled with a sudden flirtatious toss of his head. "I'll give you your present in bed. Want to see some of my Christmas presents? I did pretty well this year—how about you?"

"Nothing spectacular."

"Look here. This set of crystal glasses is mine. You know how you can tell real crystal? I'll show you." He licked his finger and ran it round the rim of the glass. A faint ringing sound arose.

"Yes. I hear it."

"People gave me some very nice things." He continued to rub the crystal. The sound became annoying.

"Does Rosemary mind sharing you?"

"Who cares? The question is, can you afford me?" He put the glass down. At last.

"No. I could never afford to put a price on that."

"Everyone puts a price on that. You think she's supporting me, don't you?"

"You do give that impression."

"Not true. She lets me stay here. Sometimes she buys a painting. Not the real stuff. The cute stuff. That's it."

"You don't provide any...uh, other services?"

"Maybe I should. She might be persuaded to part with an allowance that way. Maybe that's what our relationship really needs." He turned to stare into the fireplace. "She never lets me stay long. I always find myself out on the street again sooner or later. She can't stand to be around a real working artist. My work is too powerful for some people to face. That's why I took the name graffiti. When she kicks me out, I go stay with one of my other women friends. Yes, they're older and yes, some of them give me gifts. You can sponsor me if you can afford it. I'm not turning you away. I never pass up anyone or anything that can be of use to me. So how about it, lady?"

"No, thanks." Ingrid was outraged to discover that his presence and his hot breath near her ear had stirred a confusion of embarrassment and longing.

Okay, she told herself, we'll put a double line under last time and call it a one-night stand after all.

"Thanks for the soft drink."

"Not at all. Can you find your own way out?"

As she left, he was sitting on the sofa, dialing the telephone. "Hi. It's me—I couldn't sleep. I was thinking about you." Somewhere an older woman friend was about to have her night livened up considerably.

TWENTY-SIX

Wednesday, December 28

BY THE NEXT MORNING the wind had died to an occasional rattle of the windows in their frames. Ingrid awoke on Carmen's sofa. The sun filtered through the clouds into the room as if through a gray lampshade. The blanket was on the floor, with Mugwort sleeping on top of it. She had to talk to Carmen, whose bedroom door was closed. No signs that Spyder was there. She checked the driveway. No van. Good.

Ingrid paced the floor of the front room as she sipped her morning cup of coffee. Then she called Ben Resnick. He hadn't been able to trace the bicycle messenger who had stolen Ingrid's cameras. The messenger company had a turnover rate of close to one hundred percent every year, but the bicycle in question had been used by a female messenger until recently and then reported stolen. She brought him up to date on what she had learned, which came out sounding annoyingly like soap-opera gossip. He paused when she had finished. Then he began to ask questions. She realized that he had been taking notes.

"My police sources agree that Miranda's death has been written off as a suicide; the note was unusual but it was definitely in her handwriting. Sounds fishy to me. Just keep asking questions," he said in a tone of voice that Ingrid could only characterize as longing. "Could you give me those addresses? I'd like to send Van Horn around to knock on doors and ask a few questions about those dates."

"Sure." Ingrid read off the contents she had printed out from Miranda's diskette.

"Okay, kiddo. I'll be here, so keep me posted. This whole thing could crack wide open anytime."

"Fine. But what will come out of the shell when it does crack?"

"Just watch out for yourself and talk to these people in public places, will you? They could be dangerous." He sounded excited by the prospect.

"Sure. Thanks a lot." Ingrid was less than thrilled. She hung up and searched the cupboards for a suitably stimulating tea. Ginseng looked like the best bet. She brewed a very strong pot and knocked on Carmen's door.

A few minutes later they sat in the kitchen, where the windows had steamed up. Outside, a tree branch scratched against the pane as gusts of wind shook it and the telephone lines twitched as if nipped. Carmen wound a lock of her heavy red hair between her fingers while Ingrid described Rosemary's warning and Jason's proposition.

"I've got to admit, there must be somebody better than that for me, maybe even in San Francisco. But even if there isn't, I never want to see him again," Ingrid concluded.

Carmen stretched up toward the ceiling luxuriously; Mugwort ambled in and did the same thing horizontally. "Well, I sure can't cast any stones at an older woman with a younger boyfriend. But I don't see what the problem is. Everybody should be happy."

"I don't want to see him again. But I hate..." Ingrid gritted her teeth. It was hard even to say it. "I can't stand to *give in* like that."

"Why even talk to her again if she's such a bitch?"

"I need some information about the Flint family. I don't know if one of them hired the guy who grabbed my purse or who else might have. It's plain to me that Miranda's death was no suicide. Everybody else wants to just roll over and forget it. But there's one person who *knows* it wasn't a suicide, and before she died Miranda told that person that *I* had her files, the ones she must have used to blackmail people—she called it her scrapbook."

"*Do* you have it?"

"Please, Carmen, not you too! Remember that key you found in the pot of African violets? Someone wanted that key from Miranda badly enough to smash every pot of African violets in Flint Senior's office."

"And maybe that same someone tried to drag you away and stole your bag in the process?" Carmen sipped her tea. "So you need more information and Rosemary has it. Maybe you can turn it into a business deal—sell her the guy you never want to see again in exchange for the information you need."

"When you put it that way, it sounds rational." Ingrid nodded slowly. "But Carmen, you be extra careful too, even around Spyder." She repeated Victor's threats. "I don't know what it's all about, but I'm not leaving town. Maybe you should go to Fremont with Mugwort for a few weeks till all this clears up—maybe that would be wiser. I've got to get to the bottom of this thing. If it's connected with Victor's old business . . . I just don't know how Spyder . . ." She let the sentence trail off.

Carmen knotted her brows dubiously. "I'll talk to Spyder. I think he should tell you a few things he's held back. Maybe it will help. It's not easy for him to talk about those times. All I know is Victor helped him lease some land."

"He was in business with Vic? I didn't know that."

"Oh, my gosh. I thought you knew. I thought that was why you didn't want to go to the police."

"If I thought it would do any good, I'd talk to the police, but I don't really have any evidence. Even the memo Miranda sent me was taken by that thief. Besides, they've decided it was a suicide, and all I have right now is questions." She shrugged. "They may not be the right questions. I have two keys and a list of addresses, but I'm not sure how any of this ties together."

Carmen pushed her tea cup aside. "Ingrid, have you ever wondered why I didn't tell you where I worked or what I did?"

It took Ingrid a moment to adjust to the shift in subject. "Well, I always thought you were a cocktail waitress or uh . . ."

"Or a hooker?"

"Never that. Maybe a topless waitress."

"Close. I work the cash register in a massage parlor in North Beach. It's where I worked before I got married. It's how I met my husband, believe it or not. He said he'd reform me, but he kept reminding me that he could put me back in the gutter where he found me. Anytime. I believed that. Maybe that's why I stayed with him so long. I'd had it with the massage parlor. But after Andy died, I needed a job. I had no skills like you do. No experience. I always got along with the people there, and they owed me a favor. So I went back and asked if they had a straight job. They trained me as a cashier.''

"You never told me this before; why now?''

"The picture you showed me, that big woman in the alley. She comes to pick up the receipts where I work. Sometimes she goes to a kind of club in the back room. None of the employees are allowed back there, except some of the girls who specialize in S&M and group scenes, so whatever she's connected with must be kinkier than usual.''

"Are they all adults, the ones who go into the back room?''

"All the ones I've seen.''

"Did you ever see a small blond woman with tattoos on her wrists?''

"Oh. Her. Yes. She comes to pick up the money sometimes and talks to the manager in his office. I've never seen her go into the back room. Not her scene, I guess.''

Ingrid agreed. "Do you think you could recognize pictures of the regulars who go into the back room?''

"Maybe. But Ingrid, I'm not adventurous like you. Me, I just take orders and go along with the program.'' Carmen sighed. "If they found out I'd even talked to you, I'd be fired. They've always trusted me because my husband was on the take. There was an investigation that was about to blow up in his face when he killed himself. They felt responsible.''

"Are you sure they *weren't* responsible?''

"Yes.'' Carmen hesitated and began to twist her coppery hair around a finger again. "I wouldn't work there if I thought there was any chance of that.''

Ingrid nodded.

"Don't get me wrong—I'm not running. But if those people at the massage parlor get on our case, we'll have to put in bulletproof paneling.''

"Maybe we can teach Mugwort some guard-dog moves."

Carmen swept the sleeping tomcat up in her arms and embraced him fiercely. He awoke for a moment, then nestled against her, purring in his sleep. "Could that woman in the alley have pushed Miranda out the window?"

"It's possible. She seemed angry enough or scared enough. But I took that picture after Miranda had gone inside. Stella couldn't have gotten at Miranda unless someone let her into the building from inside."

"So that probably clears her. Let's see. You say someone saw the receptionist snorting coke with the boss's son when she said she was sitting outside Miranda's office."

"It looks like it. If that's true, either Junior and the receptionist are covering up for each other or Junior cooperated with someone else to get the receptionist out of the way."

"And the father was on the way to the airport."

"So they say. Given a little luck and a helpful person on the inside, even Victor could have gone in and done it, though it seems against his best interests of finding her blackmail book. I hate to say it, but Spyder could have done it too, although I don't know why he would have wanted to. He didn't even know Miranda."

Carmen sighed and looked troubled but said nothing.

"Of course Franklin Bates, Max Leon and Nell Scott could come and go without signing in. They all hated Miranda. But they all have witnesses to where they were at the time Miranda died."

Carmen laughed, but her face was serious. "Well, that narrows it down. What will you do after you talk to Rosemary Tanner?"

"Depends on what she tells me." Ingrid didn't want to think about it, but she knew the next step after that would be to beard Atherton Flint Senior in his den in St. Francis Wood.

TWENTY-SEVEN

Thursday, December 29

ROSEMARY TANNER grabbed Ingrid's arm as she collapsed her tripod a few moments after taking her last picture at the Professional Women's Network luncheon. They dodged through squads of waiters clearing up the North Beach Hotel's Barbary Coast Conference room. Rosemary opened an invisible door just behind the podium to reveal a small room done up in the same whorehouse red and gold decor as the conference room.

"What's this?" Ingrid asked, her feet sinking into the mud-thick carpet.

"Of course, you wouldn't have seen one before," said Rosemary, flashing a smile with enough artificial sweetener to cause cancer in several rats. "It's a VIP room for speakers and honored guests. Just a place to unwind in private before they're exposed to the rabble. We have this room for another hour. That should be enough. Sit down. Henri will pour you coffee or whatever you wish."

Henri appeared on cue with a liqueur bottle, a coffee-pot, glasses and cups on a tray. Ingrid lowered herself carefully onto an oyster-shell angled loveseat. It looked ready to snap shut at any moment but was surprisingly comfortable. Rosemary chose a straight-backed chair nearby.

"Ingrid, let's understand one another. I have no objection to working with you. You're a competent photographer. I may buy one or all of your pictures—we'll see. But I have no wish to encounter you over the breakfast table."

"I don't know what you're talking about."

"Don't you think I know when someone spends the night under my roof? He brings these women in—to find out it's a business acquaintance is quite intolerable."

"It's hardly my fault, Rosemary, that your playmate has so little discretion. Okay, he deceived both of us, so what? Lying comes naturally to him; it's part of his charm."

Rosemary was silent for several seconds. When she did speak, her voice was unexpectedly soft. "One detail you didn't find out, Ingrid: Jason Grapelli is my son."

It was hard to stay in the room. Ingrid very badly wanted to walk out. She sat for several seconds, absorbing this information. Beneath her anger at Jason for letting her think Rosemary was one of his "older women friends," a simple conclusion struggled into her mind. Jason either had not talked to Rosemary about the affair or had failed to mention that it was over. Possibly, like Ingrid, he didn't want to give Rosemary the satisfaction.

"It's very simple. If you ever want to work again in Northern California, you will promise to leave my son alone."

Ingrid managed to resist the overwhelming impulse to advise Rosemary to return her son from whence he came. She took a deep breath and concentrated on sharpening her bargaining posture.

"He may be your son, but he's of age. You don't own him."

"I own that house. I forbid you to see him there."

"You don't own me, either."

Rosemary clenched her hands briefly, crumpling the luncheon program that she had been tapping nervously on the coffee table in front of her. "What do you want?"

Ingrid wanted to smile, but said instead, "If I promise to leave your son alone, will you answer all my questions fully? It's not about you. I need some information about the Flints."

Rosemary tilted her head this way and that as if literally looking at the situation from all angles. "Yes," she said at last, drawing out the word, reluctant to let it go. "Anything you want. And you'll promise to leave my son alone. Can you keep your word about that?"

"If I say I'll do something, Rosemary, I do it."

They glared at each other for a moment; then Rosemary nodded solemnly. "It's a deal." She rose, reached out to

shake hands and stood over Ingrid for a moment. Then she
went to the door and glanced outside as though checking
for eavesdroppers. She sat down and looked at Ingrid
mildly. Now that Ingrid had agreed to terms, they could be
friends again.

"About Mrs. Flint. You knew her?"

"Eugenia Bramwell. Named for her father, Eugene. Yes,
the founder of the law firm. Jennie and I were at school
together here in town. She was no angel, but she was a lot
of fun. Until it started to catch up with her."

"Too much fun?"

"Too much money and too much time on her hands. A
terrible combination, take it from me. She filled her time
with liquor and pills and men. She just couldn't handle it.
My late husband suffered from the same need to escape his
own money and to use up all that spare time—in his case by
crawling into a bottle. It's enough to make one envy the
poor."

Ingrid nodded sagely and refrained from entering into a
discussion about problems of rich versus poor alcoholics.

"How did Mrs. Flint die?"

"She was in a sanitarium, sort of a drying-out place for
the genteelly addicted. There was a fire and she was
trapped."

"You were her friend. What did she complain about
when she started drinking so heavily?" Ingrid asked, striking out blindly.

"This may be hard for you to understand, but we grew
up in a different world in the 1940s. They taught us all
about white gloves—and nothing about contraceptives.
Jennie and I became close and stayed close later on because we both got pregnant the same year of high school.
Neither of us had parents worldly enough to ship us off to
get an illegal abortion. You can't imagine what a disgrace
it was in those days. My family had to conceal it at all costs;
we moved back to St. Louis, where we had connections. It
was a hardship for my parents, but they did it for me. And
I cooperated in turn. I didn't return to San Francisco until
I married Jack Tanner. My relatives back there raised...my
son." She seemed unwilling to say the name. "Jack never

knew the boy existed. I scarcely saw him until recently, when he came out here. Unlike Jennie, I had no constant reminder of how terrified and powerless I was back then."

"What did Jennie do?"

"Now, her father had real clout. He also had a gang of ambitious, unmarried lawyers working for him—all males in those days. Flinty was the hungriest shark in the pond. Even then he looked conservative enough to freeze a rumor in midair. That was part of the problem, I think. He took Jennie on as job insurance but he never was much of a husband to her, as she so often said."

"So Atherton Flint *Junior* isn't really related to Atherton Flint *Senior?*"

"They don't look much alike, do they. Jennie was tall and blond. Who knows? I think she had it narrowed down to about six or seven likely lads. She never said Flinty was in the running, but she never said he wasn't." Rosemary spoke flippantly, but her eyes were wary.

"I understand diabetes can cause nerve damage and impotence." Ingrid let the implication dangle.

Rosemary set down her glass and picked up a small napkin. "Jennie probably made it worse by throwing tantrums when she should have asked prettily. Maybe that was why—" Rosemary halted as if realizing she had already told too much.

"Why he likes little girls?"

"Rumors." Rosemary folded her cocktail napkin into a fan. "But there's no proof of any of it. Even if there were proof, such things are unimportant."

Ingrid held her tongue and let Rosemary ramble.

"Only three things in life truly interest Atherton Flint: African violets, legal research and money. Whenever I saw Jennie, she harped on what a bad bargain Flinty was. Not just the sex. Jennie was used to a lot of attention, and Flinty never was the cuddly type. He's got an air-conditioning unit, I think, instead of a heart."

"Well, he did protect her reputation and her unborn child." This sounded awfully melodramatic to Ingrid even as she said it, but the situation seemed to demand melodrama.

"Don't you believe it. He got that partnership in Bramwell, and once he proved himself, the old man willed him a life interest in the building. Jennie put up with his coldness and he put up with her adventures. By the time her father died, her money was tied up in some sort of trust and she was on prescription pills on top of the drinking. Flinty took over as her legal guardian and put her in that sanitarium."

"What about all her friends and relatives? Did they just stand by and let it happen?"

"Oh, her relatives had lost patience with her years earlier. They thought Flinty showed admirable restraint. As for her friends, we never guessed she was gone for good. We expected her to dry out and return next season like the monarch butterflies to liven us all up a bit. She was the only one who took it seriously."

"Was she afraid of her husband, do you think?"

"Afraid? No. Resentful, perhaps. She got it into her head that he was siphoning money from her trust account, building a private fortune for himself at her expense."

"Was he?"

"Highly unlikely. Flinty never was much of a risk taker. She wanted the trust account audited, but she never lived that long. If he really did strip the estate, he's had years to cover his tracks." Rosemary sighed. "I think Jennie's problem was that nothing very bad happened to her until she got pregnant and had to get married. She was rich, beautiful, blond, never sick a day in her life. She'd never even needed dental work—perfect teeth. She blamed Flinty for all her troubles."

Ingrid tried another tack. "The fire that killed Mrs. Flint in the sanitarium—how did it start?"

Rosemary sat still for several seconds, gazing into a distant past that seemed to be unfolding a few feet behind Ingrid's right shoulder. "An explosion in the furnace room. They thought she might have been responsible, because she was found there. I wondered if she might have been trying to escape. She talked about it so often. The basement was strictly off limits to patients, of course, but unlike the rest of the rooms there, it had a window with no bars on it."

Rosemary continued, warming to the subject. "The last time I spoke to her, she was quite distraught because one of the nurse's aides was leaving to take a better job. She was worried that perhaps no one would help her escape after all. They suspected this same nurse's aide of escorting Jennie out of the locked part of the sanitarium. So sad, really. One of the most popular women in San Francisco reduced to confiding in—well, basically, a servant."

"I'm sure she wasn't the first or the last. Did they prosecute the nurse's aide?"

"No. There was quite a scandal and they tried to locate her, but all she had told anyone was that she had a new job taking care of a little girl. No names or addresses. The police were never able to trace her." Rosemary shrugged.

"What was her name, this nurse's aide?"

"After all these years, I'm afraid— Oh, yes! I do remember that they shared that rather uncommon first name—Eugenia. That's how they started talking together, what made Jennie feel they had something in common. I don't recall the last name."

"It couldn't have been Phelps, could it?"

"It might have been; I'm afraid I've forgotten. Poor Jennie felt she had been abandoned by everyone. Of course, her husband visited regularly and brought the boy, but that just made things worse."

Probably not so great for the kid either, Ingrid reflected.

"I was the only one from our circle who visited her. Frankly, if she hadn't died when she did, I'm not sure how long I could have kept it up. As it was she died six months after she went into that place."

"Do you think she might have taken her own life, set off that fire on purpose?"

"You know, I've often wondered that. There was a tremendous explosion. If she hadn't been wearing some unique pieces of jewelry they might have had trouble identifying her; as I mentioned, she'd had no dental work. Of course, once they counted all the patients and found who was missing, that would have clinched it."

Except that two women were missing, Ingrid thought, but Rosemary continued.

"What I've always wondered was how she laid hands on her jewelry. She must have been hiding it all along. Maybe her little nurse friend helped her. Those magnificent pearls she had from her grandmother were lost in the fire, though. An old-fashioned setting of opera-length pearls. She offered to sell them to me when her husband reduced her to the penury she was expecting. I didn't take her seriously. Too bad."

"Would you recognize those pearls if you saw them again?"

"Probably. You don't see pearls like that often. The clasp was shaped like lobster claws—a little joke about the Bramwells' New England money."

Ingrid couldn't recall having seen such a clasp.

Rosemary seemed to be enjoying her recollections. She had consumed most of her bottle of Campari.

"Do you know much about Atherton Flint Junior?" Ingrid asked.

"Quite a handsome young man," Rosemary said a bit wistfully. Then she snapped to sudden attention, glaring at Ingrid distrustfully. "What about him?"

"Do you know anything about the trouble he was in a few years ago? When he lost his yacht?"

Rosemary laughed. "He's his mother's son there, all right. A South American diplomat's son—I'll name no names—was sailing with him when they had engine trouble. The Coast Guard came to the rescue and found something illicit aboard. We never heard what. Drugs no doubt. I think perhaps they were still in international waters, though. Flinty bailed his boy out and talked the other boy's family into making sure he took full responsibility. As the child of a diplomat, he had immunity and they couldn't touch him. They just shipped him home. Boyish high spirits, no harm done, I'm sure."

Ingrid declined to argue. Rosemary sat back in her chair and stretched her legs out, concluding the topic.

"What about the Bramwell Building's landmark status? Did your Preserve Our Past group get involved, perhaps use some of your personal information as leverage?"

Rosemary looked up sharply. "It was Flinty's own idea. He wanted to honor the memory of the firm's founder and restore some of the building's historical features. Of course, Preserve Our Past was delighted to do the spadework and help present it to the City's Advisory Board. It's a designated landmark now."

"A nasty little surprise for Mr. Kubler?"

Rosemary smiled. "Even if Flint himself asked permission to tear that building down, the city could block him for at least a year, and who knows what might happen in that time? Kubler just gave up and cut back on his building size."

"Why did Kubler need to build such a large structure?"

"Prestige. He wants to join the big boys downtown, to step out of the slumlord image. I say the image is well deserved—why not stick with what he does best?"

"After the Bramwell Building conflict, what happened to Flint's ties to Kubler Real Estate?"

"What do *you* think?" Rosemary stretched her arms up over her head. She glanced at her watch, then at the empty crystal decanter and her empty glass. "Ah, Flinty's well out of it. Kubler may seem like a sophisticated gentleman of the old school, but I have a feeling some of his aides carry brass knuckles in their pockets. Not that *he* would ever do anything illegal himself, but the occasional overzealous underling—well, who knows?"

Henri materialized again. Could he have been listening outside and have realized that the conversation was becoming indiscreet? He shook his head subtly as he took the tray away.

"Here, for these." Rosemary took out a checkbook and laboriously wrote out a check for three times the highest amount on Ingrid's price list. She pushed the stack of proof sheets at Ingrid, with her selections circled and numbers of prints scribbled on Ingrid's order form. Judging from her handwriting, Ingrid suspected that very little work would get done at Rosemary's office this afternoon.

INGRID HAD A FOUR-FIGURE check in her wallet and a be-mused smile on her face when she called Flint's office from the pay phone in the lobby. Tanya said he was really and truly out sick.

"If I wanted to send him a get-well card, what address would I send it to?"

Tanya hesitated. "I can't give out that information, but if you talked to someone else who wasn't so careful, they might tell you."

"I'm sure I would never remember the name of anyone who would do such a thing. Probably a temp anyway. You know how those temps are."

Tanya laughed and gave Ingrid an address on San Beni-to, deep in the protected foliage of the St. Francis Wood district. Ingrid took down the telephone number, but dismissed the idea of calling ahead. No sense in warning Flint.

"One more question: Where does he buy his African vi-olets?"

Tanya snorted and hung up.

TWENTY-EIGHT

INGRID GOT OFF the M Ocean View streetcar carrying a miniature African violet. "No relation to ordinary violets. Their real name is Saintpaulia, but they *are* from east Africa," the florist had said, giving her his card and a look that had warmed her down to her toes. She felt much more kindly now toward the little plant with the gray hair on its leaves.

Flint Senior's house was quite secluded, in the St. Francis Wood enclave of homes set back from immaculate sidewalks. A gardener's pickup truck was parked in a driveway next to the Flint home. Two men were wrestling down a huge, broken tree limb, an unfortunate victim of Tuesday night's high winds. Now it dangled, threatening the roof it had once sheltered.

A brick driveway curved up steeply from the street, linking Flint's mailbox and his house, a heavy fortress with thick, insulating walls and a roof with low eaves.

She started to ring the bell but her hand was arrested midway to the button by the extraordinary beauty of the glass panels flanking the heavy oak door. A gnarled brown oak unfolded across a field of milk-white glass shot with small patterns and explosions of colored light. Crosshatched with black, the oak stretched the length of the four glass panels, interrupted but not really broken by the door in the center. Ingrid sighed, wanting badly to photograph the doorway. At last she rang the bell.

The door swung open so quickly that she nearly dropped her Saintpaulia. She found herself staring into the impassive face of Franklin Bates. Had he been observing her from inside as she examined the stained glass?

"Hello," she said, recovering her self-possession after a second. "I was admiring the glass window."

"Tiffany." Frank Bates smiled without warmth. "I thought you didn't like windows; but then you don't have to wash this one, do you?"

"I guess you weren't fired after all."

"I guess not. Is that all you came to find out?"

"No, I had no way of knowing you would be here."

"Oh, really? I thought Miss Scott would have told you about my special status around the old plantation here."

"Have you talked to Tanya recently?" she asked carefully. "The last time I was at BSF, she was worried about you." No answer. In fact, no reaction. She continued, "I brought this flower for Mr. Flint. Do you think you could take it to him and ask if he'd see me?"

Frank Bates took the flowerpot, closed the door and left her on the porch to admire the glass panel a little longer. He returned a few moments later and beckoned her through the door. "He's in the library." He indicated a room just off the foyer.

Flint's library could have served a small law firm. The room was long and overheated, filled with heavy, dark furniture. Mahogany bookshelves with glass doors climbed from floor to ceiling. The shelved books Ingrid could see were hide-bound legal tomes, but open on the room's central table was a large volume showing a bright color plate of a flower with botanical details revealed in cross-section below. Her eye was drawn to another set of glowing stained-glass panes set into a door at the rear of the library.

"That door opens on the passageway to my greenhouse," said Flint Senior. He had been standing so quietly by the fireplace that she hadn't noticed him.

"What a beautiful house you have," she said, feeling awkward.

"Yes, it was built by my father-in-law. But you didn't come to see that."

He indicated the plant now resting on the table; it seemed a little silly to her now. The sinking feeling at the pit of her stomach reminded her of a visit to the principal's office back in grammar school. Worse. People came to this man with questions. And all the answers had price tags.

"Sit down." He motioned to an overstuffed armchair near the fireplace. She was glad to sit. After the cold and damp outdoors, the overheated room made her feel a little faint.

Flint made his way over to a chair near hers.

"I hope you're feeling better, Mr. Flint," she said, though she could see from the way he moved that he was not feeling well at all.

"Thank you for the plant," he said, nodding gravely as if the African violet were a letter of introduction. "What did you want to talk to me about?"

Ingrid opened her mouth without thinking first what she would say. "When I was looking into Miranda's records, some uh, old files came to light and I was hoping you could clarify a few points to help settle some problems about them." As awkward as she felt, Ingrid was at least lying fluently enough to keep the conversation going.

"Yes. Go on." Flint looked at her with the benign, self-contained air of a crocodile who may or may not have eaten recently. No sign of knowing about any of Miranda's files. A corporate lawyer would have to be a good poker player, of course.

"She used to work for Kubler, a client of yours, I believe. Or former client?"

Flint blinked but waited rather than replying.

"Did you hire Miranda before or after Kubler tried to buy your building?"

Flint allowed himself the ghost of a smile. "Helmut has been after the Bramwell for years—and he hasn't totally given up even now. He never does, of course; that's why he's a multi-millionaire. So I guess you could say Miranda came onto our staff *during* negotiations. Kubler is still our client in several other matters, so I'll refrain from further comment." He leaned forward encouragingly. He seemed to be enjoying himself.

"Whose idea was it to hire Miranda?"

Flint began to blush but continued to lean forward. Perhaps Ingrid's nervousness intrigued him. "Helmut recommended her very strongly. So we decided to try her out. It was the least we could do, as a favor to him."

"They wanted to get rid of her?"

"She was a liaison person, but I wanted her where I could keep track of her."

Ingrid nodded. In other words, a spy. "About the historical landmark status, Rosemary tells me it was your idea."

He nodded, marking her up a point for knowing Tanner. "Rosie was kind enough to help set up all the paperwork for me. I was glad to sign. I even talked to the committee briefly."

His hands were trembling visibly. Ingrid decided to strike her hardest blow and get out, hoping he wouldn't collapse again.

"Now then, about this very young girl seen leaving your office late at night a few weeks back."

"This *what?*"

"A girl in her very early teens or younger. Perhaps you met her. She's disappeared, and she was last seen by someone in your law firm, coming out of your office rather late at night."

"Impossible." Flint Senior seemed puzzled rather than outraged or stunned. Ingrid had expected him to throw her out.

"Well, excuse me sir, this is not the time or place to discuss your proclivities, although they are common knowledge in some circles. However, given your, uh, tastes in very young girls, it wouldn't be totally without precedent, would it?"

"Coming out of my office, late at night, you say, recently?" Still he was not angry. Instead he seemed to have trouble quite remembering where he was.

"Yes. A few weeks ago."

Flint seemed to regain control of his faculties. "Nell Scott, who keeps my time sheets, and our switchboard operators, who keep track of attendance, will be able to tell you that I haven't worked late in my office all year. Several business trips to Washington and the simple demands of work have taken a considerable toll on my health. I've been forced, against my will, to come home early each day and rest. My physician could verify that also, as he calls me each evening to make sure I'm following instructions. The last thing in the world I need these days is female companionship. Indeed, I wish I felt that well." Flint Senior allowed himself a wintry smile.

Ingrid felt foolish enough to stop immediately, but drove herself to wind it up. Flint had seemed neither surprised nor self-righteously indignant when she mentioned his rumored taste for young girls. She had expected to be shown to the door with threats of suit for slander. He treated the matter as totally irrelevant. But was it?

"Could your son have been using your office? He was the person last seen with the girl in question, after she came out of your office and left the building."

"My son? And a very young girl, you say?" Now he was angry; the brown eyes flashed but did not connect with Ingrid. He stared through the heart of the almost blackly violet flower on the table. At last he looked up sadly. "Have you ever heard of a golden handshake?"

Ingrid was taken aback. She tried humor. "Is that anything like golden showers?"

Flint laughed.

It was a dangerous sound. It stopped, then started again. She was afraid he might have hurt himself, but at last he wound down.

Ingrid looked at him cautiously. She wasn't sure what he might do next.

Flint wiped his eyes and his glasses with a white handkerchief that looked starched. "There are some similarities. My beloved colleagues are forcing me into retirement rather earlier than I had planned. With a generous settlement, of course. It all amounts to the classic golden handshake treatment, although there are some aspects of the, ahem, showers you speak of, with their, ahem, urinary connotations." He chuckled.

"But why?"

"The message is that it's worth a great deal of money to them to get rid of me. Of course, my health is an adequate excuse. I seem to be going downhill, unfortunately, almost as fast as they would like. I have no better option than to take their offer before I'm forced out, as an invalid, with no such generous settlement."

The door opened and Frank Bates appeared, whispered in Flint's ear for a moment and then bent down further so that Flint could reply, also in a whisper. Frank went out, carefully avoiding Ingrid's eyes.

Flint returned his attention to her and sighed. "Perhaps it's for the best. Things are changing too fast for my liking. Once there was some loyalty between attorney and client. Like a priest, or a doctor, a lawyer keeps his client's affairs sacrosanct." He sighed. "Well, we still do, but now half the time they're suing us or we're suing them. You'll forgive me if I cut this interview short—"

As Flint spoke, Frank Bates ushered in Tony Flint Junior and Nell Scott. Nell barely acknowledged Ingrid, but Tony smiled and fixed his eyes on her as Frank escorted her out of the room. Ingrid took one last look at the group in the library.

Flint Senior sat by the fireplace while Tony leaned against the mantel, politely bending forward as he waited for Nell to speak—although he couldn't seem to summon the energy to pay much attention. He seemed distracted. He glanced up, raking Ingrid with a hot blue glance that made her blush. Then his attention was suddenly riveted by the African violet on the table—he looked at it with abrupt, raw fascination. Ingrid remembered again that he seemed to know his way around his father's office. She thought of the shattered pots of African violets in the center of Flint's rug. Nell huddled in the chair where Ingrid had sat, but she had pulled it up quite near Flint Senior and was clearly waiting for Ingrid to leave before she spoke. Feeling like an intruder in a quiet family gathering, Ingrid turned on her heel and left.

She paused in the curving driveway, conscious of Frank Bates's surveillance through the still-open door, and scribbled a note to put under the windshield wiper of the red Porsche in the driveway.

As INGRID UNLOCKED her studio door, a slight figure came out of the dimness, and she found herself balanced to repel an attack. The figure paused out of arm's reach and puffed on a cigarette. It was Hiromasu Ito.

"Sumimasen, Inga. Just a moment, okay?"

"Oh, Ito-sensei, you startled me. Is everything okay?"

"Inga, last night a man try to break in here. Mas jumped him but he got away. Mas says he was a very tall man." He held up his hand very high to reinforce his uncertain L's.

"Blond hair or dark hair, or maybe a black man?"

Ito shook his head. "Too dark to tell. But Mas-chan knocked him into the door." He chuckled at his son's impetuousness. "I think that man has a headache now. Maybe you watch out when you see a man with a bump on the forehead, neh? That man was trying to get into your darkroom. We take care around here. It's okay."

"Oh, sensei, I'm sorry to cause you trouble."

"Doh itashi mashite, no problem, Inga-chan. But you take care yourself, okay?"

Ingrid agreed and bowed apologetically, and the two of them bowed each other out the different exits to the corridor. Her head whirled with a flood of information. Nothing seemed to form a coherent pattern. The green message light was lit on her darkroom answering machine.

"Hello," the taped voice said uncertainly. The voice had been crying. "This is Stella Anderson, from Kubler. I...I'm in a lot of trouble. Wanda gave me your card; she said...I mean—I need help. Could you meet me in Portsmouth Square tomorrow, Friday, at noon? I'll be there at twelve."

TWENTY-NINE

Friday, December 30

INGRID HUDDLED in her jacket and several layers of borrowed sweaters as she walked against the wet wind. Dark clouds moved ominously across the sky, but so far this morning it had not rained. Paper calendar leaves fluttered in the updrafts around the Bank of America Headquarters Building, and billions of paper circles saved from hole-punched paper and streamers of adding-machine tape carpeted Montgomery Street. A great mass of shredded paper hung from the Montgomery Street sign, dropped from a security-conscious bank or brokerage where all discarded information leaves the building through the shredder. People walked under the falling paper, their glazed eyes fixed on the three-day weekend that lay ahead.

Up Nob Hill toward Chinatown, Ingrid saw that the streets became abruptly clean. On Grant and farther up on Stockton the lunar calendar held sway and the year wouldn't turn for weeks yet. When it did come, the Chinese community would usher it in with red paper, firecrackers and dragons dancing to drums.

Telegraph Hill loomed at the distant dead end of the street with a sudden blank wall of concrete steps from Broadway up to the crazy quilt of pink and green roofs. Coit Tower played hide and seek behind the office buildings. At Sacramento Street it was invisible. At Clay it popped up on the right amid a cluster of signs in Chinese. When she crossed the street to Portsmouth Square, she saw it at last, standing in its thatch of vegetation next to a stacked nest of condos.

Despite the cold, it was business as usual among the old men bending over the boards on the park's sheltered tables, arguing vehemently in Cantonese as they played Chinese chess. Sometimes two men would snatch at the same small round piece, slamming it down on different squares. Perhaps they argued to keep warm.

Panhandlers worked the bright-red benches systematically. They knew better than to bother to try the chess players, and in the wet chill Stella Anderson was their only possible victim. Two men with bedrolls paused by her bench as Ingrid climbed the hill. Stella turned her head firmly away and they moved on. Ingrid shook her head even before they asked.

Stella's blue coat vibrated with intense cheerfulness against the red bench, but her face was gray with misery. Ingrid said hello and offered her hand. Stella turned her head away, much as she had a moment before to the solemn pair in grimy coats.

"Did you take the day off work?" Ingrid asked.

"Called in sick."

Ingrid sat down beside her. "Quite an art, calling in sick. When perfected, it can allow a person to endure a detestable job for months, even years, longer than would otherwise be possible."

She sneaked a look at Stella, who still had the same dogged expression on her face. Was there a slight lessening of the knotted muscles around the jaw? "It's a fragile balance," Ingrid continued, "between when to leave and why. The best excuse is generally a very physical but not too visible ailment. Timing? Let's see, the best time is right before something awful, such as taking lunch orders and delivering them to the boys in the boardroom. But you're a bookkeeper, you probably don't have to do *that*. Accountants must have other problems, though."

Ingrid let the silence lengthen. It seemed like forever, but at last Stella turned toward her as if waking from a bad dream.

"I've been taking time off every few days for weeks now, looking for my daughter. It's a wonder they don't fire me. No. I guess I know too much to be fired."

"You mean Kubler's books are not totally honest?" Ingrid bit her tongue too late. She had meant it as a gently probing joke, but she realized as she spoke that the question would have a different meaning for a bookkeeper.

Stella turned to stare at Ingrid in amazement. Her eyes were a pale, pale blue, her hair almost golden. Her mouth opened in a rosebud shape that reminded Ingrid of a baby-faced doll she had once had that cried, "Wah!" when set on its back.

"I see you're not an accountant, Mrs.—what was it again?"

"Ingrid Hunter. Just call me Ingrid."

"Well, Ingrid, if you were an accountant, you would know. No one is totally honest about his finances."

"Stella, I like you. You remind me of an old childhood friend." The doll, actually. Still, Ingrid could feel the cutting anguish in the woman and wanted to find some link between them. "You speak with the cynicism of someone who has done dozens of tax returns."

"Hundreds. Seems like thousands. Poor people cheat on their taxes. Rich people hire accountants to do it for them. It's like men. Hiring women or girls." For some reason that idea made her lip tremble, but she mastered her tearful voice. "If I'd known what men were, I would have become a lesbian like Wanda while there was still time."

"I don't think it works that way," Ingrid said gently, deciding not to mention Carmen's massage parlor. Ingrid looked for a way to put her at ease. "Believe me, I do know what you mean. I've been there. It took me years to realize that my husband wasn't going to stop beating up on me until I stopped allowing him to do it."

Stella said nothing but stared at Ingrid with shock as if she herself had been struck across the face. Ingrid wondered if she had said something wrong. This was a very tiring conversation. She took a breath to change the subject, but Stella began to speak again before she could.

"You. What do you know? Women like you. My husband and I spent a lot of time watching pretty little things like you and comparing them to me. How bad I look with how great they look. He kept at me to be like that." She was almost overcome with tears.

"What a jerk. Why didn't you ditch him?"

"Because I was afraid. And I loved him. I think he used to be nice. We married so young, I can't remember anymore. After we had Sally I thought it was better for my daughter to have a father." Now she collapsed into real sobbing.

Ingrid nervously tried to think where the nearest mental health clinic was in case Stella became truly hysterical. At least the panhandlers were leaving them alone now; that in itself was a rare accomplishment.

"What happened?" Ingrid asked when Stella seemed to be breathing steadily again. None of this had anything to do with Miranda so far, but she could see there would be no derailing Stella once she got on a particular line of travel.

"He molested her."

"Who?"

"Our daughter, Sally." Stella began sobbing bitterly again.

"Oh, no. How terrible." Ingrid felt distinctly guilty about the way she was using Stella to get more information. Maybe she could help her find her daughter, she thought penitently. She hugged Stella awkwardly and patted her woolen back. She smelled of a lemony sweet perfume. "How old is she, your daughter?"

"Just turned f-f-fourteen. Younger when my husband started bothering her. I put that bastard in jail. But when I met Miranda at the office, she seemed so nice. I thought she was a friend; but she *used* me. She found out about a place I go to, a club in North Beach. . . ."

Carmen's massage parlor!

"What we do there . . . Miranda got pictures. She threatened to send them to my ex-husband. He might not be able to get custody of Sally, but I might lose her. He would say I was unfit."

Ingrid nodded. It seemed possible.

"Well, by then I knew what Miranda was, but it was too late. She said she wouldn't tell anyone about it if I worked for her, picking up packages at the post office and the airport and dropping them off . . . other places. I knew it paid too much to be legal—that was why she kept those pictures, in case I got cold feet. Then she started talking to my kid. I wasn't worried about it. Sally doesn't usually take to adults. Half the time Sally's in a world of her own. Then Sally started staying out all night.''

Ingrid patted Stella hesitantly on the arm as she continued. ''I think that was when she met him. Or them. I don't know. Miranda introduced her to some older men. Sally started coming home with expensive clothes, jewelry. Once she realized how much money she could make, there was no stopping her.''

''Do you think Miranda knew where your daughter was?''

''Yes, but she wouldn't tell me. Besides, Sally changed so much when she started getting money from Miranda's friends—I think she may be on cocaine now.'' This last was in a small, tortured voice.

''Do you think it might have been cocaine in the packages you carried?''

''At first I didn't let myself think about it, but now I think so. I never opened one of them. I didn't want to know.''

''How big were they?''

''Fairly small. A few pounds at the most and sometimes much less. The postmarks were here in the Bay Area, sometimes Seattle.''

Ingrid stopped and thought. If it had been cocaine, a few pounds of it might have been worth hundreds of thousands of dollars, depending on the purity, but she had no clear idea. She had never followed the cocaine market; it had been bad enough watching a few of Vic's friends who had used it, abused it and then lost everything to it in a matter of a few years.

''Did you ever drop packages off at the same place twice?''

''No.''

Ingrid took out the sheets of paper she had run off from Miranda's diskette and handed them to Stella. ''Were these the addresses?''

Stella glanced at the list and shoved it back into Ingrid's hands. She leaped up and began to trot away. Ingrid chased after her, tucking the list back into her bag as she went.

"Wait. Please. We need to talk more. You must look at this photo I took the day Miranda died. I didn't point it out to the police because I had no reason to. But if you want me to—fine."

Stella stopped. Ingrid pulled out the picture that showed Stella under the fire escape in Taft Alley. She stared at it, then looked away. She refused to meet Ingrid's eyes.

"You and I together should be able to work out a way to settle this without involving the authorities. They haven't ruled out murder yet." Ingrid had the distinct feeling that they had, but she continued. "Let's talk tomorrow. Shall I come to your house?"

Stella faced Ingrid with the look of a cornered animal. "No! I mean, okay—I'll talk to you again. But give me some time to think. I have to work tomorrow, to catch up on what I missed today. I'll meet you somewhere near where you live."

"Do you know the Cliff House, out at Ocean Beach?"

"Yes."

"I'll meet you in front of the main entrance whenever you say," Ingrid said firmly.

Stella agreed to meet her on Saturday at 8 P.M. It would be New Year's Eve tomorrow, but no matter what the holiday, Ocean Beach would never be a major attraction on a cold, winter night with the ever-present threat of rain. Still, there should be enough people around to protect her in case Stella brought reinforcements. Stella seemed to be thinking the same thing. "You stay here until I drive off, okay?"

Ingrid sighed. "Sure."

It started to rain heavily as Ingrid walked back down to the Geary bus stop. The paper streamers hanging from trees and lampposts stuck together, and the masses of paper in the gutter began to turn to mush.

THIRTY

CARMEN SPENT THE MORNING shut up in her yarn room while Ingrid sat at the kitchen table, drinking coffee and trying to imagine how and why Tony Flint or Stella Anderson might have killed Miranda Falk.

She couldn't come up with any good reasons for Tony to have done it, though he certainly had been interested in finding that key. Maybe he wanted whatever was in the package Stella had dropped off. But both Josephine and Pammy could vouch for his illicit presence on the stairwell during the time when Miranda must have been murdered. Still, the very neatness of this alibi made Ingrid suspicious. As if Tony had set it up in advance. But Ingrid couldn't imagine Josephine or Pammy cooperating on an actual lie.

Maybe Miranda's scrapbook contained evidence linking Tony or Flint Senior to some unwholesome activities with fourteen-year-old Sally Anderson. Max had seen her in Tony's company, but where was she? Or had Max been lying in order to cast suspicion on Tony Flint? Max hadn't seemed particularly angry at Miranda. Ingrid couldn't work up much enthusiasm for him as a suspect.

Stella hated Miranda enough to kill her, but she didn't seem to know anyone inside the Bramwell Building who would have helped her get in to do it.

As usual, Ingrid had more questions than answers.

The mail brought an envelope from Ingrid's father with prints of her graduation class pictures. A second package arrived from her mother a few minutes later by UPS. It contained her old high school uniforms. Ingrid felt an echo of the uneasy elation that had haunted her during high school as her parents struggled toward a divorce, competing with gifts to win her affection and approval.

She took out the uniforms—the indestructible gray wool blazer, the green plaid skirt and the pale-yellow cotton dress for summer. She noted with a smile that the uniforms were very close to what every personnel agency wants the well-dressed secretary to wear.

Ingrid tried on the blazer and found she could just button it. Fortunately she wouldn't have to, but she decided to add another half mile to her morning runs. She went into the room where Carmen was sorting skeins of yarn. Her loom stood in the center of the room, baskets of multi-hued yarn lining the walls.

"You did close that door, didn't you?" Carmen said without looking up. "You know, that cat could die in agony from swallowing just a little piece of yarn."

Ingrid reached back and pulled the door handle again to ensure that it was firmly closed behind her.

"It could just knot up in his guts . . ."

"Okay, okay, the door is closed." Ingrid hung her clothes in the closet, which Carmen had emptied for her things. It was still almost empty, but the school uniforms helped a little. She closed the door as she went out with an audible click and a rattle of the doorknob from outside to prove its solidness.

Back in the kitchen, she spread out the color prints her father had sent of the shots he'd taken at her high school graduation. The small graduating class had fanned out, in no particular order, to stand in a rough circle around the edges of the school's meadowlike front lawn. They looked as if they were about to play some kind of circle game—but instead of a bouncing ball, the school faculty and small clusters of relatives, teachers and envious undergraduates bounced around the circle visiting each in turn or gathering about their chosen grad. Ingrid now saw that it was supposed to serve as a receiving line. Her memories were of enduring the uncomfortable long white dress and shoes while her parents tried to be civil to each other and a few friends and relatives spent their time taking strained photos of each other with her.

Mary Valkevich, as Miranda had been called then, could be seen in the background, complete with her original nose, looking even more forlorn and less besieged by well-wishers than Ingrid.

Beside Miranda was a younger Mrs. Phelps, wincing in pain, possibly held hostage by an unforgiving elastic girdle.

"That's Miranda Falk, isn't it?" Spyder had come in and stood looking over her shoulder.

"Have you met her?"

"Yes."

"And you recognize her from this picture? She'd had some plastic surgery since then."

"I recognize her. Vic introduced us the day she died."

"You and Victor talked to her that day?" Ingrid asked.

Carmen came out of the yarn room, closing the door carefully behind her and joined them in the kitchen. She carried her two-legged rug frame, trailing yarn, and followed closely by Mugwort, who aimed himself at the traveling mousetails of yarn. Restrained by Carmen's stern look and threatening "No! No!" he settled back on his haunches but continued to follow the yarn with the fixed gaze of the deeply obsessed.

"Okay, Spyder, what were you and Victor up to?" Carmen angled her frame near a kitchen chair and set her basket of yarns on the opposite end of the table from Ingrid.

Spyder sighed. "See, Vic told me he used to do business with this woman in L.A.—" He darted a glance at Ingrid. "He said it was just business, you know."

"Sure." Ingrid dismissed the whole pretense.

"Anyway, he suspected her of tipping the police to him. Either her or someone else—someone close to him." Spyder looked at Ingrid carefully. "He wanted to pressure her to admit it."

Ingrid stared back, puzzled. "I don't see how he could get any leverage with her. She was more likely to put pressure on *him*."

"Well, she wasn't happy to see him, but they set up an appointment to go out and talk about it. Vic told me Miranda was convinced *you'd* turned him in. He'd already had some suspicions about you. She told him you had some of the papers she was supposed to have. I told Vic he should thrash it out with you, and he said Miranda wanted to do that, too. We were going to meet you and Miranda after lunch. The idea was I could drop you three off someplace and you would get the papers for them.''

"Oh, yeah?" Ingrid said. "Did you really believe that?"

"No sense getting hostile, Ingrid. That's what Vic told me, and I believed him. Only Miranda came walking up arguing with that other woman who was so upset. The other woman refused to leave and blew the whole thing. She was supposed to just deliver a key to Miranda, but she'd lost it. Miranda said she'd go ditch her and get a spare key from the office. So Vic went off with the two of them.''

"What happened?"

"Nothing. I waited at the van."

"Did Vic come back?"

"Not for over an hour. By then a motorcycle cop came along and forced me to move the van out of the loading zone where I'd parked. I had to circle round and park in another loading zone and then walk over to stand in front of Taft Alley and wait.''

"Over an hour? It was after twelve thirty when Miranda left the restaurant." *If Vic got into the building,* she thought, *he might have waited in the stairwell, gone in and killed Miranda when she was alone in her office, then walked right out through the lobby.*

Spyder shook his head slowly. "I know what you're thinking, Ingrid. Vic acted mad enough to kill whoever sent him to prison, but I think he was cooling down. For one thing, he sure as hell didn't want to go back to prison. I think worrying about those papers woke him up to how stupid it would be to screw up his parole. Anyway he said Miranda turned him back at the door. She gave him a better idea.''

"She sure did. Did he tell you she persuaded him to burn my apartment?"

Spyder looked stricken. "No," he said softly. "I had no idea." He looked at her bleakly. "But he did come back with a paper bag of stuff he'd gotten at a drugstore.''

"So?"

"I noticed that one of the things in there was lighter fluid—he didn't have a lighter."

"I thought you were my friend, Spyder."

"You don't understand, Ingrid. Did you ever meet Amelia?"

"Once."

Spyder looked at his long-fingered hands. When he spoke again, he didn't raise his head. "Amy was with me on the farm. We kept to ourselves. We had each other. We were together two and a half years. We were saving up to get married, have kids, bring 'em up in the country. When Vic got busted, we harvested the whole crop in a day and just walked off the place. It scared Amy so bad, she left me and went back to her parents in Chicago. I was glad to see her out of it because it *was* so dangerous. She said not to call till the crop was all gone. I didn't know that would be the last thing she would ever say to me."

Spyder stared down at his hands for a long time without speaking. When he had control of his voice, just barely, he continued.

"See, Vic was our middleman. He set up several of us growers. He leased the land through Miranda's real estate company and paid most of the start-up expenses. Then we'd take the risk of living there and growing the pot. After the harvest, he'd market the crop. He got the biggest cut of the profits because he put in more and he was the one with the connections to deal in quantity."

Ingrid shook her head. "I never knew Vic had such a big operation. I thought he just had his own land."

Spyder nodded. "Yeah, that's Vic. He plays it close to the chest. Anyway, I was in bad trouble when Vic got busted. No way could I move quantity dope. So I took the crop down to the city to sell it any way I could. You don't know fear unless you've shared a van with fifty pounds of marijuana. It smells like the biggest goddamn dead skunk the world ever saw, right?" He laughed a little wildly.

Ingrid nodded, remembering her kitchen on rainy October days of harvest madness in Humboldt.

"The cops don't need a police dog to smell it, all they have to do is pass downwind. I sold most of our dope and finally found a place to stash the rest."

He sat still for a few moments as if gathering the strength to speak. "Then I tried to contact Amy. Her parents were real nasty to me. Amy—well, she'd been killed in a traffic accident a week after she got to Chicago. I wanted to send them the money, her share of the profits. I didn't tell them what it was. I said Amy gave me the money to hold for her till she got home safe. They said they spit on me and my money. Easier for them to blame me, I guess. Maybe they were right."

Carmen shook her head, pushed her rug frame aside and went to hug Spyder. He buried his face between her breasts for a moment and Ingrid looked at the table. At last he continued.

"Victor asked me to look you up when I got to the City. I don't know why I did it. It hurt a lot to see you, because seeing you reminded me of the old days with Amy, but maybe that's why I did it—I couldn't bear to think of her and I couldn't stand to forget her. I took a chance and visited Vic in prison. He said either you or Miranda had put him there. And he was betting on you. If it was Miranda, he'd be trying to get back together with you."

Ingrid stared at Spyder in shock. "*You* thought I tipped the police to Victor?"

Spyder shook his head. "It was possible, of course. You guys weren't on such good terms when you split up, and I didn't know you too well back then. But I think Victor just loves you so much that sometimes he hates you. He's got a bad temper, and he just doesn't know who to trust but he does love you. At first, when we were taking those classes at State, I didn't know you well enough. I kept wondering how you could be the sort of woman to send your own husband to prison. Once you introduced me to Carmen, I knew for sure you hadn't put Vic in prison. No one could be so rotten and get in good with Carmen." He put an arm around Carmen's waist and hugged her.

"Spyder, we should go talk to Ben Resnick. He might be able to help us make sense of some of this information.

Spyder's face was grim. "Okay. Tomorrow. I've got a few things to talk over with Victor later today. But Carmen and I will still meet you at the Cliff House before midnight, okay?"

"That's fine." Ingrid had a busy night ahead of her.

THIRTY-ONE

AT EIGHT O'CLOCK on New Year's Eve the Cliff House was full of young couples dressed like Macy's mannequins. Ingrid moved aside as a threesome walked down the steps, the man had a silk scarf hanging at the ready but clearly reluctant to spoil its drape by actually wrapping it around his throat. The women clutched their coats in an effort to keep out the cutting cold, though the sheerness of their skirts made such efforts futile.

Ingrid liked the spot for the sea lions. Although they were invisible in the dark, she could hear their baritone squabbling from the sidewalk. With her back to the offshore rocks, she watched the coast road. Above her she could see the huge windows of the Ben Butler room, named for Adolph Sutro's favorite sea lion. There, customers sat behind a curtain of warmth and music, insulated from the ocean with the wild creatures on the rocks a few hundred feet away.

Outside the darkened souvenir shop, Ingrid could see the highway where it turned south to avoid the ocean. She had walked the few blocks from Carmen's to Geary and down to the Cliff House, keeping a weather eye out for deranged bicycle messengers and black Continentals.

A few kids came up the chilly concrete stairs, exclaiming in disappointment that the Musée Mécanique had pulled down its steel shutters at dusk, locking in the antique nickel-and-dime machines and the high-tech video games. The older ones had wandered down the beach to the bonfires, where small crowds of people passed around bottles, warming their hands and building up their spirits to the peak that would erupt when they set off fireworks in the midnight fog to welcome the New Year.

She recognized Stella's orange Rabbit and waved. The greeting was not returned. Stella drove past and parked the

Rabbit in the Merry Way lot above the ruins of the Sutro
Baths. Then she trudged back to where Ingrid stood.

"Hi," was all she said, managing not to make eye contact.

"Let's go inside." Ingrid hoped her smile looked reas-
suring. She had decided to risk twenty or thirty dollars she
couldn't afford on drinks with Stella in order to relax her
and get information. What possible use that information
might turn out to be Ingrid still had no idea, but if it was a
throwaway gesture, she could chalk it up to New Year's
madness. Besides, she had a date later tonight, also at the
Cliff House. If Stella was no help, maybe her midnight
rendezvous would resolve her questions.

Stella, it turned out, liked to drink Kahlua and coffee.
Ingrid stuck to plain coffee. They sat away from the windows in a carved wooden booth with purple plush cushions. It offered a certain privacy; Ingrid did have to fend off
the occasional marauding males. But the male attention
seemed to loosen Stella up rather than irritate her. After a
few minutes of pleasantries and a second Kahlua and coffee, she collapsed back against the cushions like a puppet
with its strings cut. Ingrid was alarmed, but after a moment Stella leaned forward again.

"I don't know why it matters anyway. All this will be
over by tomorrow," she said.

"What do you mean?"

"The cleaning crew is scheduled to come in on the first
business day of next week."

"Oh," Ingrid said. "I see. Those places on that list I
showed you are all Kubler properties."

Stella nodded wisely. "Miranda must have used Wanda's key to get into the office and pick up some lists of vacant properties."

"You're the one who made the drops; you must know."
Ingrid remembered Vic's story about Miranda's carefully
insulated dope deals. "I guess she typed up one to a page
so she could sell the key and one address to a customer."

Stella glared at her and said, "We never had any keys
missing. I would have heard."

"Keys can be copied almost as easily as addresses. Or maybe someone inside the office besides you was getting part of her operation."

Stella shrugged. "Anyway, none of those properties are vacant now except the last two, and they'll be cleaned Monday or Tuesday."

"So the date on the list is the date the cleaning crew comes in, like dairy products on the shelf—use before this date. What about these locations? They have to be where she had you stash the packages—maybe she'd give you one of these sheets and then get it back from you, huh? Only she's dead now, so whatever you put there is still there. She didn't have time to sell it or go get it herself."

"So what? Whatever is in that flat, someone will get it—the new tenant, the cleaning crews, the police, who cares?" She shrugged again.

"I'm sure that's for the best. I guess you'll find out whether the police connect you with it then. It might already be in police hands, you know."

Stella looked at Ingrid with sudden apprehension. They might already be looking for her. A wary friendliness glimmered in her eyes. "Let me see that key you found in the restaurant," she said.

Cautiously, Ingrid slipped the key with its Dymo label marked 10-12 out of her wallet, careful not to show that there was another key like it in there.

Stella picked up the key and examined it closely. "Yes, it's the one missing from work."

"I thought you said none were missing from work."

"I forgot." A suddenly triumphant expression dawned on her face. "Here. I'll return it later." She dropped it down into her bra, settled a sizeable breast firmly over it and began to laugh almost hysterically. Ingrid was stunned. It was her move, and she hadn't the slightest notion of what to do. She certainly wasn't going to rip madly at another woman's bosom on New Year's Eve at the Cliff House.

"Happy New Year, Ingrid. You guys seem pretty happy already. Mind if I join you?" Ingrid looked up and saw Carmen on her own and already a little unsteady on her feet from drinking.

"Where's Spyder? I thought you two were meeting me here later," Ingrid said after introducing Stella, who was still chuckling from time to time. She seemed enormously pleased with herself.

Carmen pouted. "I've been waiting for him to come back from talking to that sinister ex-husband of yours. He called from a bar on Van Ness and said Vic wanted to come along. I said I didn't want to sit at the same table with him. After what I've heard, I just don't trust him. He could be a murderer for all we know."

"You think he might have killed Miranda?" Stella demanded.

"He's at least as hot a suspect as you are," Ingrid said, still irritated.

"Well, I don't know who killed her, but if that's the man, I'd like to shake his hand."

Ingrid and Carmen glanced at each other. They were freed from the necessity of replying to this by the appearance of the waitress with another round of drinks.

Stella stood up not long afterward and wandered off toward the rest room. She came back arm in arm with Spyder and Victor. Spyder dragged a nearby chair up to the booth and apologized to Carmen in whispers. "I couldn't stop him. He insisted on coming. He said he'll sit somewhere else if he's not welcome."

Carmen, on the spot, looked at her watch. "Half an hour," she said. "Then let's go."

"I see you've already met Spyder's girlfriend, Carmen, and my ex-wife, Ingrid," Vic murmured to Stella.

"I'm divorced also," Ingrid heard Stella say as she settled into the chair Vic held for her.

"I've been rather worried about you, young lady, since that terrible day we first met. You seemed so upset. I've wondered ever since how you've been."

Stella was only too glad to tell him, in detail, as if they were sitting alone at the table. Ingrid and Carmen cast incredulous looks at Spyder, who held up his hands helplessly. Ingrid had to admit that Vic did look raffishly attractive in a suit and tie. She had seldom seen him dressed that way when they had lived in Humboldt; there had been no occasion for it.

"My ex-wife," Vic said to Stella, not letting go of her hand, "used to take pictures of endangered species of plants. Now she destroys a tree a day churning out paperwork for lawyers." He shook his head sadly. "I think it's taken a psychic toll on her, don't you?"

Stella seemed fascinated by Vic's good looks and his eager attentiveness. He insisted on paying for everyone's drinks and twice made a special trip to get something Stella particularly wanted. Ingrid found herself staring at a suspicious bump on Vic's forehead.

"You got that trying to break into my darkroom, didn't you?" She tapped his forehead as he brushed past her to get another bowl of salted nuts for Stella.

Victor winced at her touch and moved away without answering. Ingrid tried not to meet Carmen's eyes for fear of inspiring herself to start yelling some of the choice words that were boiling up in her throat.

Returning to the table, Vic managed to spill the nuts in Stella's lap and took his time retrieving them one by one and alternately caressing and teasing Stella about the size of her thighs, pinching her in various locations. Ingrid wanted to get up and leave but felt responsible. Stella clearly liked it.

Spyder, who rarely drank more than a beer or two, got uproariously drunk. Ingrid could tell that Carmen had forgotten her half-hour deadline and had begun to worry about getting Spyder safely home. There was a dangerous electricity in the air—half sexual, half violent. Spyder began whispering in Carmen's ear as the evening wore on toward midnight, and Ingrid got the impression they were about to depart to usher in the New Year in bed.

Ingrid got up and headed for the rest room. Surprisingly, Stella followed her.

"Look, Ingrid, I can see you don't approve of your ex-husband flirting with me. Well, butt out."

"Stella, you told me that sad story about how *your* ex-husband abused you so badly. Well, Victor's warming up to the same thing. You just met him and he's already getting rough with you. Hey, if that's what you want, fine. But I feel like a fool for listening to you whine about it.''

"Hey, whatever he wants to do, I like it. Have you got that? He's a very sexy man, and he can say any damn thing he wants to so long as he follows it up with the appropriate action. *I'm* not planning to marry him. All I want is a decent night in the hay—is that too much to ask? Maybe I don't mind a little rough treatment within limits. Maybe I get off on it.''

"This is San Francisco. You're an adult. It's none of my business. I just don't want to be responsible.''

"Well, you're not. Maybe you think I'm some kind of monster because I can enjoy myself without knowing where my little Sally is, but I've got to break out of this depression somehow. And here's a man who's offering to help me do it. You should know what it's like in this town. There aren't that many men to go around, so if you don't want him, the least you can do is give me a crack at him.''

"Stella, I've never warned a woman about a man in my life and I'm not about to start now. Just watch out for yourself, that's all. Remember what happened to Miranda. I have no reason to be sure that Vic wasn't involved in that.''

"You should keep your mouth shut when you're jealous, Ingrid. It doesn't improve your looks in the least.''

Ingrid gritted her teeth, silently got her coat and went outside, waving farewell to the others. There was a thin manila envelope in her shoulder bag. For a moment she forgot what it was; then she remembered that it was the picture of Stella under Miranda's window as Flint Senior passed by.

More limousines than usual were swarming down the Great Highway. Usually there were none, but tonight they seemed to cruise past every few seconds. A tan stretch limo stopped outside the Cliff House and an impossibly young Asian couple got out, looking as if they had just arrived from the senior prom. They went into the bar next door on street level, where an indifferent rock band was playing. It was nearly midnight.

Ingrid wandered down a few yards from the sidewalk and leaned against the wall behind Cliff House. She felt slightly removed from the occasional couple passing by, yet she still stood in the well-lit area. Below and stretching off to the horizon, the ocean roared, black as a tar pit come to life. The moon froze a path of gleaming black rock among the waves. Ingrid wished she could run out to that swatch of white light, walk the glittering path right up to the horizon and disappear. But if it was chilly on the concrete, it would be even colder out there and definitely wetter.

"What are you thinking?" She had moved away from the approaching figure, seeing only his fine topcoat and thinking it must be one of the men she had fended off inside. But it was Flint Junior. So quiet on his feet for such a tall man.

"Tony!" She was a little unnerved, as usual, by his imposing height and glowing fitness.

"I read the note you left on my car. You said you'd be at the Cliff House at midnight. I came early—I didn't want to miss you. What's on your mind?" He slouched back against the wall amicably.

She mimicked his posture, leaning against the wall as she turned away from the ocean. "Well, just now I was thinking that I have never seen so many limousines in this neighborhood. You didn't come in one of those things, did you?"

"No. No. Very cheap to rent, though, for a group."

They stared out over the nearly empty stretch of Ocean Beach parking spaces. One limo had parked facing the water. Its inhabitants were no doubt drinking and carrying on, as were the crowds around the bonfires down on the beach.

The strains of "Auld Lang Syne" resounded from the bar at the Cliff House and faint yells of celebration could be heard all around. From the beach explosions of fireworks shook the sky into a garden of giant sparks. Red. Green. Blue. White.

As she turned to wish him "Happy New Year," he embraced her. She returned the hug. It turned into a very gentle kiss, which with a sudden thrill of surprise and dismay she found herself enjoying. She started to move to free herself, but he insisted on drawing her closer and she felt herself responding, against her better judgment. The warmth was so wonderful that she realized how chilled she had grown in the past half hour of being outside. She broke away when she heard a hiss of accusatory shock.

"That man." Stella emerged from the stairway of the Cliff House with Victor in tow. Carmen and Spyder followed behind them. Stella pointed at Tony Flint and whispered something urgently to Victor. Vic narrowed his eyes at Tony speculatively. He moved back to say a few words to Spyder and then returned to Stella, drawing her close to whisper in her ear. He led her down the block to her car, making a carefully wide path around Tony and Ingrid on the broad sidewalk.

"Do you know that woman?" Tony asked, releasing Ingrid from his arms but keeping a hand on her shoulder.

"Slightly. She seemed to know you."

"Really? I don't remember where I might have seen her." He shook his head, as if clearing it, then smiled at her with the air of one returning to an abandoned treat.

"Kubler Realty maybe?"

Tony removed his hand from Ingrid's shoulder casually and took a folded piece of paper out of his pocket. "In your note you mentioned African violets," he said, guiding her closer to the streetlamp so she could read it.

The note read: "You seem to be interested in the contents of certain pots of African violets. Come to Cliff House at midnight on New Year's Eve if you wish to discuss."

Ingrid nodded. "I found a key in an African violet pot you must have missed. That was a big shock for your father, you know, having his plants emptied out on his rug."

"Yes. It was too bad, but I saw her hide a key in a pot once, and I thought she could have sneaked one up there with the rest as camouflage."

"So you trashed your father's office?"

"Why not? After all, I do own the building."

"How can you own it? I thought your father owned it."

"Clever girl, but understandably ignorant of my father's interest in the building. It's called a life interest. He can't sell what he doesn't own. When he dies, it's mine."

Ingrid remembered that Rosemary had used that term, which had meant nothing to her. She said nothing, not wishing to seem more confused than she already was. But Tony clearly intended to lecture her on the legal intricacies.

"When my mother married, old Grandpa Eugene settled the property on Dad for as long as he lives. But he can't sell it outright, because when he dies it reverts to me. True, the landmark status will hold me up a little while, but once it's mine I'll be able to get around it and turn it into a parking lot if I want to. It's just a matter of time."

"One thing I don't understand. With a team like Pammy and Josephine giving you an alibi, why kill Miranda? It would seem to have been more profitable to have killed your father."

Tony laughed, his voice ringing in the chill night air. Ingrid felt she had been left out of the joke, but she noted the sharpness with which he stared at her when he had finished laughing. He was not smiling.

"What an idiot you are, Ingrid. I didn't kill her. Right there in the office? She probably killed herself. Kubler put her into the firm as sort of a loyalty test for my dad as well as a way to get his hands on that property. She worked hard enough at it, but her tactics were deplorably crude. She kept blathering about her little scrapbook of blackmail evidence. Come on—blackmail? In this day and age? Anyway, she did convince me that Kubler wanted that site pretty badly. So I went over her head and talked to Kubler myself. Of course that made her superfluous. She failed Kubler, and that's not a wise thing to do. If he didn't have one of his buddies knock her out the window, maybe he threatened her with worse and she just took the easy way out. As for my father: no need to rush the process."

"Still, it was a very interesting coincidence, your making yourself a perfect alibi by choosing that moment to decoy Pammy onto the stairwell for a cozy little snort of cocaine and then manage to be seen by a woman who would give you an alibi out of sheer lovelorn, ladder-climbing necessity.''

"What can I say, Ingrid? I'm an opportunist. When a pretty woman is standing next to me and I have a perfect excuse to kiss her, I'll do it. Just because it might have been convenient for some theoretical killer to find Pammy away from her desk at the same time I happened to have a little coke to share with her, it doesn't mean anyone murdered Miranda.''

"Speaking of corrupt kiddies, the question around BSF lately is: Did you and your father share the services of Sally Anderson, or were you the only one with her? The last time anyone saw her, she was in your company. Maybe you're running a halfway house for underage girls in your spare time?''

Tony reacted with the sudden, instinctive coiling of a snake about to strike.

Ingrid realized that without thinking she had shifted her weight to her back foot and had raised her arms to protect herself.

Flint seemed to bring himself under control bit by bit, as if commanding each set of muscles to relax. His voice was harsh.

"The first time I saw you, Ingrid, you were displaying your pathetic store of martial arts training. It turned me on just a little, actually. I like a woman who can put up a little athletic struggling. But you know they say around the dojo that the most dangerous student is the green belt, because he thinks he knows something. But he doesn't know how much he doesn't know. Maybe you *are* dangerous, at least to yourself.''

Ingrid forced herself to walk past him and up the wide sidewalk toward Carmen's house. She looked back for any sign of pursuit. Tony Flint stood where she had left him, thoughtfully igniting a cigar with a small butane cigarette lighter that illuminated his face for a second. A moment later his Porsche pulled up. She couldn't see who was driving. He got in, and the sports car made a perilous U-turn on the blind curve in front of the Cliff House. Ingrid wondered if they might be circling around to intercept her at Point Lobos.

THIRTY-TWO

FROM THE SIDEWALK Carmen's house appeared deserted. Spyder's van was nowhere in sight. Perhaps Carmen and Spyder had gone to find an open store that sold ice cream, they got that sort of mania sometimes. Ingrid stood staring at the house for a moment, scanning the sidewalks for dangerous animals. No sign of a red Porsche.

She entered the house and found the Christmas tree lights blinking on and off forlornly. Mugwort didn't come out to greet her. Had the cat discovered a neighbor's New Year's party with a low buffet table? She glanced down the hallway and saw the door to the yarn room gaping wide open.

She hurried toward it, racking her brain in an effort to remember when she had been in the room and hoping that the tomcat was not writhing on the floor in agony with a skein of yarn knotting up his intestines. She seemed to remember that there was an all-night emergency pet hospital across the park—was it on Irving?

The yarn room was dark. She found the light switch and paused at the door, casting about the room for small movements that might betray a potentially fatal feline yarn frenzy.

Nothing. The room was still. Ingrid walked over to the closet. Mugwort was an expert at hiding. She had to search for a tail sticking out of a box or a crouched figure in an unlikely little hole. She looked carefully through the shoes and boots on the floor of the closet. No Mugwort.

Ingrid jumped. A pair of green eyes appeared in the gloom of the top shelf.

"Mugwort! You sneaky cat!" she called out in relief. She pulled his substantial body down off the shelf, as he protested with his low-pitched meow. He gripped her with his claws as if a little spooked. She took him into the center of

the room and examined him under the harsh overhead
light.

There were no telltale fibers anywhere on him. He
showed no other signs of distress. "Okay, kiddo," Ingrid
sighed in relief. "First we take you out of the room. Then
we'll have to keep you around to make sure you're all
right." She switched off the light and stepped out into the
dim hallway, holding the cat with one arm and closing the
door firmly behind her.

Mugwort's claws raked her arm and shoulder as he
scrabbled his way out of her grasp with a strength that she
had not imagined he possessed. She looked down to see
bleeding scratches along her forearms.

A viselike grip closed over her wrist, and she turned
around to look into the broad face of the man who had
mugged her. The face receded abruptly as someone came
from behind, knocked her feet out from under her and
flipped her over backward on the floor. A moment later
Tony Flint's face appeared above her, and she found herself looking down the barrel of a large, businesslike hand-
gun.

"Let's quit the kidding around, Ingrid, and hand over
that key. The one you found in the flower pot. I saw her put
it there."

"I'm not sure I have it with me."

"I think you do."

Ingrid turned her head slightly and watched Tony load a
clip into the gun. Time to take action and defend herself.
But she stayed motionless, stunned as a rabbit in the head-
lights of an oncoming car.

"Otto." Tony prodded the muscle-bound bike messenger. Otto pulled Ingrid roughly to her feet, and Tony
grabbed her other arm, cocked the gun and pressed the
barrel against her cheek.

She noted that the safety catch was off. That knowledge
formed the core of the gun lore she had picked up in Humboldt. Somehow, at the moment, it seemed enough.
"Okay." He released her, and Ingrid found her shoulder
bag and, in her wallet, the key.

Tony took it and pocketed it. "Okay, Otto, let's walk her over here to the fireplace and sit her down. Fine. Keep hold of her. Good. Now." He squatted in front of her and put his face very close to hers. "Ingrid, what I want is the location of the door this key opens. Miranda must have given that to you. She told me she had given her scrapbook to you. Also, there is this." He took the memo from Miranda out of his pocket and waved it under Ingrid's nose.

Ingrid sighed. She didn't know why she wasn't just giving him everything she had. But some small part of her brain was looking for a door out of this mess. Resisting Tony gave her time to think; she came up with desperate plans to run or lash out and discarded them. Every muscle in her body was bathed in adrenaline. But there was nowhere to run to, and physical strength was not indicated. "If you read that memo more carefully, counselor, you'll see that she only says she *told* everyone I've got her scrapbook. She didn't actually give me anything. Think about it and you'll see that's much more consistent with Miranda. She never gave anything away, did she? Why should she give me her scrapbook?"

There was a flicker of doubt in Tony's eyes, but it vanished almost immediately. "Otto, dump out her purse here on the coffee table—let's take a look."

It didn't take them long to find the list of addresses, one to a page. Tony thumbed through them and held them up to Ingrid. "You mean to tell me this didn't come from Miranda?"

"It came from a computer diskette she left at Wanda's hidden in some magazines. Stella Anderson says they're Kubler locations."

"Good work, Ingrid. Well, we've got Kubler waiting up for us, so that's fine." Tony laughed, examining the sheets of paper. "Dated in chronological order. Must be the last one. The date on it is today. Let's go."

Tony had parked the Porsche around the corner.

"I'll get the old man and meet you there."

"Well, try not to get lost," Tony said.

"With the old man in tow, not likely. Think you can handle this bitch? She's kind of mean. I told you I'd knock her around, and I ain't finished yet."

"I'm glad you mentioned that, Otto. I've been keeping in mind that you didn't finish that job. Don't worry." Tony opened the glove compartment and brought out a set of handcuffs. With a practiced gesture he snapped them on Ingrid's wrists.

Tony found the Fulton Street address as easily as if he regularly commuted there. He parked next to a fire hydrant near the house, which proved to be an old Victorian. Tony got out of the car and walked around to the passenger side. He hauled Ingrid up out of the low seat by her cuffed hands. Ingrid wondered if any neighbors were watching.

As Tony locked the Porsche, Otto pulled up in the black Continental, followed by a Rolls Royce with Wanda at the wheel.

"Hello, Wanda. Taking the invalid out for a spin? Come on. Join us." Tony's grip on Ingrid's arm increased.

The back door of the Rolls popped open and a very old, grasshopper-thin man unfolded himself up onto the pavement. Tony bowed to him formally, his grip on Ingrid compelling her to dip as well.

"Herr Kubler," he said.

Otto parked his large black Continental in a nearby driveway and joined them.

"Shall we all go in?" Tony took on the air of a host at a party.

The Kubler Realty sign in the front window was the newest thing about the decrepit Victorian. "Leased" had been pasted over the sign reading FOR LEASE OR SALE.

The hallway echoed with their footsteps as they all walked in. Tony looked at his list. "This place has a date of December 31. Does that mean anything to you, Wanda?"

They all looked at Wanda. She nodded grimly. "Yes. That's the last day before the cleaning crew comes in. I think we made a deal with these tenants not to clean up, in exchange for a discount on the first month's rent. Normally we would have a crew in here Monday and the tenants could move in a few days later. You see, the electricity is still on. The service was never broken."

"Upstairs fireplace," Tony read. "There's a fireplace down here—must be the room above this one."

They filed upstairs slowly. Even with Wanda's help, it took Kubler five minutes to get up the stairway and into the front parlor off the hallway. As Kubler reached the landing, Tony waved everyone over to one side of the doorway. He unlocked one of Ingrid's handcuffs.

"You go in there and get that thing out of the fireplace." He turned to the others. "We'll wait out here. It could be a bomb, you know. No sense in all of us getting killed." He waved her into the room.

The upstairs floor was in even worse shape than the downstairs. She made a wide berth around rubbish heaps that seemed to conceal weaknesses in the floorboards. The fireplace was blocked up with old boards and chunks of plaster. A brand-new Macy's shopping bag, its handles neatly pulled through each other, sat among the trash. She brought it out into the center of the room. In the bag was a file box covered in soft black leather. She picked it up by the handle. It was padlocked.

"Open it," Tony said. "Remember, you're still in easy target range, Ingrid."

"It's locked."

"Otto, get the tire iron."

Otto didn't hesitate—clearly he was not afraid of bombs. Ingrid wanted to cry out in protest as he levered the case open, scarring the fine leather. Tony directed traffic with his pistol.

"Hand it back to Ingrid, Otto—we'll let her take inventory. Okay, everybody inside and move together where I can see all of you. Fine, what's in there?"

Ingrid drew out two envelopes and an old-fashioned leatherette scrapbook that fell out of her hands under the weight of the photographs and negatives stapled to the pages. The group flinched collectively, but Tony simply motioned with the gun. She caught the book, but one print, unstapled, slid out and hit the floor.

"Pick it up. Slowly." She bent and retrieved the print, its negative strip in a glassine envelope stapled to the back. She held it awkwardly on top of the scrapbook, with the envelopes in her hands as well.

The print Ingrid had picked up was of a nude girl, very young, mouth and eyes wide open in pleasure or pain. She had been photographed from above, her body framed by some sort of white-sided box. Not a bathtub; the corners were too sharp. There was a series of marks all over her body, like irregular tattoos or—

Tony ripped the print out of her hands roughly, almost causing her to drop everything. He folded the print in half and put it in his coat pocket. He glanced at the scrapbook briefly and set it back into the black leather file box.

No one seemed to have any doubt that the photos were the raw material of blackmail. Somewhere in there, Ingrid supposed, must be the picture that had ensured Stella's co-operation.

Tony nodded at Ingrid to open the envelopes.

The thinner envelope held two passports, one with Miranda's picture and one with Tony's. The names were different, but the passports looked slightly used, with entry and exit visas from the Bahamas. There was also a folded sheaf of papers from a Sausalito yacht broker, ownership papers on a thirty-six-foot sloop. Tony examined them briefly, nodded and slipped the documents and the fake passport with his picture on it into his inside breast pocket. He held out Miranda's passport to Kubler.

"Want a memento of your little girlfriend, Kubler?"

Watching Helmut Kubler under the weak overhead bulb, Ingrid began to understand something about Miranda, who had never had anything given to her for free. Ever. "Are you the one behind Miranda's scholarship?" she asked.

Wanda stepped forward and jerked the passport out of Ingrid's hands.

Kubler nodded, unperturbed. "Yes. I paid for her education, as much as she would take. I put her in a ballet class when she was nine. That is the age that intrigues me most. A few hours of her time after class, some extra playtime with me, a little after-school job. Why not? She was still a virgin when I finished with her. No real harm done. Ach! All this sentiment over children. But who else offered to pay for her ballet lessons or her high school and college? She dropped out of college before she completed her first year. But I have helped her with a job whenever our paths crossed. That much of an obligation I accept. Alas, she did not turn out to be trustworthy."

"Of course, you will never admit that you might have made her untrustworthy," Ingrid said indignantly. "I guess being rich means never having to say you're sorry."

Kubler addressed himself to Tony as if she hadn't spoken. "I have no wish to own a forged passport with a picture of some old woman in her thirties. Worse yet, purchased with money she embezzled from me while risking my property in patently illegal enterprises."

Tony Flint gestured impatiently to Ingrid to open the large envelope.

It rattled as she opened it. She poured out a handful of small, yellowish, transparent stones. A faint sigh filled the room. Even Kubler's face took on a slightly more lively appearance. Ingrid deduced that these must be uncut diamonds. Nothing less could produce such a reverent pause from this group.

"What would you say?" Tony asked Kubler. "More than a million? Less?"

He shrugged. "Hard to tell without a jeweler's loupe." He reached into his inner breast pocket but brought out only a silver cigarette case. "You will, of course, turn those over to me as reimbursement for the money I advanced you for those rights to the Bramwell Building, which were not yours to sell."

"On the contrary, you owe me. Having Miranda in our office cost our firm a great deal. Some of us paid for the damage out of our own pockets," Tony replied.

Kubler smiled slightly. "Yes?"

"I have no doubt she smuggled these into the country in our client's company pouch. She was so crooked, she had to find an angle for herself everywhere she went. What did you expect her to do?"

Kubler shook his head angrily. "It's what I expected you to do that bothers me, Tony. You have been a perpetual disappointment to me. I turned to you when I realized that your father wouldn't cooperate. Then after I had put out a great deal of earnest money, what do I discover? These property rights will not be valid until your father—my old friend and current stumbling block—dies. He may easily outlive me. So tonight you inform me that I may be able to recoup my losses. Well, I say this does not even come close to my losses on you alone. There should be more."

"That's why I offered you the passport. With it and a little help from Wanda, you may be able to tap her Bahamian accounts. I doubt it, but as your former lawyer I think it's your best bet. Of course, the risk of detection by the law might be too much."

"I think I would prefer the diamonds as well." Kubler raised his cigarette case and Ingrid saw now that the lighter was a very small automatic pistol. It made a deafening explosion in the small room when he fired. No. A sound came from Tony's gun as well. Tony stood unhurt.

Kubler fell to the floor. Wanda moved to support him. Blood flowed down his pants leg and he groaned in pain.

In the ringing silence Otto came as close to Tony as he dared and hissed, "Where's that other grand, Flint? You promised me two thousand dollars to grab that chick there."

"And you admit you blew it. If you'd done your job the way you were supposed to, I'd have had a lovely few days with Miss Hunter and picked her brain clean. You'd have your money and we wouldn't have had to involve your boss. Right now I'd advise you to help Wanda get Herr Kubler to his car and to whatever medical attention seems appropriate and hope like hell she doesn't tell him you've been free-lancing. See that you leave me strictly alone in the future. I'll make it easier for you by leaving town. Ingrid and I will, however, wait till you leave. You can go now."

Ingrid and Tony stood by the window until the two cars disappeared down Fulton Street. She expected to see a formation of police cars—or at least one—in answer to the two shots, but nothing had happened.

"New Year's Eve fireworks," Tony said in explanation. "Besides, this neighborhood is used to everything. If they called the cops every time they heard a gun or a car backfiring, they'd never get any sleep. Let's go."

"Where?"

"My place, of course. Wasn't that the idea? Then we'll follow Miranda's original plan and head for South America, you and I."

THIRTY-THREE

ONCE THEY CROSSED the lobby of the old San Francisco hotel, Tony steered Ingrid into an elevator with only one destination button: PENTHOUSE.

"The place hasn't been renovated much since 1929," Tony explained. "Of course, they did things so well back then. Not much is needed."

Ingrid would have agreed, had she been calm enough to appreciate the fixtures he pointed out. The beaten-bronze ceiling, the mirrored doors to the bar with art deco designs etched along the edges. He opened the doors and offered her a drink as well.

"No, thanks," she said automatically, "I don't drink."

"You. Will. Drink." He lashed out a fist and knocked her down. Ingrid almost lost consciousness. As she fought her way up from darkness, a slow animal cunning began to coexist with the fear.

"Help me up and I'll join you in a drink," she said.

Tony heard something different in her voice. He sipped his own whiskey and looked at her cautiously, one animal to another. "No." He whispered. But he reached down and helped her up, then kissed her gently on the lips. Ingrid restrained herself from kneeing him in the groin with great difficulty. She had to get out of the apartment.

"Look around, explore. Maybe you'll find something I haven't seen here yet. Go ahead."

Ingrid walked around the apartment as Tony flipped through a rack of cassette tapes, selecting one and then another. Ingrid saw something on the counter in the large kitchen, just to one side of the bar.

It was one of the cameras she had lost in the mugging. She recognized the strap Carmen had made for her with her name woven into a bold red-and-gold design. The strap itself was caught around the door handle of a large freezer.

Ingrid looked around to make sure Tony wasn't watching. She felt as if she were stealing her own camera as she pulled the strap free with a jerk and dropped it into her shoulder bag. The freezer door flew open. Ingrid found herself staring into the open blue eyes of a naked woman. No. A girl, she was that young, with blond hair. She was screaming but there was no sound. This was the reality of the picture Miranda had used to threaten Tony. The one he had put into his pocket. There were cuts and bruises all over her body. Sally Anderson had died in pain.

Music suddenly blared from the speakers in the living room. Ingrid turned around. She saw that Tony Flint had come up to look over her shoulder with the mild inquiry of one whose taste in interior decoration has been questioned by someone whose opinion he does not respect.

He sighed. "Might as well get started." He slammed the door to the freezer shut.

"That was Sally Anderson, wasn't it?" Ingrid did not know whether it was better to talk about it or not to talk about it. But it was too late to call the words back.

He sighed again. "I guess that's her name. I didn't pay much attention. She told me how old she was. Doesn't look fourteen anymore, does she? I was going to pack her up and take her along with me—you know, drop her in the ocean way off shore. But I just don't have time. I've just got enough time to do you up right, and then it's off to sea for Barnacle Bill the Sailor." He took the handcuff and went for Ingrid's other wrist.

She blocked him but gently, ducking under his arm, pulling out of his grip, "Wait." She didn't want to anger him. She knew he was stronger. She wanted him to listen.

"Wait. There's something you should know. About yourself, I mean. If you spend this time doing what you've planned, you may never get to meet your mother."

"My mother is dead. She died when I was five." He moved toward her purposefully.

"No. Someone died in that sanitarium fire. But not your mother. The woman who died was a nurse's aide who took your mother's jewelry. Think about it. The body was burned beyond recognition. There were no dental records.

Neither woman had ever been to a dentist. Your mother's pearls were never found, but I know where they are. There's a woman who calls herself Eugenia Phelps. Sounds like Eugenia Flint, your mother's name, doesn't it? This woman has those same pearls. All your mother's friends would recognize them. The pearls with the lobster claw clasp she got from your grandmother."

"It's impossible." But he had stopped. He was thinking.

"They looked for the nurse's aide but never found her. If it hadn't been your mother, hiding out, don't you think that woman would have come forward to be cleared of suspicion?"

"I don't know—it . . . it sounds incredible. Where is this woman?" He turned on her suspiciously.

"Only a few blocks from here. We can go talk to her."

If we can sober her up, Ingrid silently added to herself.

Tony patted each pocket as they went out the door. Worried about his diamonds, his passport, his photo, his yacht papers. He even picked up the scrapbook in its black file box and brought it along. The lid didn't lock anymore, so he carried it under his arm.

The open handcuff jabbed Ingrid's thigh with every step. She held it out from her body in her cuffed hand, hoping someone would notice it and come to her aid as they walked down Jones to the Paradise Hotel. Lower Nob Hill gave way to the Tenderloin. Somehow the sidewalks seemed grimier under the yellow halogen streetlamps.

The street was deserted except for three men (Ingrid counted) shivering in doorways along Eddy Street. One looked up from his nest of blankets, newspapers and cardboard to mutter a request to Tony for spare change so halfheartedly that he seemed to know there was no chance of a reply. They might hear her cry for help as Tony dragged her back to his apartment, but locked in their own tragedies, what could these men do?

The lobby of the Paradise Hotel seemed like a safe harbor now. The street door was locked, but an old man loitering in the lobby responded to the twenty-dollar bill Tony pressed against the glass. He opened the door a crack, snatched the bill and let them in. They walked up the stairway, their footsteps muffled by the dusty carpet.

It took a long time to rouse Mrs. Phelps. Ingrid was convinced that it was Tony's elegant suit that tipped the balance. There could be money in this, the old woman must be saying to herself. She sat on the bed as she had during Ingrid's last visit.

She was shaking, not violently but with a steady tremor. Tony stared at her, weighing the grim possibility that this could be his flesh and blood.

"Can you wake her up a little bit?" he asked. "I have a few questions."

"We'll have to get some alcohol down her—that's the only thing that can stop the shakes in the short run."

Mrs. Phelps, perking up a bit, nodded. "Yes, I'll be okay with a little drink."

"Well, now where do you propose to *get* a little drink at nearly five A.M.? The bars have been closed for hours."

"A man on the fourth floor sells it anytime," Mrs. Phelps said. "He wants an arm and a leg, but he sells it anytime."

"You'll have to show us. Do you think you can make it?" Ingrid said, instantly realizing it was a ridiculous question. Mrs. Phelps would obviously have crawled on her hands and knees if necessary at this point.

The man on the fourth floor was awake, more or less. A few other customers lounged on his floor. They took the bottle of gin back to Mrs. Phelps' room, where she drank off a hearty measure and then another. Gradually the shaking vanished.

"You call yourself Eugenia Phelps," Tony said.

"That's right. Eugenia after my father, Eugene."

"What was your maiden name?"

"Prentice."

Tony cast Ingrid a significant look. "You're sure it wasn't Bramwell?"

"Of course I'm sure."

"Did you ever know another woman named Eugenia, Mrs. Eugenia Flint?" Tony's face was taut with suppressed emotion.

Mrs. Phelps took another long swallow from her gin. "Maybe."

Ingrid interjected a question, "The bartender at Mac-Harg's Bar over on Gough Street told me you often wear a beautiful set of pearls—"

But Tony was already going through her purse. He found the pearls and held them under Mrs. Phelps' nose. "Did you steal these?"

"They're mine. They were a gift. Okay, okay, the lady who gave them to me did have the same name. She was a patient at this sanitarium down on the Peninsula, where I worked. We got to talking. She told me all her problems, and I told her I'd get her out of the place if I could because there wasn't nothing wrong with her a good day of working wouldn't cure. Took her down to the main floor the day I left. I told her which way to go, but she must have taken a wrong turn and got down to the furnace room. I ran into her husband and kid as I was leaving and I had to run for it. Didn't want to be around if they found her trying to escape. Then that fire happened and she died. My god. Good thing I had a live-in job. I had to lay low after she died, cuz they come looking for me. Couldn't find me, though. Must have stopped looking." She looked up in sudden doubt. "Unless that's what you're here for, looking."

Ingrid looked at Tony and saw he was staring at the pearls with their gold lobster-claw clasp. "This is Eugenia Flint's son. If she were alive somewhere, I know he would want to see her. You see, he was only five when—when the fire happened.

"Well, it was too bad, but she died. Say, I do remember that little kid." Mrs. Phelps took another pull from the bottle. "He was a mean little bastard, the bane of her life. She said she caught him with some bugs once—god, I don't even want to think about it. A five-year-old kid, yet. Wait a minute. I remember. The kid was there the day the fire started. Damned if I didn't always think he started it."

"Let's get out of here." Tony threw the pearls on the bed as if they had suddenly turned red-hot. He grabbed Ingrid by the uncuffed wrist and dragged her out the door.

Ingrid was suddenly seized with hysterical laughter, which infuriated Tony as he dragged her back up the Jones Street hill and threw her into the passenger side of his Porsche.

"I've had enough of you. I don't want you in my apartment. You're garbage, and I know exactly where to dump you. It's on my way. I'm docked in Sausalito." She could hear the muffler striking intermittent sparks off the roadway as he gunned the Porsche up the hills and along the stretches on the approach to the Golden Gate Bridge.

As they drove, he snarled at her, speaking in broken fragments. "I'll catch that morning tide. I have everything I need. These diamonds won't leave my pocket till I'm a hundred miles out."

As they passed Fort Point, Ingrid's hysteria left her. The bridge was deserted and wind whipped before dawn on a winter morning. The traffic lanes were set up, three in each direction. Today was a holiday. On workdays they moved the lane dividers so that four went in the most traveled direction—into the city in the morning and out to Marin during the evening commute.

He pulled up the Porsche just short of the San Francisco tower. *The middle of the bridge,* Ingrid thought. *Deeper water.* She threw open the door and scrambled out of the Porsche as he rushed around the front of the car. She didn't get more than a few steps away before he grabbed her arm and hauled her toward the water, up over the low fence between the roadway and the sidewalk on the east side of the Bridge. Ingrid began to shiver violently as the harsh winds hit her.

"I said you're trash," he repeated, dragging her along, "and I'm going to throw you right off this bridge."

"Tony, this whole bridge is under constant police surveillance." Ingrid's teeth were chattering. She had no idea whether what she said was true or not. The cold handcuff was like ice on her skin. "They have t-t-t-television monitors and everything."

"Won't take long. You'll be dead. I'll sail before they know what hit you."

He was insane, of course; they would probably catch him. But it wouldn't do her any good if she died falling from the bridge. She wondered if he could hear how short of breath she was, from terror. She was shaking as much from the cold as from the roar of the bridge, shuddering under the impact of the moving water two hundred feet below. But Tony seemed to take on an inhuman energy from the vibration of the walkway under their feet.

Both of them were breathing heavily now. Tony dragged her over to the railing. Ingrid clung to it desperately. It wasn't until he grasped her around the waist and hauled her away that she realized resistance would be most danger-ous. He was too strong for her. Abruptly she slumped to the ground, slipping out of his grip. As he bent to tumble her over the rail, she desperately kicked up toward his groin, putting her whole weight behind the blow.

And missed.

Her foot glanced off his thigh and did very little dam-age. Ingrid stood up slowly as Tony staggered back, stunned by the impact. It took him a moment to get his feet under him. Her aim at his crotch enraged him further. He came at her with a bellow, and Ingrid forced herself to stand in place until the last moment. Then she dodged aside.

Too late. He bowled her up onto the rail, and they grap-pled for a moment before overbalancing and rolling over the edge together.

They fell.

Ingrid stretched her arm as wide as she could, the hand-cuff snapping up and whiplashing as she strained to grasp the thick, orange cable. It seemed years away. For an in-stant her right hand connected with something.

Then, pain. Her whole weight pivoted on the open handcuff as it caught on the cable and swung her in from the water. She lost sight of everything for a few long sec-onds in the pain, as her arm seemed wrenched almost out of its socket and she bounced violently against the rails of the bridge. She felt the open handcuff slide down the ridged surface of the cable. She dropped heavily onto the repair-men's catwalk a few feet below the roadbed. Immediately and instinctively, she reached up to cling to the railing from the outside.

She waited to feel the pain recede from her left leg, which had struck the railing as she had landed. It was numb at first, then seemed to be broken. But soon she could feel it, solid underneath her. Her cuffed hand responded when she tried to move the fingers, but she decided not to put much weight on it. Then she looked up to see how far she would have to climb from the catwalk up to the road.

She clambered up over the rail without knowing quite how she did it and stood unsteadily on the sidewalk, well back from the rail. She took a few steps and hugged the large orange lamppost, gripping it tightly. Then she looked around for more danger. She saw nothing. She edged toward the rail and looked down.

Only the cold steel water of the Bay in the winter morning light. Nothing showed on its surface but the tide. No sign of Tony Flint, gone with his picture and his precious package.

She found her camera bag near the rail and uttered a silent prayer of thanksgiving that, broken though it might be, her camera had not gone into the Bay. She hadn't even noticed when it slipped off her shoulder.

Ingrid walked back to the Porsche. The door was still open, keys in the ignition. It never occurred to her to drive his car. She wanted to get as far away from it and him as possible. She reached into the back behind the driver's seat and took out the black file box. She put it under her arm, the scrapbook inside rattling forlornly. She began to walk slowly, favoring her left leg. The orange pedestrian gate was still locked for the night. She walked around it, out into the deserted traffic lane, toward the city.

A horn honked frantically on the opposite side of the road and Ingrid looked up, recognized it and trudged across the highway to Spyder's van, dodging an orange repair vehicle, which slowed for her obligingly. A moment later she gratefully squeezed into the front seat with Carmen and Spyder, wincing as she was immediately hugged in several sore places at once.

THIRTY-FOUR

"WE FOLLOWED YOU as soon as we could," Spyder said, when they had all calmed down. "Victor got busted last night."

"Why? What for?"

Spyder shook his head sadly. "He got a little crazy in prison. I didn't realize how crazy till last night. It was revenge he wanted. He told me he's been in touch with the narcs, trying to throw them a victim."

"*Victor* did that?" Ingrid could hardly believe it.

"Honestly, Ingrid, I had no idea. I was afraid of something, but not that."

"You were afraid he pushed Miranda out that window."

"Well, I wondered. Vic still wasn't sure you hadn't turned him in. He said he agreed with me when I told him it couldn't be you. But Miranda convinced him you had her blackmail files and you were going to send him away for good this time. That really drove him crazy. Last night Vic told me they had set you up to deliver a package of coke to a customer for her. All Vic had to do was tell the narcs what and where, and they'd pick you up for possession with intent to sell. Then Miranda died and he couldn't get at you. The cops wanted results. So he grabbed Stella last night and had her take him to the last place she'd made a cocaine delivery for Miranda. He called his cop friends and tried to set her up for the bust. But she refused to touch the package unless he went in with her. She made him carry it. The cops arrested both of them."

"Did you bail him out?"

"We called his lawyer. Let the lawyer bail him. The woman who got busted with him looks like a real solid citizen. I'm not worried about her."

"Oh, she's got a rich boss. He'll take care of her. He'll have to—she knows too much about his accounts." Ingrid sighed, thinking about the daughter in the freezer. There was no way to be bailed out from death.

Carmen gently took up Ingrid's wrist, which was beginning to swell under the handcuff. "Say, speaking of law and order, do you mind my asking about this, uh, police bondage equipment here?"

"Oh, god, how will I get rid of this?"

"We'll go see Ben Resnick first."

"It's not even seven. Will he be there this early?"

"Ben is on Eastern Standard time."

They surprised Ben in the act of brewing a large pot of coffee, which he shared with them while they explained the complicated choreography of the night before. Carmen was persuaded to have some orange pekoe tea, the closest thing to a noncaffeinated beverage in the place.

Ingrid gave Ben the scrapbook in its black file box. "I'd have thrown it in the Bay, but I was afraid it would float or wash ashore." She turned away as he glanced at the photos.

"What I don't understand," Ingrid asked Spyder, "is how you knew to look for me on the Golden Gate Bridge."

Spyder explained. "All the doors to Carmen's place were open, so we checked with Resnick to see if he knew the address for that big blond lawyer we'd last seen you with. We decided to try his place first and to check on you. For all we knew, you were just starting a meaningful relationship."

"Van Horn had everyone's addresses after the first day. He's very good at that sort of thing," Ben explained.

"That was when Vic called from the Hall of Justice, which delayed us," Spyder continued. "About the time we got to golden boy's address, we saw you two go roaring off in this Porsche heading north, so we followed the best we could—he must have been hitting eighty on those hills. We finally passed the Porsche on the Bridge. But no one was in it and we couldn't see either of you. We went on up to where we could turn around, and that's when we saw you walking back toward the city."

"Intervention would have been welcome a little earlier, but better late than never." She held up her handcuffed wrist to Ben, who had put the scrapbook aside in distaste.

Ben was equal to the assignment. "Let's see, is it eight yet? The Joy of Bondage should be open by now. May I?" He held the scrapbook meaningfully in front of the door to his wood-burning stove.

Ingrid nodded and watched as Ben fed the photos and documents into the stove, one at a time, until the scrapbook was empty. Then he dropped the book itself into the flames and stirred it with a poker until it sank into embers.

THE BARTENDER at the Joy of Bondage squinted a moment at the cuff and whipped out a key from under the bar. It fit. The cuff dropped open, and Ingrid could at last rub her wrist, which had begun to throb steadily.

"I usually charge a sawbuck for that service, Ben," the bartender said.

"How about a free ad for a month—that's worth about fifty times that."

"Not to you, it ain't," he grumbled, "but all right."

"Ingrid," Ben said as they walked back to the *Gadfly*, "my receptionist quit. I have a proposition for you. I've been thinking of taking on a photo stringer."

"Those two statements don't quite add up to a proposition," Ingrid said suspiciously.

"Let me finish. I also need some lab work done now and then. I only pay my receptionist the minimum wage, but if we combine the receptionist job with some photo free-lance fees and you do all our lab work, you could just about live on it. We can negotiate for ad space if you want to do some commercial work for extra money." At Ingrid's uncertain expression, he continued, "Look, kid, there's a plus, and it's a big plus: I'll pay any lawyer's fees that arise out of the Flint affair."

For a moment Ingrid was too stunned to take it all in. She looked at Spyder, who shrugged helplessly. "You can have it, Ingrid. You've got all the bargaining chips, and I'd make a lousy receptionist."

"What's the catch? Aside from making the coffee."

"*The Gadfly* gets to scoop the dailies with your exclusive story on murder in the shadow of the high-rises. Think it over, Ingrid. Digging you out of this will take specialized legal skills, and I think you're going to need that little fringe benefit, possibly as early as this afternoon. I'm going to call my police contacts and suggest they send the homicide boys over to Junior's apartment. They'll remember you from before, you know."

"I think I'll accept, Ben, but I've got one more place to go first."

CLAUDE SULLENLY EXAMINED Ingrid's pass and waved her toward the Bramwell Building elevators. She realized from the looks people gave her as she limped through the halls that she had not dressed for success and her bruises showed.

First she went to the basement. The friendly Irish janitor was nowhere in sight. A young man in a similar coverall was moving into the office. "The old guy's left," he said with some amusement.

"Wasn't that rather sudden?"

"He didn't seem too unhappy about going. I never would have thought he'd leave without those union pension benefits. He just picked up and went back to Ireland. He used to say he'd retire to Florida, but he didn't even want to wait for that. They made it worth his while. He said he cashed in his insurance policy."

"I don't know what that means either."

The boy grinned. "I wouldn't know myself if he hadn't been looking through Miss Scott's desk the day she moved last week and turned up with a bunch of little bits of paper. Those small memos, you know. Didn't look like much to me. Every one of them just had one line written on it and a signature, but he said they were pure gold."

Ingrid thanked the new janitor and pressed the UP button on the elevator.

In Nell Scott's office the mag card typewriter was hard at work, feeding in new cards automatically as it needed them, clattering away unattended, severely unaware that it was obsolete. Ingrid picked up the log reel of paper feeding through the machine and coiling into a box behind the unit. She nodded. It made sense.

"Morning, Nell," she said when Nell returned with a sweet roll and a cup of cafeteria coffee.

"Oh, hello, Ingrid. More time cards? I thought we had your final bill."

"Not quite. I see your mag card's at work. You can probably run a hundred pages before you need to press another button."

"Probably. Was there something—"

"I figured out how you did it. You collected the memos she kept sending you till you had one that sounded like a suicide note. You turned on the loudspeaker on your dictaphone and put on a tape of Flint Senior. Then you ran your mag card to keep the janitor from coming in."

"Why should I want to do something like that?"

"Sit down, Nell."

"I prefer to stand." Nell had a wary look. A few new wrinkles seemed to have crimped into her face overnight. "What do you want?"

"Tony's probably dead. He fell off the Golden Gate Bridge a few hours ago while trying to throw me off it. Even if he survived, the police will be searching his apartment soon. You must know what's in that freezer."

Nell sat down. She expelled a long breath. "I told him to get rid of it."

"Well, he didn't. I saw the body at Tony's apartment. And when they fish him out, he'll have Miranda's picture of Sally Anderson in his pocket. This scandal is going to come out, Nell. It wasn't worth your effort to try to stop it."

Nell pushed her steaming cup of coffee and sweet roll to one side as if they were someone else's. She put both arms on the desk and breathed deeply twice, almost as if in relief. "Maybe you're right. Still, I came pretty close, don't you think?"

"Goddamn it, why should you cover up for them?"

"Affection." Nell smiled sadly. "And skill. It's what I do best. We almost got away with it. I've been taking care of Tony since everyone else gave up on him. I'm just stubborn that way. I won't give up, even if someone kicks me in the teeth repeatedly."

Ingrid sighed noiselessly. "I know what you mean."

"He was quite mysterious for several weeks. Miranda had struck a bargain with him to sail her to South America, where she could buy herself the indolent life style she'd always dreamed of. His price was the boat. She bought it for him, and he would have kept it. Then suddenly he started dropping into my office again, looking melancholy. It seems that she introduced him to that Anderson child and it didn't go well—or perhaps it went too well. Tony had...done that before. We managed to cover up the death in South America pretty well. Everyone assumed Tony was carrying drugs on that boat." Nell sighed with the air of a woman whose work is never done. "Anyway, somehow Miranda found out about that prostitute and how she died on that boat with those boys and their rough treatment. We were lucky that ambassador's son was aboard. He played the gentleman and took the blame. They honored his diplomatic immunity. Perhaps Miranda decided she needed some insurance if she was going to be alone with Tony on the high seas. So she pushed him too far."

"Tony said he didn't kill her."

"No, he didn't, poor baby. He was nearly in tears in my office. Said she wasn't going to give him the boat after all. Her plan was to blackmail him with that for the rest of his life. I suggested he wait five minutes, then take the receptionist out on the stairwell and do whatever he wanted, as long as it took at least half an hour. He managed to keep her there fifteen minutes but that was enough. His luck seemed to be picking up, because he ran into Josephine Lewis and she gave him an alibi.

"You're right about the tape. I called Miranda and told her to listen to it on that ridiculous speaker phone of hers. Until I broke the connection, her phone would remain engaged. Then I put the receiver against the machine, set the mag card to run off a few hundred pages and went upstairs. The janitor just assumed I was in there when he heard the machine running. I frequently visited him in his office, but he hated the noise, so he never so much as knocked on my door when the machine was printing. Later I dropped by for some coffee cake, and when the police talked to us I promised the janitor I could vouch for him because *I* was there all afternoon. It never occurred to him to doubt it.''

"Until he found the other notes from Miranda that you'd saved. The ones that wouldn't quite do for a suicide note, but sound pretty similar. When he brought those to your attention, you knew he could turn you in, so you gave him a handsome cash settlement and a one-way ticket to the old country,'' Ingrid surmised.

Nell nodded. It seemed important to her to explain, to have someone understand. "When I got upstairs, Miranda was still listening to the tape on her speaker phone. She looked surprised to see me. Of course, I wouldn't let her Do Not Disturb sign stop me. She must have thought I was either typing or listening to the tape as well, back in my office. I shoved that stupid cart of flowers out of the way and opened the window. She was surprised at my rudeness because I always made it a point not to show any anger around her. 'Come on, just look at that,' I said, as if she might be afraid. When she reached the window and leaned out to look . . . well, I just pushed. I almost went out after her, it was so easy. The tape was still blasting away, of course. Mr. Flint's plan to protect the building's landmark status, just the thing Miranda was trying to prevent. After that, I took a pencil and used the eraser end to turn off the speaker phone. I used my hankie to take the receiver off the cradle—it always pays to have a clean hankie, my mother used to say. I pressed the end button, calling out on Miranda's private line, and dialed the number for time.''

"And you left the door slightly ajar, knowing the draft from the open window would slam it the minute anyone opened the outer door.''

"That's right. After all, I occupied this office for a year; I know its little quirks. Then I went back to my office in the basement. When Tony dropped by to tell me he'd finished with the receptionist, I hung up the phone that disconnected Miranda's line. I told him to get upstairs and work all afternoon as if his life depended on it." She grimaced in pain at the phrase. "I then called up Personnel and tried to get through to Miranda as if I thought she were still alive." Nell smiled grimly. "Her private line was lit, of course, so little Pammy wasn't about to disturb her. I ran off more pages of the form manual for another quarter hour or so, mainly to give myself a chance to calm down, I think. Then I went over to the janitor's office for a little coffee break."

"Why did you ask to see Miranda's body when the police were there?"

"Sounds very cunning, doesn't it, anyone who would make that much of a fool of herself couldn't be a murderess. Actually, I think it was failure of nerve. I got a little overwrought. I thought if anyone could have survived that fall Miranda would have—out of sheer spite. I've often wondered these past few years if she was quite human."

"I'm sorry, Nell," Ingrid said truthfully. "What do you propose to do now?"

"You think I have no further options? Well, think again. Look!" Nell went over to the window and cranked it open, leaning out over the sill, as if the hinges were stuck.

Ingrid hobbled across the room, her new sprains and old bruises turning her attempt at a run into a disjointed trot. Nell watched her approach for a second, then gazed back out the window. "Well?" Her voice was harsh and challenging, but she smiled sadly and stepped over the sill.

Ingrid leaped forward as she disappeared. But by the time she got there Nell had gone out. And down.

Ingrid reached the window and grasped the frame. This time she looked away rather than down.

She turned back into the room and picked up the telephone to call the paramedics. Then, she knew, she would call Ben Resnick to take him up on his offer of the job and his free legal aid.

Her hand shook and she held the receiver with both hands. She breathed carefully for several moments before she could manage to say anything. Nell's smile would stay with her for a long time.

Cat's Cradle
Clare Curzon

A Mike Yeadings Mystery

OLD LORELY PELLING WAS AS QUEER AS TWO LEFT BOOTS....

She's a reclusive eccentric with a checkered past and dozens of cats, and her shooting death is first believed accidental, the result of local boys' target practice. But Detective Superintendent Mike Yeadings of the Thames Valley Police Force believes darker motives are behind the death of the old woman.

The villagers are astounded that Lorely has named her neighbor's children sole inheritors of her estate. For Yeadings, it means unraveling the tangled skein of deception, scandal and desperation in Lorely's long, frustrated life—and the secrets she shared with a killer.

"All the right ingredients." —*Booklist*

Available in September at your favorite retail stores.

To order your copy, please send your name, address, zip or postal code, along with a check or money order (please do not send cash) for $3.99 ($4.50 in Canada), plus 75¢ postage and handling ($1.00 in Canada) for each book ordered, payable to Worldwide Mystery, to:

In the U.S.	In Canada
Worldwide Mystery	Worldwide Mystery
3010 Walden Avenue	P. O. Box 609
P. O. Box 1325	Fort Erie, Ontario
Buffalo, NY 14269-1325	L2A 5X3

Please specify book title with your order.
Canadian residents add applicable federal and provincial taxes.

 **WORLDWIDE LIBRARY**®

CRADLE

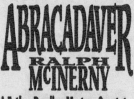
ABRACADAVER
RALPH McINERNY

First Time in Paperback

A Father Dowling Mystery Quartet

NOW YOU SEE HER...NOW YOU DON'T

A magic show at St. Hilary's one snowy night proves entertaining for the stragglers who braved the weather. Aggie Miller allows her ring to be used in a disappearing act and Father Dowling chances to notice the inscription. Oddly, the ring belongs to Frances Grice, the missing wife of a local millionaire entrepreneur.

The ring's new wearer had found it at a garage sale, but it clearly brought bad luck—poor Aggie is brutally murdered. What was the connection between the death of Aggie Miller and the disappearance of Frances Grice?

"Dowling fans won't be disappointed."
—*Kirkus Reviews*

Available in September at your favorite retail stores.

To order your copy, please send your name, address, zip or postal code, along with a check or money order (please do not send cash) for $3.99 ($4.50 in Canada), plus 75¢ postage and handling ($1.00 in Canada) for each book ordered, payable to Worldwide Mystery, to:

In the U.S.	In Canada
Worldwide Mystery	Worldwide Mystery
3010 Walden Avenue	P. O. Box 609
P. O. Box 1325	Fort Erie, Ontario
Buffalo, NY 14269-1325	L2A 5X3

Please specify book title with your order.
Canadian residents add applicable federal and provincial taxes.

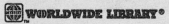 **WORLDWIDE LIBRARY®**

ABRA

THE DOWN HOME *Heifer Heist*

Eve K. SANDSTROM

First Time in Paperback

A Sam & Nicky Titus Mystery

THIN ICE

Rancher Joe Pilkington, neighbor to Sheriff Sam Titus and photographer wife Nicky, is run down when he interrupts rustlers during a heist. Aside from tire tracks in the snow, the only clue is the sound of Mozart heard playing from the killer's truck.

Two more grisly deaths follow, and it looks as if a beloved member of the Titus ranch may be accused of murder. Sam and Nicky grimly set out to corner a killer...before they become victims themselves.

"Sandstrom makes the most of her setting...."
—*Publishers Weekly*

Available in October at your favorite retail stores.

To order your copy, please send your name, address, zip or postal code, along with a check or money order (please do not send cash) for $3.99 ($4.50 in Canada), plus 75¢ postage and handling ($1.00 in Canada) for each book ordered, payable to Worldwide Mystery, to:

In the U.S.	In Canada
Worldwide Mystery	Worldwide Mystery
3010 Walden Avenue	P. O. Box 609
P. O. Box 1325	Fort Erie, Ontario
Buffalo, NY 14269-1325	L2A 5X3

Please specify book title with your order.
Canadian residents add applicable federal and provincial taxes.

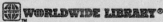 **WORLDWIDE LIBRARY** ®

HEIFER